Robophobia

Matt Hayden

Contents

Dedicated to

Terry Gilliam
Guillermo Del Toro
Mary Shelley
Tove Jansson

Thanks to

Garrett
Em
George

Introduction

Welcome readers, welcome.
This is the world, the very strange world, of
Robophobia.

Find yourself a comfy chair, maybe partake in a
warm beverage, or simply snuggle by a fireplace
somewhere familiar. But do make sure you're
relaxed and comfortable.
For I want you to let me open your imagination,
and transport you on a journey of madness and
mayhem. Within the pages of the book you hold
within your grasp, you will encounter revengeful
robots, lonely trolls, freaks aplenty, homicidal
lovers and other entities that hide in the shadows
of our realms.

Come discover the rich, imaginative, warped and
beautifully written tales and you will encounter
lives that cannot fail to charm and chill.

Robophobia is not a world to be discovered - but
instead, unmasked.

Sumire and the Robot

As the train hurtled its way down to Tokyo, Sumire was deep in thought. He used to love his journey to work. Mr Kazuki had treated all his staff like family, remembering birthdays and the important issues for everyone. The atmosphere at the Sunrise Sushi restaurant was so friendly, and it wasn't like a chore to be at work.

But that had changed since Mr Kazuki had passed away and the restaurant had changed owners. Sumire still loved his job, it was only the new boss he had felt disappointed with. New owners had brought fresh problems.

Whereas before he'd felt like a valued member of the team, Yoshihiro Masuda treated him just like a regular rice-maker, an anonymous cog in a wheel.

If he hadn't been so young and without any other qualifications, he might have considered trying to find other employment, but he had made so many friends, the thought of leaving left him feeling despondent.

He sighed. Luckily, he had recently changed his days and now tended to only work weekends when Mr Kazuki wasn't there too much.

A small red robot stepped onto the train, breaking Sumire's thoughts. It seemed to be by itself. At first, Sumire thought it must be a prank, but as it came closer he saw that it was alone. In fact, it looked heartily happy that it was in its own company.

The robot was comprised of four main sections. His head, a flattened globe, was at just below Sumire's waist height but seemed flexible enough that it could look up and about. His body was a complex box, smaller than the third unit, another box, forming its lower half. This tapered into the fourth unit, his mobility unit, which appeared to be two clunky feet pads that looked like they had been fashioned on small shoe-boxes.

The robot stepped down the aisle, stopped by Sumire and gave a few low beeps. Then it climbed up on to the seat beside him. Before Sumire could react, it had snuggled up beside him and seemed to switch off.

Sumire looked around sheepishly, wondering if he had suddenly become the mark on one of those prank reality shows. Any moment now, a camera crew would jump out and 'Surprise.' But no, it appeared that the robot was a genuine commuter. So Sumire sat there bemused.

"Make yourself comfortable," he said, chuckling, unable to resist patting the robot's head.

It seemed odd to suddenly have company. Normally Sumire rode the train alone, and being solitary had become somewhat of an unhealthy habit. For a while now, his life was an up and down affair. Some of it was interesting. Some of it was not so interesting. Most of it boring. Long slow periods of nothing much, with occasional periods of working.

A few moments later, as the train began its long descent, the robot climbed down and went to stand by the door. When the train pulled in at the next station, it got off. The conductor didn't seem at all bothered; it was as if he was perfectly normal.

Sumire might not have given it a second thought, but exactly the same thing happened the next day. The robot sat beside him, enjoyed the attention, then got off a couple of a few stops later.

After the third weekend it happened, he gave in to his curiosity and asked the train conductor if he knew anything about the robot.

"Its name is Donnie, I think," he told Sumire. "When I started my job the other conductors said to look out for it. It's been getting on this train for nearly a year.

"Apparently, it travels all different routes - but always this one on the weekends. It's like it knows where it's going."

"Have you have any idea where it comes from?" Sumire asked.

The conductor shook his head.

"You should follow it one day," the conductor joked.

Sumire laughed, but once that idea had been suggested and once he started to think about it he couldn't get the idea of his mind. On Sunday morning he caught his usual train as if he was going into work. Now, when the robot got off, he might follow it.

Only it didn't show up the next weekend. It wasn't there the following Sunday, either.

*　*　*

The next Saturday morning Sumire told the conductor what had happened.

"Do you think it knows what it is doing?"

"I wouldn't be surprised. Robots are very clever machines."

The train pulled into the next station.

"Look. It's here again today," the conductor added.

Spending time with the robot, even for a few moments, made a big difference. Sumire began to enjoy his journey to work.

Then, one weekend, it was raining hard and the train was busier than usual. An old man took the seat next to me, and Sumire didn't feel he could ask him to move.

Sumire didn't see the robot that day. The journey into Tokyo wasn't the same without the unusual companion.

By the time Sumire got to work, he had come up with a plan. He would ask his boss if he could take the weekend off, then he could follow the robot wherever it was headed.

If Donnie had a home to go to, fine. If it didn't, Sumire might put into place some kind of ownership.

"Is it an emergency?" Mr Masuda asked when Sumire finally summoned up his nerves to ask him. "We've some busy weekends coming up, as you know."

Sumire could have invented an excuse but he didn't approve of being dishonest. So he opted for the truth instead - after all, he could only say no.

"A little robot has been getting on my train every weekend. I want to follow him and see what it's about. If it turns out to have no owners, I might be able to claim it."

Sumire stood, shoulders tense, waiting for his boss to tell him off for wasting his time. Instead, his face broke into a big grin.

"I didn't take you for a robot fan!"

He reached for his mobile phone and for the next half an hour showed Sumire hundreds of photos of his visits to conventions and robot shows.

Sumire had never even heard of the robot conventions and said as much.

"You don't know what you're missing," he said.

"They're so much fun. Such lovely people. My wife works for Toshiba, and they host some great shows in Kyoto. Why don't you go along one time? You'd be more than welcome."

He printed off a flyer and handed it to Sumire.

"And let me know how you get on following that robot, won't you?"

"Thanks, Mr Masuda," Sumire replied, too taken aback by his boss's unexpected relaxed attitude.

"I'm glad you told me about the robot. It sounds fun. I've been having trouble settling into this new job. It's so difficult having to follow Mr Kazuki.

"I felt I needed to put my mark on things, but I think I may have gone a bit too far." He gave Sumire a smile. "What do you think?"

Sumire wasn't sure what to say.

"Maybe it just takes time?"

To Sumire's astonishment, Mr Masuda chuckled.

"I need to try to not go over the top. I'll have to work on that," he said.

For the rest of the day, Mr Masuda didn't stop smiling. It was as though his hard exterior had softened, allowing a much friendlier persona to come shining through.

It wasn't just Sumire who thought so, either. Koji, one of his colleagues, remarked on the change during their morning break.

"What happened to the boss?" he asked. "He came back into the kitchen and asked how things were going. He called me Koji!"

Sumire chuckled.

"It's my fault, I think." He told his colleague about the robot.

"Well, let's see if it lasts," his colleague replied. "I was thinking about jacking this job in last week."

"I guess we'll have to see."

Sumire considering telling Koji had said about difficulties of following Mr Kazuki, but in the end, decided not to. Better to let things develop.

✳✳✳

The next weekend, Donnie got on at his usual stop. Sumire gave him a big smile.

"When you get off, I'm coming with you," he whispered.

As the train began its long descent into the Tokyo, robot and man headed for the door together.

"Good luck," the conductor called as the train slowed in at the station.

"Thanks," he said. "Have a good morning. You'll have to let me know."

The moment the doors opened, the robot stepped off and headed for the lift down to the street. After a while, it paused at various intervals as if to make sure that Sumire was following it, before setting off again.

It wasn't long before they reached a small motorbike workshop.

"There you are, Donnie," the mechanic said as he tapped the robot on the head. "I see you've brought a companion home with you."

The man turned to Sumire.

"Fancy a coffee? I've got some brewing."

Why not, Sumire thought.

"Thanks. That's very kind of you," he said as he took a seat on an old plastic chair.

"Yukie Kitamura," he said when he brought Sumire a coffee. "Pleased to meet you."

"Sumire Yakusho," he replied. "Is Donnie your robot?"

"Yes. I found him languishing in an old factory. It was as though it was waiting for me. It gave me a project, and also kept me company," Yukie blushed. "I'm not very good at making friends, so Donnie helped me get through some lonely times."

He then apologised for perhaps being too open and honest. He tapped Donnie on the head.

Sumire nodded. "I know how you feel. I am too, sometimes."

Yukie's girlfriend emerged from the back of the workshop and was introduced. They sat around and chatted for nearly hour. Sumire talked about working at the Sunrise Sushi restaurant, and Yukie talked about creating motorbikes.

"Donnie has this way with bringing people together," she said.

Sumire nodded.

"I think it's doing a good job. I spend too much time on my own."

Yukie and his girlfriend both nodded as if they understood what Sumire was talking about.

The next morning, Sumire told Mr Masuda what had happened.

"Wow, that sounds quite a story. If you ask me, it sounds as if the robot is creating a weird network of people."

Sumire's boss chuckled.

He fiddled in his desk drawer and pulled out a flyer for a robotic show in Tokyo the following month. He gave it over to Sumire.

Sumire smiled.

"I know, it sounds daft, doesn't it?"

"Actually, no. I've been wanting to invite you to a Sci-Fi convention, and my wife says I should expand my friendships. It never seems to be the right time." He paused. "What would you have said? If I'd invited you, that is."

"I would have said yes," Sumire replied with a moment's hesitation. "Since my parents died last year, I've found myself living alone. It's hard to make myself get out and about."

***

As the train pulled into the train station the following weekend, Sumire could see the robot, waiting as usual, but this time it didn't get on the train.

"Looks like it plans to catch the next one along," the conductor said. "So, did you follow it home last time?"

"I did. And met some interesting people."

"Sounds nice."

Sumire looked away for a moment. He took a pause to think about all the new people he had come into contact with over the past few days.

As the train pulled away, Sumire looked back down the train station to where the robot was stood, watching the train as it went on its way.

If he hadn't known better, he could have sworn that the robot was nodding with satisfaction.

The Troll Whisperer

It was June 25, 2035, and Elisabet Gisladottir, the troll keeper at Isafjordur Wildlife Park, watched the female troll as she prepared to give birth to twins.

Elisabet had developed a special bond with the collection of trolls and become known among colleagues as something of a 'troll whisperer'.

Having been asked how her special relationship with the trolls developed, Elisabet explained the dynamics.

"The adults warmed to me after I'd been their primary keeper for a year," she said. "If they saw me they'd let me come over - not because they thought I might be food, but because they are naturally curious creatures.

"I've earned their trust. They are skittish in nature, so if they don't trust you, they won't interact at all.

"I've got a relationship with the adult male, but he can be a bit grumpy. The others will let me stroke their chests or rub their tummies. They don't play, but they'll follow me around and come and sit with me, on the other side of the fence, obviously."

Andrei, the male troll, and Agustina, the female, came to the park from other Icelandic collections and were both ten years old when their cubs were born.

They were part of an Arctic-breeding programme and keepers hoped they'd bond and produce a litter of their own. Two years later, Agustina gave birth to three female troll cubs: Nina, Jonina and Oddny.

"In the wild, trolls rear their babies in seclusion and will often reject them if they're disturbed,"

Elisabet explained, "so we kept contact to a minimum. Andrei, the male, remained in the neighbouring enclosure but was never too far from the cubs. He took a great interest in his new family.

"After the first few weeks, and after a few shaky starts, the cubs mastered the art of standing on their own. Within a month they were striding about.

"A few weeks later, they left the cave and went into the outdoor enclosure. Mum was dragging them back in again to start with, but after one or two months, they were going in and out at will."

At three months old the cubs were successfully introduced to their father, Andrei, in the main outdoor enclosure.

"We'd been monitoring them and there was no friction between the male and his brood, so it was time to introduce them. Elisabet said, "The mother went out to meet Dad first. She said 'hello' in the way trolls do, and they got all lovey-dovey. It was like she was saying, 'I've missed you,' and he felt the same.

"The signs were all good. Then the three youngsters came out and had a sniff. It went well, so they all got shut into the main enclosure as a family. The mother continued to be very protective and was edgy towards the keepers. I had to build up her trust again. It took a bit of time, but it worked out in the end.

"The cubs were suckling their mother's milk for about nine months," Elisabet continued, "and after five months they started eating solid food as well.

"We gave the adults extra food, and the mother would get hers and let the cubs have a go, then finish it herself. The father wouldn't let the cubs anywhere near his food.

"It's the mother's job to provide food in the wild.

"At ten to twelve months, the special treatment where Mum shared her food had passed and it was every troll for herself. In the wild, they'd be out in the mountains hunting with their mum."

I caught up with Elisabet as the troll cubs were reaching adolescence.

"They're growing up fast and are like teenagers now," she told me. "They're spending time with the family and trying to annoy Dad, poking and prodding him while he grumbles at them.

"They're definitely more independent now; they sit in a separate patch of the enclosure from Mum and Dad and are spending more time play-fighting amongst themselves. Agustina will always be a protective mother, but now they're off exploring and more independent lives."

Normally by the time they reach two years a wildlife park would be looking to move them on to breeding programs.

"We plan to do that, too, but there are other options: we've got three female trolls, so if they don't come into season - it can be slowed with medication - then we can keep them for a bit longer.

"Ideally, we'd like to find new homes on outer islands for them, though, where they'll be paired up to breed."

The Wildlife Park does have its opponents though. Troll conservation can be a hot topic at times. Being online, I find a letter to the Icelandic populace warning that if trolls numbers are encouraged, 'Deaths will occur!... dismembering, abductions... I don't want trolls in my backyards any more than they (troll advocates) would want serial killers or rapists in theirs.'

I find it sad but understandable. Standing at over eight feet high, covered in mangy brown fur and smelling of rank sweat, they look like walking grizzly bears in a way. With fierce reputations, the likeability of trolls is difficult. Most tales tell of fierce creatures and horrors of barbaric confrontations. In truth, most trolls are shy and will do pretty much anything to avoid human contact.

I mention this to Elisabet.

"It's a human perception problem. You have some people who think that bloodthirsty trolls wait behind every ridge top or behind walls waiting to jump out and eat them. Then you have you have ones who associate the trolls with everything they don't like about 'interfering' government."

No one ever said coexisting with troll would be easy.

***

Helping Trolls In The Wild

Icelandic trolls are now among the world's rarest troll species. Numbers have fallen dramatically in the past 50 years, almost to the point of extinction.

They once occupied much of the Arctic/Scandinavian area, but now they're only found in Northern Iceland and in patches of Greenland and some remote Faeroe islands. At the lowest point, there were only 60 of the trolls left in the wild.

In September 2020, the 16th Iceland Troll

Census, covering much of the Arctic continent, estimated that 315 Icelandic trolls now exist, consisting 190 adults males, 100 adult females and 25 cubs. Human intrusion and hunting or an epidemic of disease could still spell the end of the species.

Conservation work, including breeding programmes like the one at Isafjordur Wildlife Park, continues today and the trolls are classified as endangered by the Conservation Union of Nature and Tourism Service.

For The Love Of Gimps

Tracy had never felt despondent because she had not married. She had many lovers, men and women, and although she hadn't had many friends, her rewarding career as a very successful university lecturer had been full of friends. Some of them were central in her life as lovers.

There were young folks she had met in various ways. One of her favourite friends was a twenty-something Samantha, whom she got to know when the young woman began working at the university library.

Tracy potted around in her kitchen while she waited for her guest. She felt despondent. Despondent with her life. Despondent with being alone. In between her pottering, she thought she could feel her own heart aching. Tracy felt like she was starting to disappear - seeping, fading. There was little evidence of her old life.

Depression and loneliness was a terrible ailment. She woke up alone and in silence. Sometimes she would lay in the bath without turning on the bathroom light, and cry until the water got cold.

Samantha had said she would call by today, and suddenly there she was, coming up the path with her dog beside her. Both of them seemed oblivious to the dank autumn weather.

Tracy couldn't help but feel uplifted. Since retiring, she could do what she wanted but had started to become somewhat of a recluse. She chose to make the most of Samantha's visit.

She opened the door that faced the street.

"You should have waited for better weather!"

Samantha and her little boxer dog ran the last few paces and shuddered their way into Tracy's hallway. Samantha slid a large pack off her shoulder and put it on the floor.

Tracy held out her arms and they exchanged a warm embrace. It was hard not to hug Samantha - she was a real head-turner, with golden long wavy hair and seemingly endless legs in tight jeans that just displayed a cute pert bottom.

Though Tracy held her own in the beauty department. At sixty-nine, Tracy was still strikingly beautiful and she could still, Tracy knew, turn heads when she made the effort to spruce herself up.

"I hope I haven't disturbed you today," Samantha apologised.

"Don't be daft. It's too dreary to be out in the garden, and with my early retirement, I am at a loss some days. I'm pleased you made the time to come by and visit."

Tracy smiled, mainly because she loved having visitors and seeing old flames brought back a spark of mischievousness that her life was lacking these days. She did wish, now her life was less busy, that she had a lover. She and Samantha had sometimes discussed it. Samantha, like most young people, loved company. She found it difficult to understand how Tracy could live on her own.

"You should get a lover for the company. You'd love it. A young girlfriend like mine would be perfect."

"I'm not sure I have the patience for a lover," Tracy had told her. "All that love making and cuddling. At times I'm too slow to take a brisk walk… let alone anything else."

Both of them laughed. Four or five years ago it had been a different story. Samantha had known all about Tracy's stamina.

"You should join one of those online swinger sites. You could find yourself a nice middle-aged couple looking for a third."

"No." Tracy had said this more than once. "Those websites attract too many weirdoes. I do miss that swinger club we used to visit in London though. That place was always very entertaining."

Tracy turned to Samantha now as she was drying off her dog with an old towel.

"I do enjoy your visits though during the holidays. I'm going to miss your visits when the next term year starts." The little boxer skipped across the room and stopped by Tracy's old-worn armchair.

"He wants your company so he can sit with you," Samantha told her.

"He'll have to wait until I get our coffee sorted." Tracy headed for the kitchen and her voice floated out over the rattle of mugs and the boiling of the kettle.

"Are you all ready for another term in the library?"

"Yep," Samantha called back. "Getting geared up to mingle with all new students and lecturers."

"You'll be kept busy I'm sure."

Tracy came back into the lounge bearing a tray of coffee and cake.

Samantha stood up to lend a hand.

"Here, sit down. I'll take it."

Tracy let her take the tray to the table and she settled into her chair. The boxer jumped on to her lap. Tracy rubbed its back with love.

"It wasn't that long ago that you obeyed me." Tracy grinned. "You used to like me being in control."

"I know," Samantha smirked. "I used to think that I'd always be your sex slave."

Tracy took the mug of coffee Samantha offered and put it on the small side table. She wagged a finger at Samantha.

"You hush now." She blushed a little at fleeting memories. "You were the nearest thing to a wife I was ever going to have. You were a great joy to me, Samantha. I'm going to miss you. Have you got someone special in your life at the moment?"

"Well, there is someone." Samantha launched into a spiel relating to recent love interests. Tracy listened to her rapid chatter and watched, with amusement, how she could still manage to drink coffee, start on a piece of the cake, and talk seemingly at the same time.

What a wonderful thing it had been to watch Samantha grow from a shy nineteen year old to a young, confident woman. She was headed into adulthood now, but she still hadn't forsaken the enthusiasm and coyness that had always been part of her personality. Tracy hoped that it would always stay with her.

"I had to make sure I called in today," Samantha added after telling her all about the new flat that she was moving into. "There'll be little time for the next few months. You know what the new year is like. Always a muddle."

"It's good of you to visit." Tracy smiled. "It's always good to rekindle the memories. Why don't you have some more coffee."

"No, thanks. I've been trying to scale down my intake lately. I reckon I'll be drinking plenty in the next few months."

Tracy suppressed a small laugh.

"I'm sure you'll be having plenty of lunchtime

coffee dates, Samantha. No need to worry about that."

Samantha flushed a little. She had forgotten just how she and Tracy had first met outside the university campus. First a coffee, then supper at the house… then. Samantha flushed again, feeling a familiar warm glow of lust tingle between her legs.

"Well, I'm not sure about that," she protested in jest.

"Yeah, right," Tracy smirked hastily.

"Anyhow, there is something I would like to do for you," Samantha told her solemnly.

"Is there?"

"Would you keep an eye on the dog while I go sort it?" It's a fun surprise, you see. It's in the garden summerhouse. I want to make it ready before you take a look."

"In the summerhouse?" Tracy frowned. "A fun surprise?"

"It's brightening up outside so I'll dash out for a moment." Samantha stood up.

"Yes, of course. A fun surprise! You are a mystery. Can't imagine what you're up to."

Before she had finished her last remark, Samantha was out in the hallway and retrieving the large pack she had arrived with.

"Just stay there, Mistress!" she laughingly called.

Whatever was she up to, Tracy wondered. What had she brought in that pack? And why was she suddenly calling her Mistress, a name not used in quite a while? She felt suddenly nervous.

The boxer suddenly turned over in her lap and barked softly.

"She'll be back in a moment," Tracy told him. "Then we'll go out to the summerhouse and see what she's been up to."

Tracy thought back to the times spent in the sunshine of the summerhouse with Samantha and the way things had felt so relaxed and sensual between them. A lot of naughty afternoons had been spent in that summerhouse.

It was the type of raunchy memories that would remain with her always, as dear to her as the memory of being introduced to swinging by a late husband. It had been a few years after his untimely death that Tracy had decided to explore her Bi-side. That had been when Samantha had entered her life, in more ways than one.

She rubbed the young pup behind his ears.

"Your mummy is a woman full of surprise," she told him.

Samantha's voice called suddenly from the hallway.

"Come outside and see what I've arranged!"

The dog was off Tracy's lap and barrelling down the passageway and out into the back garden. Tracy heard his little feet scamper on the kitchen tiles as she got up to follow him out to the back garden.

Samantha was standing on the path.

"I know that you miss having a lover, but not a swinger or someone from the internet -"

"I'd love either one of those," Tracy protested, "But they don't suit -"

"I know... I know," Samantha interrupted. "But I think this will."

Damn... Tracy thought. Surely she hadn't set her up on some kind of weird blind date!

She stood on the pathway that curved across her small lawn to the summerhouse. The lawn was peppered with old benches and seats. Tracy, to her relief, saw no one in sight.

Samantha noted her eyes searching in bewilderment.

"Look in the summerhouse," she said, pointing at the end of the garden.

Tracy walked down the path, with Samantha eagerly following. She stepped around Tracy and put a hand lightly on the door.

"You said you always liked having younger lovers, and I think this will bring even more fun into your life."

Samantha slowly pushed open the door to the summerhouse. Tied by a long chain to the back wall, a young woman, no older than twenty at a guess, sat in a leather cat suit. A ball-gag and blindfold added to the costume.

"Samantha!" Tracy's voice was full of surprise and delight. "A gimp!"

"She's not as good as I was, I know, but I want to lend her to you while I'm working. Kind of like having the old times back."

"Samantha, she's wonderful. I shall so enjoy her!"

Samantha's face glowed. From behind the ball-gag, the gimp blushed.

"I hope you will. She'll need training, but you'll manage that I'm sure."

Tracy turned back to the garden, beckoning behind her with one hand and a cheeky smile. She had a stride in her step like a young child - as if everything that was happening was new and fascinating.

"Let's make the slut wait for a while."

Tracy felt a rekindling of lust. She had felt this lust all along but had buried it under the bustle of retirement and trying to grow-old-gracefully. She hadn't wanted to risk igniting the old habits. But maybe it was again, she thought. She wouldn't let this opportunity go to waste.

Samantha followed her back up the garden oath, her face lit brightly because she knew her gift had been appreciated. A bit of planning was all that was needed. Her young lover had gone around the back of the house earlier, and Samantha had the outfit and chains in her bag. All had gone smoothly.

"I won't have too much time to visit; just mainly in the term holidays. But you won't forget me, will you? Not with the gimp out there in the summerhouse."

Tracy pulled Samantha into a hug. Samantha held and kissed her.

"Samantha, I couldn't forget you even if that wonderful surprise wasn't chained out there! And as soon as you've gone, I'll get to training the slut."

"Great plan, Mistress." Samantha grinned. "Great plan."

Yamamoto's Wish

Yamamoto had wanted a robot for as long as I dare to remember. The word 'Robot' had been scribed on every Christmas list and birthday hint since he had started writing. Yohji and I had tried our hardest to dissuade him with numerous reasons why we couldn't have a robot and we secretly hoped that it was only a childhood phase that Yamamoto would grow out of.

When I picked up the crumpled birthday list from the kitchen table I knew that we had been foolish ever to have thought that. Yamamoto was just about to become a ten year old and the only thing he had decided to scribe on the piece of paper was Robot. Only this time he had sketched out a basic drawing of a robot with a sad face beside his request. I suspected this was his way of telling us that he knew his request would fall on weary parents once again.

As Yohji made supper, I sat at the kitchen table and mentally went through all the excuses we had used over the past years to try and fob-off Yamamoto and his persistent requests. It had begun with the fact that we were living, at the time, in a tenth-floor apartment and simply had no space. But we had since moved to a house on the outskirts of the city. Another reason was that we hadn't considered Yamamoto mature enough to look after the machine properly, but I knew that to no longer be the case as he owned two rabbits and a canary and had shown himself to be caring and diligent. Last year had been tough, with the loss of job for Yohji and a stressful promotion for myself, and Yamamoto had been understanding back then. Despite my reservations, I could not help but feel it may have been time for reconsideration.

After supper, as I washed the dishes, I muttered to Yohji about Yamamoto. "His birthday in two weeks," I said. "What do you think we should get him?"

Yohji put aside the book she was reading and sighed.

"Another canary? It seems sad to have the one on its own."

"I was thinking more along the lines of something he never stops asking for."

Yohji sighed again and she knew exactly what I was referring to.

"He's really matured this past year, and has become a great young man."

She twiddled the ends of her hair, as she does when she really gives something some serious thought.

"I understand what you're saying. But what happens if he loses interest after a month or so and we end up having to maintain it?"

I laughed.

"I'm not convinced that would happen. Besides, I found this in his school bag yesterday."

I gave over a tatty magazine.

Yohji flicked through a few pages and I let her study it for a moment.

"It's an old robot catalogue. I've not seen one like this for years," she laughed. "I wonder where he got it from?"

"I think he could manage, you know. And maybe it would be good for him. He's got some difficult growing-years coming up."

Yohji nodded.

"I've noticed him becoming quieter. Not like

the young Yamamoto."

Her weariness of motherhood lifted to a grinning smirk.

"Maybe we could get a new member of the family."

A fortnight later and I could not be sure who was more excited, Yamamoto or myself. I couldn't wait to see how he would react when we went to choose his present. I could see mixed emotions on Yohji's face. She was still a little weary on the addition to the Maki family.

Yamamoto looked confused as parked outside a row of local warehouses. I could see his mind trying to work out why we had driven to the industrial sector of the city, and having told him we were having a birthday surprise.

"Just wait, sweetheart," Yohji said encouragingly.

Yamamoto looked on as I gave him a new robot catalogue that I picked up a few days earlier. His eyes grew wide as he flicked through the pages and the realisation slowly drew in his mind.

"Really?" he asked.

Yohji grinned as I nodded.

"What are we getting?" Yamamoto shouted, practically bounced up and down in his seat.

Yohji smiled.

"Well, that's up to you. You don't think we would pick out a robot without you, do you?"

Yamamoto threw his arms around my shoulders from the back seat.

"Thanks, dad, thank you… thank you."

"Well just wait till Grandpa gets here. Then

we'll go find you a robot!"

Yamamoto grinned.

"Grandpa is coming?" he beams with a genuine joy.

"Yes, of course. He wouldn't miss joining us!" I smiled reassuringly at him.

His grandpa has been downbeat lately, and I knew that Yamamoto has been worried about him. It had been difficult to explain to him that grandpa was still in mourning following the death of Yohji's mother six months earlier. It was taking everyone some time to adjust. Grandpa himself was in a sort of a malaise; not a dark place exactly, but in a kind of lacklustre area that we hoped Yamamoto might help shift him from.

I looked over at Yohji and smiled.

"You think this is okay?" I asked with a sly smile.

Yohji realised she'd sighed.

"I hope so." She gave me a peck on the cheek. "Just remember, no big robots. We want a nice small, manageable size." Yohji notions to her knee and gives me a marker.

The old warehouse was crammed with aisles and aisles of second-hand robots, a sad reflection of a throw-away society. Yamamoto strolled from aisle and aisle, studying each robot carefully. His eyes sparkled with enthusiasm. He grinned, for to him, the warehouse was a treasure chest of excitement and possibilities.

Finally, after an hour, we got to the last aisle.

"One man's junk is another man's..." started

Yohji.

"…Junk," I muttered with a smirk.

Yamamoto shot me a look. Yohji scoffed and turned away to suppress a laugh.

"Well?" I asked Yamamoto.

"I'll find one… just give me some time."

Yamamoto put his hand to his brow and looked the very image of his beloved grandma when trying to make an important decision. Grandpa gave a wry smile when I caught his eye. Yohji, too.

We watched as Yamamoto turned his attention to a stack of parts that are mingled with circuit boards and robotic limbs of varying sizes.

He poked and rummaged at everything with his hands, pulling at parts and studying it with intensity, as if it is the most wondrous thing on earth - which it is.

Yohji looked at me, her expression uncertain. Will this take long?

Without saying a word Yamamoto made his way back down one of the aisles. He paused in front of one of the shelves that housed the biggest robot I had ever seen. I felt the anxiety emitted from Yohji. The robot that Yamamoto studied by no means fitted her criteria of a 'manageable' size.

Yamamoto turned and waved over his grandpa. He joined him by his side.

"So much for my advice," Yohji muttered to me.

I gave a weary shrug.

"Don't you think it's a little large for you?" I suggested.

Yamamoto turned and looked at me like I was being a dunce.

"I kinda like it," he said. "It's perfect to fix up."

I tried not to sigh. I had wanted him to take responsibility and make his own decisions, but I was worried my empowerment had backfired. I was not sure that we had room for a robot that could be mistaken for a towering giant! Only then did I realise that Yamamoto had his eyes fixed on the next shelf.

The shopkeeper hobbled along the aisle.

"Oh, I don't think you want that robot," he said in a voice that was slightly condescending. Fortunately, Yamamoto had been raised to be polite, so he gave his best smile.

"Actually, I think I do."

Yohji rolled her eyes, and I knew that we were thinking the same thing. Shoved into a corner and boxed, all we could make out was a bundle of metal and electronics.

"Can I take it out and take a look?" Yamamoto asked, hopping from foot to foot.

"I'm a little cautious. I'm not sure it's suitable for a youngster. Sometimes robots are so broken that they can be dangerous," the shopkeeper said.

Yamamoto looked quizzical.

"He means you might get a cut or electrical shock from it," his grandpa said with a look of knowledge.

I sighed. I desperately wanted to give Yamamoto what he wanted this time around.

"It came in broken and in a bad shape," the shopkeeper said sadly. "It was found in an old laboratory and we've not had time to fix it up."

"I'm sure it'll be okay. It just needs someone to spend some time on it," Yamamoto said firmly and touched the robot. He straightened his shoulders and stood his ground.

He put his hand into the box and lifted up the robot's arms and his grandpa, with inquisitive eyes, reached out to gently stop the youngster.

But then he stopped. I could see that my father-in-law is studying the dishevelled machine which is starting to make low beeping noises. Yamamoto's curiosity was infectious. We all soon leaned over to take a closer look.

Yamamoto smirked and clapped his hands at hearing the old robot starting to make noises. I watched his eyes darting about like the thoughts in his head, constantly moving, never still.

"Just be careful," Yohji said with a clear warning tone.

I kept my eyes on what Yamamoto was doing.

"It's okay, Yohji. I don't think he'll do anything risky."

I tried to suppress my anxiety. I could not imagine a worse way to celebrate Yamamoto's birthday than taking a trip to the local hospital to get him patched up following a cut.

It was two weeks later and I began to see that the robot was some sort of companion machine. I watched, holding my breath, as it started to power-up following a basic clean and rewire.

"I can't wait to download some new coding for it," Yamamoto said with a glee. He beamed a smile at Yohji expectantly. Yamamoto was becoming more and more like his mother with every passing day. His smile would melt the hardest of hearts.

Yamamoto's grandpa gave his shoulder a squeeze, and then fiddled with a control panel so that the robot began to move limbs.

"You might have something here, Yamamoto."

I looked over at Yohji. She was looking on with amazement.

I almost couldn't bear to watch. I so desperately wanted this to work out, but it wasn't just for Yamamoto. It was also for the family as we came together to fix and look after this robot.

It even passed my wife's size restrictions.

Yamamoto's grandpa was smiling, as if he knew something we didn't.

Beside me, I could see a silent tear roll down Yohji's cheek.

"I can't wait till we totally rebuild it Grandpa!" Yamamoto stated.

Grandpa smiled and nodded. "I've got lots of tools we can use," he said.

"It's a perfect robot, Yamamoto. A great choice."

"I'll be careful with it, I promise," Yamamoto said. He gave his mother a smile of reassurance.

I saw his mind already working from one idea to idea, now venturing into a new prospect. Inevitably there would be ups and downs, but I hoped Grandpa would help Yamamoto smooth out any difficulties. The pair of them always seemed on the same wavelength.

With the enthusiasm from Yamamoto and Grandpa, I realised there was so much joy in the world, and lots of it in such basic, simple things that we all too often take for granted.

I felt Yohji's arm around me, and I knew that everything was going to be okay, both for us and for the newest addition to our family.

Vilborg And The Troll

Vilborg stood at the backdoor. It was early in the morning and another dreary autumn day. A few seabirds paraded across the pewter sky. Everything looked so dank, so dismal, and Vilborg felt the same dull greyness in her heart. She missed the summers. She missed the warmth, the rich colours in the nearby mountains and the beauty that radiated from the hours of basking sunshine. It all seemed such a time away now.

She sighed, and then quickly cursed herself. She had no more tears.

She stood up straight, lifted her chin and breathed deeply. She hugged herself against the chill.

"You have no right to be so sullen, Vilborg. You are really very blessed to live in such a beautiful land." Her melancholy felt quite pitiful.

She thought fondly of her summertime trips down to Reykjavik. The time spent in the capital had broken up the harsher living in the northern edges Iceland. Enjoying time around lots of other people had done her good, especially now she was alone and getting older, and she was very grateful to have her facilities still.

Living in the small coastal village, where mountains butted against buildings, was not easy though. In the summer months her guesthouse heaved with visitors, both Icelandic and foreign, but once autumn took hold the home became starkly barren. Vilborg had tried to keep herself busy by repainting the downstairs rooms and working on the porch area out front. Iceland can be such a foreboding place!

"I must remember that once the snowy mists lift in spring, the greens and yellows of the mountains will emerge, and with it the warming sunshine. It will just take time and I must learn to be patient," she muttered.

Vilborg did not know anyone in the village well enough yet to impose. Life was so different here and she felt shy, and sometimes anxious at the wildness of it all.

Back on the southern edge of Iceland, life had always been lived with others. There had always been city folk from Reykjavik and visitors for most of the year; always things going on in the community, always friendship.

Here, everyone seemed to live in their own little houses behind closed doors. Of course, the harsh weather didn't help. Vilborg thought, not for the first time, whether moving had been such a bright idea.

Vilborg chuckled as she pictured herself having garden parties and cocktails in the morning fog and rain.

It was not that it didn't get cold and wet down on the south of the island, of course it did, but at least it tended to only last a day or so each time. Here, it could be shroud in icy fog for weeks or rain for day after day. Such a wild part of Iceland.

"Just wait till the spring sunshine," locals had told her. "There will be picnics and tourists again."

Despite the supportive words she got from locals, she still woke with a knot of anxiety in her stomach.

There seemed to be a large number of families

living in the village. Vilborg enjoyed seeing the mums scampering to get their children to the school bus in the mornings. After an early breakfast, she would stand on the front porch, sitting and reading as not to appear to be nosy, and watch the village men going off to jobs in their 4x4s. Again, every day at four she would look from the living room window at the people on their way home, shivering and scurrying through the icy weather.

People always brought a smile to Vilborg's face. She loved people. Vilborg and her husband had been pillars of the community in the previous village, but since her husband's death, a change had been much needed. Sadly, the new village had not yet blessed her with many friends.

Being new though, of course, was also the problem. These relationships take time to develop and it is not easy to settle into a different community. She wasn't sure she even had the heart for it.

A local friend had taken her along to a village meeting where she introduced herself and explained about her ideas for the guesthouse. Everyone had been welcoming and friendly enough, but Vilborg had felt vulnerable and awkward. All through the meeting Vilborg had the melancholy of performance, as if she were imitating her past self. She was not as confident as the younger villagers about just mingling and had left early feeling anxious.

"Perhaps it is too soon, Vilborg," her friend kindly said. "Perhaps you'll be queen of the town when you feel more at home here."

"Yes, maybe." Vilborg had tried to smile. "Perhaps you are right. Give it time."

Vilborg did not know how to say to people that she was lonely right then standing next to her friend, that, like the Icelandic chill, she could feel the ache of loneliness seeping into her.

**

Vilborg sighed as she swept some old leaves from the back doorway. She looked across the garden. The young troll stood against the back shed, watching, waiting.

Vilborg's heart skipped a beat.

"Oh," she said. "Here you are again, young troll, out on such a bitter day, and I have been keeping you waiting. I am sorry."

She put her broom down and went into the side store room. She lifted up her freezer lid and pulled out a thin, long slice of whale blubber.

Coming down the back steps carefully, she called to him.

Vilborg continued to chat away soothingly in her soft, calm voice. Slowly the nervous troll drew near, shuffling in the shadow of the shed until at last, it made a little skip into the open of the backyard.

She watched on as it walked slowly, nervously, her heart thumping in her chest.

The old lady continued to whisper gently to her grand, young friend. All the weariness and dankness of the day seeped away. The troll understood her. Language was not an issue to him. He returned over and over again until he had had his fill of whale meat. Then off back into the mountains he would scurry.

As she turned to back into the house, Vilborg was aware of a small figure watching her.

There, peering around the side of the house, stood a young girl in dungarees. She was petite, and the hand-me-down clothes draped over her in the wrong places. She look like some kind of war-child who had stopped growing. Freckles shone on her cheeks like scattered pebbles. Vilborg guessed her to be about eight years old.

"Hello," she said with a smile. She was aware of how odd the troll encounter may have been for the youngster.

Like children do, the little girl asked the first question that popped into her mind.

"You live alone?"

"Oh, yes," answered Vilborg. "Quite alone."

The little girl looked at her with uncertainty and then ran off, without replying, back into the street.

"What a funny little miss," she said to herself. "What a fright she must have had."

The following day the troll came again for his fatty breakfast and Vilborg was once again aware of the same figure keenly watching from around the side of the house as she fed the creature.

This time when she said "Hello," a timid smile came to the little girl's face. She was intrigued by her little troll friend. Vilborg could see that.

***

The following week was blistering cold and blizzards and there was a stark chill in the air. Winter had arrived in full force, and had begun to bite. Many animals had left to hibernate, but the little troll would remain.

Although Vilborg was glad that her mountain friend with his winter coat of silvery grey would be staying, she was also concerned that he wouldn't go hungry. So much so that Vilborg had to order another whale from the local hunter, much to the hunter's bewilderment.

"Really, really? You're sure?" Rinker the hunter had asked.

"Why do you care so much?" Vilborg had replied with a slight huff. Moments later, Vilborg having apologised, Rinker did the typical Icelandic thing and averted his eyes while accepting. He didn't seem to ask Vilborg if she had any problems. She wouldn't have said yes, but it was somewhat humiliating that he didn't bother to ask.

Vilborg had left hurriedly. She had walked quickly, her shoulders folded inwards. Rinker had watched her cross the street and turn into a shadow. She had looked dejected.

As often as the troll came searching for a meal, it seemed that the little girl from down the street was here, too. She didn't run away now when she saw her. She smiled, and the girl's smile brightened her day.

One morning, as Vilborg swept the front porch, she saw the little girl was standing in her garden already. In her hand, she held a large ham. The autumn dungarees had been replaced by a heavy parka and deep blue skirt. She wore a red wool hat that the girl had pulled down over the tops of her ears.

She looked over at the girl. The young face was smiling at her. She stood waiting for Vilborg with blithe confidence, the way little girls announce their princess ambitions for life. What was Vilborg supposed to do?

Vilborg beckoned to her to go around the side of the house. Vilborg met her out back and waited in quietness on the path.

"We'll just wait." Vilborg whispered, looking down at the little girl and smiling.

The little girl nodded.

"You don't speak much, do you?"

The little girl looked up and smiled, the kind of smile that could erase every melancholy ache. They both stood in quiet synchronicity.

When the young troll emerged into the garden, they held out their offerings.

"Come on, young troll. Here is my new friend come to feed you today."

Slowly and cautiously, the troll edged nearer and nearer. He hesitated a few feet away from them. Even at his young age, he towered over them both. Vilborg continued to speak gently and reassuringly.

The little girl naturally stood close to Vilborg. "Is it safe?"

Vilborg rested a reassuring hand on the girl's shoulder.

Then it happened! The troll reached out gingerly and took the ham from the little girl. He hurriedly took a large bite before reaching out for Vilborg's whale blubber and rushing back into the safety of the shadows of the nearby shed.

The little girl turned to Vilborg, her eyes wide with wonder and joy of it.

"He came to me!" she gasped.

"Yes." Vilborg nodded. "He did."

"It's like something out of a story book," the girl whispered.

Without a prompting, the young girl added, "I'm Steinunn."

And then, quite unexpectedly, she gave Vilborg a hug and skipped back off down the side of the house. Her long blue heavy skirt shimmed in the breeze and she twirled, spinning it wider. The village suddenly seemed a little brighter.

Vilborg wiped a tear from her eye.

"Thank you, young troll," she said.

All would be well now. Vilborg had made a true friend.

The following day, as she watched the young mums scurry their children to the school bus, one little girl, turned and waved at her, a big smile on her face. All the way to the school bus she kept looking back and waving, until she was ushered onto the bus.

Vilborg turned with a smile. Perhaps it was time to rethink her attitude. After all, if she was going to share her adventures with new friends, she would need to learn to be more positive. And Steinunn would help her, she felt sure of that.

Now, just to slice up the new whale carcass she had in the freezer.

Good Fortune

The goblin was there again. "Look, I'm sorry, Goblin," Selma sighed. "It's no use just popping around on a whim. There's no way you're moving in with us. I struggle to feed the two of us, let alone having a lodger."

Selma felt a compelling mixture of compassion and fascination. She barely moved, for fear of startling the creature.

The goblin sat stolidly on the small wall outside the backdoor. A tremulous whine came from deep in its throat.

He wore a light open-necked shirt and a pair of cargo shorts. The randomness of the outfit was somehow endearing as if he was making an effort to keep up with the human world. His fury legs were sparsely sprinkled with grey hairs, his feet were in red socks and leather sandals.

"I can't keep spending time with you," Selma exasperated in irritation.

The goblin had been sitting on her back wall every day for the last fortnight when she came in from picking up Anders from playschool. It didn't grumble, plead, fuss or tease at her, or run about at her feet, or cause mischief in proper goblin fashion. It just sat and stared at her.

Today, as she popped Anders in his kitchen chair while she popped the kettle on, she looked out of the back window of her cottage.

The goblin seemed to sense her gaze and swivelled its head around, making it look like a fat cat. The yellow eyes glared at her and she knew what it wanted.

"Goblins don't use much vocal communication amongst themselves," she recalled from somewhere, "they use body language instead." The goblin outside was conducting a body language conversation with her, and she was having to force herself to ignore it.

Maybe it was somebody's much-loved pet or an escapee from an animal sanctuary. Hopefully it would go home when it got bored.

She made some supper for herself and Anders, and got ready to settle in for the evening. While Anders spooned in his supper, Selma began to read him a short story that she had been working on.

"I don't know, Anders," Selma informed her son as she cleared up. "They all said we'd never manage, but we do, don't we?"

Anders agreed with a beaming smile, thankfully unable to register the wobble in his mother's voice as she made her brave declaration.

She gave him a glass of juice and, after a final hug and kiss, laid him down him in his bed beside her own in the small cottage.

There was nothing on television worth watching and she'd managed to catch up with her writing and preparation for her book as a local author.

So now she would enjoy the rare luxury of writing, absolutely nothing involving childrearing.

"Stop being lazy!" she scolded herself, half an hour later, as she fussed around the cottage trying to keep things clean and tidy.

It was no use, she couldn't settle to a steady rhythm, no matter how eager she felt to finish her book. There was a heavy sense of having to keep going, never being able to settle. Then her phone rang.

"Hello, Sis." Selma held the phone at arm's

length and frowned, preparing to listen in resigned silence as her older sister launched into her usual diatribe of Selma's struggles and their mother's thoughts on the subject.

"So I told mom, 'Selma will manage just fine,' I said."

"Wait?" Selma could hardly believe her ears. Had her sister actually said something positive about her? Had she stood up for her? Not mocked her failures to their mother?

Was there a genuine interest in her voice when she asked about her only nephew?

Selma put the phone down gently, feeling a warm, friendly glow suddenly towards her sister, whom five years older had spent most of their upbringing sprouting sarcasm and mockery.

If her sister was coming round, then perhaps Mom would, too. It had been hard on them, Selma knew only too well, having their youngest daughter leave the home town to live alone in the north of Norway. Irresponsibility in love had caused scorn, and so Selma had practically fled, though she had always stated it was to focus on her writing away from distractions.

She wanted to be Selma, their successful daughter, the happy sister, the family pride and joy, their glittering achievement.

Selma managed, during the daytime, to put a brave face, to manage, but at home, alone, when Anders was sleeping, she sometimes felt the weight of melancholy looming.

And now, maybe, just maybe, it looked as though her sister was rallying to her cause, and maybe, just maybe, her family would welcome Selma back into the fold.

Her warm glow of optimism made her want to embrace a new sense of hope. She needed some

fresh air. She went and stood out by the back
door. A cold, brisk wind was blowing down from
the hills.

In the murky gloom of the evening she saw a
movement by the side of the shed.

The goblin was still there.

"Of, for fuck sake," she sighed. She stepped out
into the night and confronted the persistent
creature.

"I can't really be managing any more things in
my life, but if you promise to behave yourself
and do not get too comfy, I suppose you can
come in."

She had actually succeeded in taking the goblin
off guard. It stood upright in the breeze and
stared at Selma, eyes narrowed, looking for the
catch.

Ok, no catch.

It stretched, shook its arms and legs and
skipped nimbly over from the shed, watching
Selma all the time as it strolled casually across
the backyard and up to the door. On the doorstep,
it paused and looked Selma over, took her
measure and decided that she was on the level.

The goblin came in. Selma shut the door, gently
but firmly, not wanting to frighten the creature
with too sudden a movement, but being tough
and wild, it ignored her.

Selma grabbed some old towels and rubbed the
sopping wet fur, feeling the thinness of the
creature under the ragged coat. It was hungry.
She could tell, though the goblin still disdained
the usual goblin ploys to seduce her into feeding
it; sitting there on an old chair beside her in
scruffy dignity. But Selma could tell what it
wanted.

Body language again.

"I'll reheat some vegetable stew for you," she told the goblin, pointing it towards the kitchen table.

She got little response from the goblin.

"How do feel about homemade bread?" she enquired, rummaging in her small bread basket, and not even knowing if goblins ate bread. She seemed absurdly chuckled by her inquires,"No, hang on, here's something. I got some ham chunks in the fridge. I'll add it to the stew."

Once Selma had heated the food and deposited it into a big, deep bowl, the goblin rapidly disposed of half of it in an immediately rush. Then, realising it must be making an obscene sight, slowed itself and ate in a relaxed and comfortable manner.

Keeping an eye on Selma as she made up a bed on the spare sofa, it happily took in the homely surroundings, even taking in a moment to have an idle wander about in the neighbouring lounge, before slumping in the bed that was on offer.

"Goodnight, Goblin," Selma murmured, tired herself by the unexpected evening activities. She felt a strange giddy sense of contentment, what with her sister's call and now the goblin's company...

A mumble and shuffle was all she got in reply as the goblin stirred and resettled itself.

***

Next morning Selma woke to the sound of Anders mumbling away cheerfully. He had shuffled out of his bed and gone into the lounge, and he and the goblin were communing happily.

Selma had realised, slightly guilty, that she had

overslept right though dawn. Feeling really rested for once, she went along to the lounge and sat watching the other two making friends - Anders sat on the floor with his back resting up against the sofa, while the goblin gazed on from its position on the cushions.

Then Anders squealed with delight as he spotted his mum and got up for a quick cuddle before they launched themselves on a new day.

"It's no use acting all tough!" she teased at the goblin. "I saw the way you looked at Anders; you're a tough sweetie underneath!" And she rubbed the affronted goblin on the top of its head.

By the time she got to playschool, Selma was conscious of an itch on her neck which she fought to ignore. Only tension, she told herself. But by lunchtime she had admitted to herself that it might be more than a stress rash. She felt herself itching again when she was in the library.

"What if it's fleas!" she muttered aloud.

"Huh?" She hadn't noticed that Angelina Nystrom, assistant librarian, had sat down beside her on one of the library's couches.

The town gossip said that her husband of several years had gone off with another woman a couple of months ago. Selma had felt sorry for her but had schooled herself to remain unreceptive to idle gossip.

She had only enough energy to divide between work and Anders, there wasn't room to pry into the lives of others. Today, however, she seemed buoyed and less oppressed, so today she could cope with other people.

"I hate to admit it, but my new pet might have given me fleas!" she repeated and when the lady laughed, Selma couldn't help but laugh along.

"Sorry. What a thing to say to a stranger."

Angelina shook her head and waved it off. "No issues here. I have a dog. The thing can be a damn nuisance."

"I've kind of got it saying for a short time. Think it might need a treatment and spruce."

"The sooner you do something about it, the better," Angelina advised, smiling and beaming a sparkle.

"You're so right, of course. I should." Selma was touched at her concern. "Does your dog cause lots of problems?"

A shadow fell across Angelina's face. "At the moment, yes. It's getting old."

Selma was warmly sympathetic and they chatted amicably for a few minutes before Angelina got a cold look from her supervisor that hinted at more-work-less chat.

***

Once Anders was back at home from playschool, Selma had time for a quick tidy round. Then as the evening began, she begun to wonder about Angelina. It must be hard to be the target of town gossip, and then Selma wondered whether people talked about her. A part of her didn't care, but she was only human. No one likes to be gossiped about.

"Well, Goblin," she mused, "at least you're here tonight to keep me company." The goblin dozed happily by the fireplace.

There was a gentle knocking at the front door, and when Selma went to find out who was calling, found Angelina standing there. Tucked under her arm was a plastic bag and a bottle of wine.

"Hi!" she puffed, divesting herself of her various burdens. "I guess this is kind of weird, but I found the flea powder I use on my dog and thought I'd bring it by."

"And the wine?"

Angelina laughed. "Well, I just brought the wine and was going to go home for a dvd and wine night." She waved it before Selma. "I don't mind sharing though."

Selma laughed. "Oh, no. I couldn't do that."

Angelina shrugged. "I've the time. You got company?"

Selma thought of the goblin, then laughed. "No. Just me, come on in."

"Thanks. That's nice of you. Nobody really likes drinking alone anyhow."

"Sure you don't mind drinking with someone who's flea infested?"

Angelina shook her head and smiled.

As Selma hastily went off in search of glasses, Angelina stood awkwardly in the lounge until Selma told her to stop standing and sit down some place. Angelina laughed and slumped in a chair.

"How's your dog?" Selma asked. For a moment there was no reply and when she looked over, Angelina was looking sullen.

"Getting old. I took him to the vets today. He's got arthritis," she explained. "I don't think he'll have long."

"Oh, no. I am sorry," Selma genuinely said.

The goblin sat, frozen-like, surveying the scene while they drank, sizing up this new visitor.

About an hour later the phone rang. It was Selma's sister again, sounding oddly nervous.

"I was wondering, if... whether..." she began

dithering "… if I could possibly come and visit for a day. Maybe we could go somewhere for lunch?"

Selma was slightly taken aback. She knew how hard it would have been for her sister to have called. Her sister's Aspergers made any social interaction awkward, but with their odd relationship lately adding to it, Selma took a pause.

"That… that would be nice," she gulped. "There are lots of nice places here for lunch."

Her eyes were shining with emotion as she put the phone down and smiled at Angelina. Suddenly life seemed brighter instead of bleaker; she had turned the corner, she and Anders.

Selma wondered if she could meet up with Angelina after her sister went home following their lunch. An evening drink perhaps? She'd already suggested a curry-night when she discovered Selma hardly went out. Sorting a babysitter would be easy enough.

***

The goblin didn't bother to pretend it was going to go back out into the yard, and jumped up into its makeshift bed on the spare sofa.

It snuggled down contentedly.

Selma yawned and curled up in a warm, happy ball on the other sofa. For the first time in what seemed like forever, she had a week or so of things to look forward to, a sisterly visit, a new friend…

"Thanks, Goblin," she muttered sleepily. "We'll have to start thinking of a name for you, won't we?"

***

Selma slept, and the goblin pondered. It hoped the woman would sleep well, and that good things would come her way. It was just a shame that it would not be here to see its work come to fruit.

When it was done with the daydreaming, it sat back against the sofa and hung its head. Its mind ached, and his thoughts were all jumbled. For a time there was only silence in the cottage. Even the sound of the countryside outside had faded, and it had a sense of the boundlessness of the universe, of dreams racing away into the vacuum, colonizing the void, and of itself piecing fragments of fragile lives, in this great dark universe of dying light and distant, spiralling galaxies, while it was merely a temporary positivism in nature, a torch upon the system.

It snuggled into the creases of the sofa. Exhaustion overcame planning; it curled itself into a little ball and dreamt.

In the morning it would sneak out before Selma woke, and take to the hills to venture out and find others in need.

A visit to the coast and a trip abroad afterwards seemed like a better idea than ever. Then it would go for a solitary retreat. *If* it felt like a good idea.

In the goblin's mind, it was already journeying up the road. For that night though, it stretched languidly then curled up, dreaming happy dreams.

Sailing For Sunshine

"Okay, then, Bella, we'll just grab a coffee and then we'll lock the boat and head home."

"Did you just call your troll Bella?" An American accent stopped Hafdis in her tracks.

The owner of the accent emerged from the cabin of a nearby boat, a sheet of sandpaper folded in his hand. He stood there, one foot on the prow, with a cheeky grin on his face.

This was no suave Tom Hanks debonair type; instead, Hafdis found herself face to face with a Colin Farrell lookalike with mousey brown hair, a scattering of wrinkles and an attractive smile. He had just the rough-and-ready look she always fancied in a man.

"Don't you think Bella is a terrible name for a young troll? Do you not want a strong Viking-type of a name? I'm Todd, by the way."

"Hello, Todd by the way," Hafdis replied playfully. "I'm Hafdis and this is my young troll, Bella."

"Pleased to make your acquaintance, ma'am," he drawled. "When I had a troll, I always called him Loki. Sounded the most Viking I could think of. Pretty idiotic now I guess."

Hafdis laughed.

"Here in Iceland, we are a little fed up of old Viking names."

"My wife thought the same. Always gave me hassle about it," he laughed. "Still, she was somewhat of a mean sonofabitch back in the day."

Hafdis shocked herself on two counts, firstly because she felt bitterly disappointed that Todd had mentioned a wife, and secondly because she had recognised that this stranger was bringing a warm, fuzzy feeling to her stomach. Had she been flirting, she thought.

What would Emma have to say about this outrageous behaviour?

Todd continued in his already endearing manner.

"At the risk of sounding clichéd, do you come here often? It's a grand spot to have a boat."

"Grand spot - I like it." Hafdis chuckled with that girlish giggle that frightened her. "It's not that grand, but I like it. I used to come down here to the harbour all the time, but I haven't been for ages. Too many memories…" Her voice tailed off.

Todd was no longer standing on his boat. He had deftly stepped off onto the quayside. He didn't pry into what Hafdis had meant by 'Too many memories.'

"Well, it's certainly brightened up my day that you came down here today," he replied, keeping the same light, and somewhat flirty, manner. "It's nice to have chatted with a local. I only motored in yesterday. Haven't had time to mingle in the town."

He extended his right hand to shake hers, displaying his stoic muscles and well-worked hands. A true working-man, Hafdis observed.

Hafdis' heart skipped a little as she shook his hand.

"I hope you enjoy Hafnarfjordur, Todd."

Just at that moment a truck rattled by them by the quayside. Hafdis strained to hear what Todd was saying.

"My wife… Iceland… fifteen years…"

Hafdis seized on the last part of what he had just said.

"Did you say you've been here fifteen years,

Todd? You've not lost any of your broad Irish-American accent. You sound just like Colin Farrell."

Todd laughed.

"Yeah, I get that a lot. A few folks have mentioned I look a little like him. I wish I had the talent and money.

"Also, I hear he quiet a ladies-man." he added, looking right into her eyes as though searching for a glimmer of mischief.

Hafdis felt herself blush and turned away to hide any embarrassment.

"I've not given it much thought to be honest," she flustered. Her smile, Todd noticed immediately, was self-conscious. She smiled at his comment but then turned her face slightly sideways.

Deep down she was churning away at all emotions she had not felt in some years. Was he flirting with her even though he had a wife somewhere? Was he looking for a girl in-every-port scenario?

She pulled herself together.

"Well, I should be going. It was nice to meet you, Todd. Come on, Bella!"

But Bella was no longer lingering behind her. Most unlike the shy troll. Why did she not have it on a lead?

Hafdis was annoyed with herself. How had she managed to forget about her mischievous Bella? How had she failed to notice that it was no longer lingering about them?

She began to panic and set off to look about the old fishing huts beside the quay. The old metal huts had been broken into many years before, and empty doorways and collapsed huts provided many a hiding place for a playful young troll like

Bella.

It really was most unlike Bella; it always hung by her side. It was normally nervous of people and terrified of crowds. It also got startled easily, and this really worried Hafdis. A terrified young troll was not what she wanted scampering around near the town. Hunting trolls is forbidden in Iceland: as they roam in the wild, a troublesome troll in a public place would not be so lucky.

Todd was upset, too.

"Gee... I feel kinda bad. It's my stupid fault for taking up your time," he said, following her around the old fishing huts.

Tears and worry began to wash over Hafdis' face as she panicked.

Thankfully, Todd made no rash attempts to quash the emotions or try to calm Hafdis. No platitudes like 'It'll be alright' either.

"I'm sorry, Todd. You must think I'm being daft. It's just that Bella is so special to me. I really don't want anything to happen to it. Emma gave it as a gift."

"Then we'll find it," Todd stated quietly but sternly. "Let's go look near the old part of the quay. It's quiet there. Maybe it just wanted to play away from us people. It won't have gone far. It's not stupid, even if it happens to be called Bella."

He winked at her, teasing her a little to ease the sudden tension. Hafdis couldn't control the slight smile that she replied with. Todd had a kind and concerned face that immediately put Hafdis in a positive mood. It was a stoic face.

"I'll stick to the quayside," he continued. "How far do you normally walk with it? As far as those old buildings?"

He pointed to the derelict, broken-windowed,

buildings that were once the main canning and fishing hubs at the end of the harbour.

"Yes," Hafdis replied, "It's very quiet about there. Hopefully, it'll be hiding about in the old buildings. I hope we find it soon. I really don't want to be calling the authorities."

"Me, either," agreed Todd, with a voice that resonated warmth and calmness.

Hafdis was touched that he was treating her crisis with sympathy.

"See you back here in thirty minutes. It shouldn't take much more than that," he added as he departed swiftly.

**

Thirty minutes later, a golden glaze of twilight had lit the quayside. The evening drew in early in Iceland, and it would not be long before nightfall.

"No sign of it?" Hafdis asked Todd, growing even more concerned.

"I'm sorry, Hafdis," he replied. "I had a good look about and asked a few passers-by.

"I even searched inside the old canning building, though it was a bit of a scramble because most of the walls are crumbling now. There was a lot of old machinery and rubbish about. But no Bella I'm afraid."

Hafdis sat on a mossy wall, ran her fingers through her hair and wiped away the line of sweat, then decided she would have to make some phone calls. She wasn't panicked, she was annoyed with herself for letting Bella get lost.

A young boisterous pet troll was not what they wanted running amok in Hafnarfjoydor, and certainly not towards the suburbs of Reykjavik. Although only a year old, Bella was already a 140-pound predator. Trolls aren't really looking for human intrusion, and tend to flee from people. But then trolls come in all kinds of moods.

Trolls tend to set off such a range of emotions, they run the gamut from playful wild creatures to dangerous foes that needed to be hunted. Ask anyone in Iceland where the boundaries for troll protection ought to be drawn, and you get opinions about predators, property rights, conservation laws and a creature's rightful place on the planet. Having an anxious youngster causing trouble in the suburbs would not be viewed positively though.

Damnit, he thought. Not the kind of trouble to try and contend with at the end of the day. He worried about the repercussions for the woman he had just briefly met.

Hafdis was shivering by now with the late-afternoon chill and her shoulders were trembling.

" Damn… Hafdis, you're shivering," Todd remarked. "It's gotten so cold. Let's just go back to my boat for ten minutes. I can make some hot chocolate, and we can decide what to do next."

"Won't your wife be getting back soon?" Hafdis wondered apprehensively, "I don't want to be intruding."

"There's no intrusion. It's a mug of hot chocolate for a fellow sailor. We can then think about how we're going to call the authorities.

"I know it's going to call some heartache and trouble, but it will be for the best…"

Hafdis nodded. I'm screwed, she thought. A long line of troubles came to mind, things like the police, the public backlash, and the newspaper. Getting out of this mess was going to be a long series of formalities.

Todd suddenly stopped talking and began laughing. Before Hafdis could object to the inappropriate humour, she followed Todd's out towards the old fishing huts where they had first met. Bold as brass, there was Bella. Sat up against one of the huts as if waiting for the two of them to return to the boat.

Hafdis ran up to the young troll and hugged it close to her chest.

"You bloody pest! Where have you been?" she cried with relief. "I'd better text Emma and let her know Bella is safe. I sent her a stressful message earlier."

Todd walked onto his boat and went below to put the stove on. Hafdis chained Bella to one of the railings and followed Todd. Hafdis followed Todd's invitation to sit down and sighed with part exhaustion and part relief. While Todd saw to the stove, Hafdis looked about at the cabin. It was all very minimal and tidy, and she observed that there seemed a lack of cosiness - missing a feminine touch.

She imagined homemade blankets, cozy cushions and a scattering of books perhaps. A potted plant wouldn't go amiss, either.

"I'd better be making my way soon," she said as Todd passed her a hot mug of fresh hot chocolate. "Won't your wife be surprised that you're entertaining a lady onboard? I've taken up enough of your time." The boat had an air of loneliness.

"I don't have a wife, Hafdis. She and I, well…" He looked away. "It's still a bit difficult to talk about."

The cabin fell silent and a moment of

awkwardness descended over them like a heavy cloud.

Todd offered her a piece of home-made shortbread.

"Oh, I love shortbread. They look yummy." She took the smallest piece from the tin.

"It was my wife you taught me how to bake." He avoided eye contact and looked away sullen.

The silence in the cabin was palpable as Hafdis and Todd sipped at their chocolates.

The only sound to be heard was their loud chomping on the shortbreads and the flagging of the rigging of the nearby boats. It was so peaceful and cosy on board.

"Have you had your boat for a while?" Hafdis asked brightly.

Todd shook his head. "No, not too long. About eight months. My wife and I had dreamed about sailing a boat from our home in Newfoundland to Scandinavia. She had thing for the Norway and the fjords you see."

Hafdis began to recite a poem.

"Blow you solar wind
Across the universe within
From dancing lights
In magnetic storms
To where our souls cede
And the harbour fires warmed
Those Icelandic nights
Where voyages at sea bites
Where souls are formed
On seafaring storms."

They were lines from a famous Icelandic poet.

Todd smiled and she could almost read his thoughts: What a crazy day I've had! Could life get any more bizarre?

Embarrassed by her openness to recite poetry to a man she hardly knew, she realised she was taking up way too much time.

"I'm so sorry, Todd. I've suddenly realised the time. I've used up way too much of your time. You must think I'm a weirdo."

She flushed with embarrassment. Hanging about with this stranger - talking poems and intruding into his personal life. He must think I am a nuisance.

"I'm sorry about the poem. I couldn't resist it. I tend to babble on when I get tired."

Todd smirked.

"Think nothing of it. You've certainly livened up my day."

"You said you were planning to sail to Scandinavia…" Hafdis prompted.

"Well, that was the plan. With my wife… but, well. Life had other plans."

Hafdis was polite and pretended not to notice Todd getting emotional. The tears in his eyes were gathering.

"Well, you're here now. On your well."

"Yes, but it doesn't feel the same. My wife would have loved Iceland. It's so pretty here."

Hafdis looked out at the harbour. Certainly, it was a lovely place to live. The mix of wild mountains and cosy fishing ports made Iceland a special place to live. She looked at the mix of boats in the harbour, the golden glow of dusk setting in.

"It is certainly pretty."

Her phone set out a tune, and Hafdis rustled in her coat pocket to answer it.

"That'll be Emma replying."

"No doubt she's been worried about you. Shall

I walk you back to your car?"

Hafdis took a last sip of chocolate and stepped up onto the deck. Todd followed.

A ladies voice carried out across the quayside.

"Hey, there! Is that you Hafdis! Are you okay!"

"Emma!" Hafdis threw her around the young lady that came to hug here. Hafdis was caught off guard.

"Phew, Hafdis! Your message sent me into a panic. I was worried. Are you and Bella okay?"

"Yes, yes. We're fine now. Thankfully we had some help from this gentleman." Hafdis pointed her hand towards a quiet Todd.

Emma stepped forward and shook Todd's hand.

"Thanks for helping my Hafdis. I appreciate it very much." She turned back to Hafdis, then nodded to a shivering Bella. "Let's get both of you home."

Hafdis and Emma left Todd standing on the quayside, looking somewhat forlorn and bemused.

***

The following week, as Todd was rubbing down the side gunnels, he was surprised by a visit from Hafdis.

"Ahoy, there! Anybody on board?"

Todd stood up and couldn't help but beam a smile.

"Nice surprise. Not lost your troll again?" Todd joked.

Hafdis blushed. "Ha, Ha. Very funny." She held out a small package to Todd. "It's just a little thank you for your help the other evening." She'd felt somewhat embarrassed by her previous interest in the sailor. Though she could not recall all of the stressful evening, she did feel ashamed that she'd imposed herself on the gentleman.

Todd unwrapped the parcel to find a small book of Icelandic poetry inside.

He blushed. Then followed it with a laugh.

"I was just thinking about your impromptu poetry recital from the other day."

It was Hafdis' time to blush. She stared, feeling a little unnerved, until he smiled in an open sort of way.

"It's not every day you get a beautiful Icelandic woman serenading poetry for you. Emma's a lucky lady." His yearning for her over the past days had surprised him. He felt somewhat overwhelmed by it - caught off guard. If only she knew what I'm thinking, he thought.

Hafdis suddenly looked confused, then had a fit of giggles.

"Oh god, no. You don't think... you don't think Emma and I are a couple?'

Todd looked bewildered. " Well, I saw that she was very worried about you. She came rushing down to the harbour to find you. I just thought..." He stopped, realising he had totally misread a situation.

"Sorry, I just presumed that you and Emma were a couple. Sorry."

Hafdis laughed. "It's okay. Emma is my sister. We're close... but not that close."

"But you can't be single?"

Hafdis gave a quizzical look. "Not sure how to take that?" She laughed, "But yes, I am single."

"It's been a while since I discussed such things," Todd said.

"When did your wife pass?" Hafdis asked.

There was silence for a while and Hafdis hoped she had not misjudged the moment. A little on edge, she waited.

Todd muttered something vague in response, then laughed a little.

"Oh no, she didn't pass away. My wife left me for her tennis coach. Clichéd but true.

"As you can imagine, I've not dealt with it too well. Hence my desire to sail away from it all on our boat."

"I'm sorry to hear that," Hafdis lied, but inside her warm butterflies churned and her heart was beating feverously. There was no wife on the scene, and she felt she might be in the mood for some company in her life.

What was more, she had Emma's prompting. And she was normally the cautious one. She told herself not to be so silly though.

"It takes some time to get over these life changes. But your heart will heal, Todd. Especially if you're sailing to Scandinavia." She laughed.

He pointed down into the galley. "I was going to put the stove on for a drink. I don't suppose you fancy another hot chocolate?"

"I reckon that's a great idea," Hafdis giggled, holding out her hand to let Todd help her aboard.

The hot chocolate drew them in. The boat, each others company, made them cosy. It soothed something deeper than they knew. And so they were quiet for a while.

"Wait till I tell Emma," thought Hafdis.

Robot Rumble

Charlotte closed the front door to her terraced house, went next door, then hesitated, her hand raised to press the doorbell.

Should she risk another excuse? From recent experience, she was pretty sure that Jasmine, the new tenant beside her, simply liked being on her own and wouldn't welcome being dragged out for evening drinks with the girls.

Yet she'd seemed so friendly at first. It was just since that evening at the bowling with Charlotte and her friends that she had changed.

Now, whenever they encountered each other coming in or leaving our houses, Jas barely spoke, and obviously wanted nothing of Charlotte - her company.

As Charlotte hesitated she heard the faint noise of music playing from inside. Alone just Adele albums for company on a dark, late November evening?

The next moment, before she could back away and change my mind, she was knocking on her door.

"Hi, Jas," Charlotte said brightly as it opened. And the sprightly bombshell walked out.

She was blonde - which Charlotte thought suited stunners best - with a wavy mass of golden hair spilling down to brush a very impressive curvy figure. The face boasted sparkly blue eyes with an innocence in direct contrast to the short skirt and tight white tee-shirt that she wore.

"Oh, hi, Charlotte."

She didn't look especially enthusiastic to see Charlotte standing on her step but Charlotte persevered.

"Some of the girls are meeting up at the corner pub, the one that's just had the revamp. Fancy joining us for a drink or two?"

"Ah, thanks but I can't. I'm trying to save for Christmas."

The door started to slowly close but I put my hand out and stopped it.

"Don't worry about it. We're all a little skint at this time of the year. We buy our own, so there's no pressure. Just one drink."

"But you lot all know each other, and -"

"It's only because we all went to college together," Charlotte interrupted. "Don't feel left out because of that. We're a good bunch. Well, apart from that Emma… she can be a bitch sometimes," Charlotte laughed at the unwarranted joke. "I only joke. No seriously, we're a friendly crowd.."

"Well…" she began and then it suddenly struck Charlotte that she looked a little sullen.

"Come on Jas, be a sport," Charlotte said impulsively, beaming a wide smile.

"Oh, well, all right. Thanks… But I can't stay out too late." She gave me a timid grin and cutely blushed a little. "I'll just go grab my coat."

***

Three hours later, and all a little tipsy, they had tumbled out of the pub and stood huddled in the doorway.

"Damn… it's so cold." Charlotte shivered and pulled in her coat around her against the evening bitter chill. "Could be snow, don't you think, Sam?"

Sam, the daughter of a local garden centre owner, was their expert on all things outdoors.

"Could be. Well, it's nearly the end of the year. Not long till the holidays. How's your nan doing, Charlotte?"

"She's great, thanks. She and her fella are sunning it up in Spain somewhere. Lots of sunshine apparently," she replied, then, to fill Jas in, said, "My nan found herself a toyboy with money. They've gone to winter over in the south of Spain."

"Have you heard much from the bloke... Rob?" Paige asked and Charlotte pulled a face.

Charlotte was a beautiful young woman. With a tough, athletic body, her swagger oozed confidence and sexuality. Her eyes were nut brown and lively, her mouth plump and succulent and quirked at the corners. Charlotte had an air of dominance and strength. She was feisty and strong and didn't need to hang on to anybody that didn't treat her right.

"No, I haven't. Thank goodness. Talk about inflated ego. It's no loss I can tell you."

It was too cold to hang about, so Cathy, another of the group was the first to make a move home.

"Well, I got to get off. Early start at work tomorrow. Is Friday bowling on as usual?"

Charlotte nodded automatically and was turning to Jas when she suddenly let out a groan.

"Fuck, I forgot. I'm not sure I can make this week. Sorry."

"You what! But, Charlotte, you have to come along," Janice chimed in. "You're one of our best players. The team needs you."

"Yeah, I would. But it's Black Friday this week. I really need to pick up a bargain I've had my eye on. So..."

"Black Friday… what the fuck's that?" Cathy raised her eyebrows. "My Fridays are always Gold Friday… when I get paid."

"I think Charlotte means the American shopping idea," Jas began hesitantly. "It's the week after their Thanksgiving I think. All the shops have bargains. A bit like the January sales, but before Christmas."

"Oh, yeah, that's right." Paige was nodding "It's kind of catching on over here. My boyfriend got me loads of cheap butt plugs last year." The girls that weren't stunned into silence all laughed out loud.

"Paige! You're so wrong," giggled Janice.

"Anyway," Charlotte said, "there's something in that new Silicone City shop I saw advertised online."

Silicone City was a new Adult store that had opened at the far end of the latest mall in town. It was very much in the headlines for being the largest Adult shop in the country. Three floors of naughtiness was how their tagline promoted the store.

"I really want to get a bargain, so I'm going to queue," Charlotte finished.

"You mean queue outside? In this weather?" Cathy looked bewildered. "What time are you going to get there?"

"I'm not sure." Charlotte tried a nonchalant shrug. "All night, if necessary."

"Lawdy. You must be mad. I'm sure you can pick up the bargain online."

"Not for this, I can't," Charlotte said stubbornly. "And anyway, I might always seem something else I might like."

The girls all giggled at their friend's sauciness.

"What is it you're after?" Paige asked.

"Oh, maybe you'll find out soon, "Charlotte said evasively. "But Rob may have outlived his usefulness."

"Well, good luck. Night, darling." She held Charlotte tight for a moment and gave her a smacking kiss. "Bye, girls. Cheers, Jas - nice to see you again."

Jas and Charlotte walked home together. Charlotte thought she was coming out of her shell during the evening, bemoaning the misfortunes at her workplace and sharing jokes about men and about her new hobby of trail running.

But now she was silent, almost constrained, so that having chatted openly all evening and with others, Charlotte, too, fell quiet.

It was only when they approached their houses that Jas suddenly spoke.

"I'm going to the queue for the Friday sale as well."

"Really? Great. Why didn't you say earlier?"

"I… I just didn't want to embarrass myself," Jas said.

"Maybe we can go together."

To be honest, Charlotte had not been totally sold on the idea. She loved her warm duvet too much, and the thought of standing about in cold weather didn't appeal to her that much. But she wanted her bargain.

"What are you hoping to get?"

"I want to look at their robots. Like you said, Silicone City are the best in the country, and their sex robots are pretty good."

Charlotte smiled.

"Yes, they do look pretty good don't they."

"What is it you're after?" Jas asked as she stood in front of her house.

Charlotte hesitated.

"I didn't want to say in front of the girls - especially Paige. There would only be teasing. But there is a Latino robot who comes with a big…, well you know. It looks gorgeous.

"He's about six foot, all muscles and has a tight butt. And, well, that big cock on it, so…"

"I see. You dark horse, Charlotte."

Charlotte flushed with embarrassment. Jas just giggled. She took out her keys, then over her shoulder said coolly, "About five on Friday morning, do you think?"

"Absolutely. I'll bring some coffee and some folding chairs.

"Five on Friday it is then."

Charlotte was intrigued by her newest neighbour. There was something intimate and vulnerable about the woman. Charlotte isn't sure how to take these emotions.

There was an odd silence between them so complete Charlotte thought she could hear Jas' heart beating. She wondered if her neighbour guessed how she felt. Charlotte felt a twinge in her groin.

Charlotte's heart was going to jumble - she could feel it - then she met Jas' gaze. Her lips curved, just a little, and her eyes stayed on hers as she went to open her door.

"Sounds great."

"And we'll keep our shopping ideas to ourselves, yeah," Jas added

"Of course." Charlotte was already walking up to her front door. "Goodnight, then."

"Goodnight, Charlotte," Jas replied and, feeling strangely uplifted, went into her house with a slight smile on her face.

***

The alarm on Charlotte's phone was ringing as they met outside their houses at just before five in the morning. They shuffled their weary selves down the street and towards the mall.

Outside the Silicone City store, there were already a couple of people who announced that they were after some discounted bondage gear, and an elderly man balanced precariously on a weathered picnic chair.

"Well, I guess we should hunker down," Charlotte muttered to Jas, who was still in that sullen mood. In fact, she'd barely spoken. Charlotte got out her scarf and hat set and sunk into her folding chair, feeling somewhat despondent. All her fizz and excitement for the shopping had withered.

Jas obviously wanted to be somewhere else, and where were the jostling crowds, the vendors, the jovial mood. Maybe Cathy had been right - everyone would be buying bargains online.

"Tipple?"

Charlotte realised that Jas was holding out a miniature bottle of brandy. They snuggled up close. Charlotte caught the scent of Chanel. She tried to hide a smile.

"Oh, good idea. This cold is quiet biting. And I've brought some fruit scones. I made them yesterday evening."

Charlotte dug them out from her bag. She offered one to the old man that was sat beside them.

"Thank you, Charlotte. It is Charlotte, isn't it?"

Charlotte almost chocked on her mouthful of scone.

"Yes, but -"

"Mr Sandford. Doctor Sandford."

"Of course, wow." Charlotte turned to Jas. "Mr Sandford was our family doctor when I was growing up. Good heavens - how weird to see you here after all these years."

"Would you like some coffee, or a little tipple?" Jas asked politely. "Might keep away the chills."

"Well, perhaps a top up in my hot chocolate might be nice - it is rather cold out here after all." He gave a cheeky grin. Jas reached over and poured a little of the brandy into his flask cup.

"It's such a surprise to see you out here, after all this time," Charlotte repeated.

He'd been older than most of the adults in her life when growing up. In fact, he had retried by the age she had reached her teenage years. But Charlotte had never forgotten how well he had looked after her family through their various ailments.

The hours passed surprisingly quickly, and in any case, Charlotte was so numb with cold that she couldn't think of much. Jas, though she still didn't have much to say to Charlotte, was lively enough with Mr Sandford - or Doctor Sandford, as she'd called him through her childhood - and they discovered a mutual interest in books.

Jas was engrossed as he told her about his interest in writing his memoirs and his wish to get to the bookstore to pick up some How-To-Write-A-Bestseller books.

"I'm not here just for the bookstore though… there are lots of interesting shops in the Mall," he stated.

Jas and Charlotte gave a cheeky glance to each other. Neither were going to tell the old guy why they were here. Jas couldn't help but let out a childish giggle.

Charlotte was bewitched. She began to feel the strong warmth of attraction welling up inside her. She found this very interesting. They sat close in the dim light and watched the crowd slowly grow.

It was not long before the scene looked like the beginning of a football game. A couple of families staked out with their entire camping set, sun-lounges and gas stove included, a group of college guys who looked like they were all nursing hangovers and a couple dressed in matching sports attire, preparing themselves for the rush with an, almost military, plan of action.

As night turned to dawn, gradually more and more people started to arrive so that as opening time approached Charlotte folded up her chair and worked out her strategy.

They'd surely let them in the Mall in order of queuing, so it would be two to the bondage department, Mr Sandford to the bookstore - and Charlotte and Jas to Silicone City. The other stragglers would fight it out amongst themselves in the surge of limbs.

The magic moment came at 08.00.

Two Mall assistants, flanked by two security fellas, appeared on the other side of the glass doors, turned the keys and let the doors slide open, then fled. So much for an orderly start.

A cheer rang out from the crowd, feet were stamped, limbs were shaken and everybody surged forward.

And as Mr Sandford stood up, someone bundled into his right shoulder and pushed him, sending him sprawling headlong.

Jas managed to grab Charlotte and stop her from tripping over the old man as the crowd pressed in from behind them.

"Are you okay?" Charlotte asked Mr Sandford. He struggled to get clear of the rabble, and sat himself up, nursing his left hip.

"So stupid," Mr Sandford said faintly. "You two get on. I'll be okay in a moment."

Just for a moment, visions of a Latino sex robot drifted across Charlotte's mind, then she pushed Jas onwards.

"You go and grab your bargain toy. I'll stay here a moment with Dr Sandford." He had after all been there for all her ailments. Now it was time for her to care for him.

"But your robot," Jas whispered.

Charlotte shrugged wearily. Maybe today was going to be another disappointment to add to the growing list in her life.

"He's probably been snatched up by some gay pervert by now." Then, as Jas still lingered. "Go! Honest, I'll be okay here."

Charlotte put her hand reassuringly on Dr Sandford's shoulder, which seemed quite bony and frail, and she felt a surge of worry seep through her.

"I'll just go and get some help."

But then she heard the reassuring voice of a security guard. "It's okay, miss. Let us give you a hand."

***

Charlotte was sipping at a cup of water outside the Mall Management office when she detected someone rushing up to her.

"Fuck, where have you been? I looked everywhere, then one of the security staff told me you were sat here."

"They just took Dr Sandford to get checked out at the hospital. I was just getting some water," Charlotte answered.

"How is he?"

Charlotte looked up from where she was sat. "They said he'll be okay. Maybe a fractured hip."

"Well, that sucks. At least it was nothing serious." Jas sat down on a chair next to Charlotte.

"Yeah, I'm sure he'll be fine. Did you get your bargain?"

Jas shook her head. "I wanted the Swedish Viking Man robot, but it had gone by the time I got there."

"So I guess our trip to the Mall was a waste of time." Charlotte pulled a grump face and looked away.

"Well, not quite."

"Oh?"

"Look, I know you wanted to perve for yourself, but I took a liberty."

Maybe Jas was making the effort to be friends after all.

Charlotte turned around and looked at Jas who was holding out a receipt. Charlotte took it from her and read it. Her voice tailed away as she read the piece of paper.

"You brought it?"

Jas laughed. "Yes. I went straight there and got it."

"And that's why you haven't got yours?"

Jas shrugged.

"Well, there's always next time."

"Oh, Jas." Charlotte lifted her arms to hug her. "I'm so grateful," she added. "Can't wait to spend the winter with him." She laughed, but saw a faint of sadness flash across Jas' face.

Charlotte read the receipt once again, then looked at Jas. "Oh, it'll be so much fun. I'm so grateful, Jas. I -"

Jas was going to mutter something, but she never finished the sentence. Charlotte had taken her by both hands to pull Jas into her arms and was kissing her. And what was more, Jas was kissing her.

"When did you know I fancied you?" Jas muttered.

Charlotte looked guilty. "Not till just now. I've been such a dunce."

She looks at Jas with a mix of astonishment and lust. Charlotte was not expecting this vulnerability and rush that made her feel as her mind was adrift in a thick mist.

Charlotte would be hard pressed to say what made her swallow up Jas in her embrace. It just seemed as if lust had enveloped them both.

Jas' lips were warm, and there was a strange powerful thrill in feeling them warm against hers. The full-throttle surge of the kiss jolted Charlotte's erotic system into drive, churned in her belly, punched through her veins. Charlotte wanted that strong, curvy body, the shape of it, the taste and scent of it.

"What about the robot?" laughed Jas, as she eased away from Charlotte for a moment.

Charlotte paused for a moment. "Maybe we could share him?"

Jas blushed and giggled.

This girl could snog, thought Charlotte, and she wanted to hold onto the dizzy sensation of having her own lips, her tongue, ravish hers.

"Is he as big as the advert boasts?" Charlotte

asked.

Jas laughed out loud. "Oh, yes."

"There must be something wrong with us," Charlotte joked.

"Yeah," whispered Jas, "probably."

Charlotte had been trying to maintain a cautious distance toward Jas. But her imagination skipped a beat when it came to her new friend, her fantasies; her longing grew every time they had met.

Charlotte drew Jas nearer and laughed out loud too. And Charlotte knew that Jas was going to be trouble.

The Quarry

Of course they threw stones at it. What else would three ten-year-old boys do with a freshly discovered robot? Later, when the fascination had faded, they would have probably have gone home to tell their parents about the machine, but at present, at that first moment of discovery, they had a new toy and it had to be carefully examined before it would be taken away.

Their parents would probably call the police, too. Certainly that was what they had agreed would happen, but for now they were just happy to prod and poke their new toy. Then all of the rules drastically changed when the robot moved.

"Fucking, shitballs!" Mark's voice wavered as the robot beeped and turned its head in the afternoon sunshine. The others were all so shocked that nobody questioned Mark's choice of cuss words.

Every last one of them took one step back when they heard the noise. They were all watching when the arms began to lift and the head slowly turned. Their adrenaline was kicking in at the thought of how close they were to this thing.

The lankiest of the three scuffled back so quick that he stumbled over his own feet and fell onto the rough gravel. It took a moment for the joke to register, but then smiles and sniggers rolled round the group and his humiliation was complete. To his credit though, he took it and managed a cheeky grin and a shrug. He hid his embarrassment manfully.

One of the boys wasn't sure if what they were doing was a good idea, but there was the thrill, that warming shiver that danced up and down the spine as he thought of all the things they could learn about life if they just mucked about a bit.

The quarry wasn't a place they ought to be anyhow, but caution was made for grown-ups. Kids tend to leave caution in the dust.

"What are we gonna do with it, lads?" Mark again. He had to ask. They couldn't just leave a cool robot lying about on the ground. They needed someplace where older kids wouldn't ruin their new plaything.

Mark glanced nervously about, checking to see if there were any grown-ups around. At that moment, he couldn't decide if the lack of them made him happy or nervous as hell. None of them were supposed to go playing at the quarry, but that had never stopped anyone before. The big bonus was that their parents were out at work and so couldn't check on them much.

And still, what could happen to them in this quiet corner of Cornwall?

-

The two men looked remarkably alike, big-square-faced over-the-hill officials in cheap off-the-peg suits with middle-aged men guts hanging over their leather belts.

They had just driven through Heartsdean village and had briefly parked in the main square so that they could receive their latest instructions. Two charity shops angling for local trade; an outdoor café with weathered table, empty in the later afternoon sunshine; a hardware store; a post office that doubled as a newsagent. A normal, anonymous Cornish village.

Tom had parked up to use the public bathroom. Travis went in search of some coffees. They passed by locals - everybody smiling and nodding hellos, all unaware of the tragedy about to occur in their quiet corner of life.

Picking up two coffees to go from the café, they had listened to their new mission and set away, leaving the village in their rear-view mirror. Feeling a little adrenaline, they headed further west, then north into the hills of Cornwall. They stopped at a wayside track, where a disused mining road started off into the woods.

They took their time walking over from the parked car, looking at the quarry pits from the high ridgeline.

They had an unusual protocol to follow, designed by Military Intelligence years ago, in case the feared network was in danger of exposure. Nobody liked killing civilians, but their primary concern was in cleaning their own mess.

Travis watched as the robot tried to sit up, then as one of the boys jabbed a stick into its chest plate and pushed as hard he could. Travis shook his head. You do stupid things and you end up paying a price, he thought. That was one of the simple rules that dictated life.

Tom watched the young boys through the scope. "My God, my God. We're gonna do this?" Sweat broke out on his neck. He felt slightly nervous; he couldn't hold his colleague's gaze. His body and mind were leaden with a weight he could hardly bear.

He couldn't voice his unease of course. Travis had a temper, and Tom didn't want him moody for the journey back to base.

Travis shrugged; he didn't care. He carried himself with an impatient air. His phone rang on his pocket; he excused himself with a quick wave of his hand, received some more instructions, and rejoined the quick survey of the situation.

He stood beside Tom and rested his hand on his colleague's shoulder. Leaning in, he whispered their orders.

Travis then looked up into the sky, and instinctively, Tom did also. Both men could picture in their minds the military Predator drone that was circulating at 50,000ft and watching their every move. Tom wondered how many agents were stood about in the control office and observing.

Tom took a couple of deep breaths to calm himself. The feelings of the next thirty seconds pitched him back to when he was just starting. His stomach lurched a little and he lost his colour from his face to his feet. Or it felt as if he had. He covered this frowning by looking down the scope.

Travis cleared his throat. "Taser first." Then he nodded to the lake. " Then we will drag the bodies into the water. The boss wants to make it look like they drowned. Avoid any obvious foul play. We'll make it look like a local tragedy." He took a stick of gum out of his pocket and started chewing.

Ronnie Goes AWOL

Rinko gathered up the last of her CDs from the shelves and dumped them in the cardboard box. At least Simon hadn't taken any of hers, as far as she could see, and he'd even left his books of Singapore they'd spent so many evenings pouring over, choosing their dream trip away.

"Oh, Ronnie, I'm so miserable," she said to her companion, who was gazing at her with those cute robotic eyes she loved.

Her own eyes filled with tears but she wiped them away.

She wouldn't shed anymore for him, she thought, and began stacking her books into another storage box, although all she really wanted to do was lie under the duvet all day.

When all her belongings - clothes, books and clutter - were gathered, she carried them out to the van, then went back into her apartment one last time. She stood, slowly looking around at what had once been her life, tears threatening to appear again.

This had been home, where she and Simon had been happy for nearly a year. There was still a crack in the ceiling plaster where the champagne cork had ricocheted before drinking to the happy years that had not come.

And there, if she looked carefully, were the tiny imprints of their hands by the front door, symbolising their little sanctuary.

This was to be their year for getting engaged and to go travelling, with him promising her sunny skies, emerald seas and exotic sandy beaches.

But now that he had moved out - to be with

someone else - she couldn't bear to remain here. This was just an empty flat… certainly not a romantic sanctuary. Other people would soon be living here, arranging their possessions and lives to suit a new start.

Rinko stood, swinging her car keys and letting the memories sweep through her. Then she took a deep breath and turned to her companion, who was still gazing at her fixedly.

"It's just you and me from now on. I know we programmed you for this area, but you'll get used to the new neighbourhood."

She picked up the sturdy box with the robot in, walked out of the apartment and locked the door. She then put the keys in an envelope and dropped them into the supervisor's door. A new stage in her life had begun.

***

Rinko dumped her handbag on the side cabinet in the hallway.

"I'm home, Ronnie."

But the little robot did not appear, as it had done for the past few days.

Poor Ronnie had taken the move quite hard, refusing to spend any time outside the communal areas unless Rinko went, too.

Maybe he'd finally shaken off the old programming, she thought, but when she went to take a look no little white Ronnie was sunning his solar panel on the central lawn.

She opened the window.

"Ronnie. Updating time!"

Nothing.

When she looked at his laptop in the living

room she saw that he had not logged on at all during the day.

Anxiety and worry spiralled in her mind. There were more people around here, for it was a more central neighbourhood in Tokyo. Perhaps he'd been hurt on these unfamiliar roads…

She slumped into a chair and burst into tears. She couldn't handle any more heartache in her life.

***

Chen Kun came home from work in a thoroughly bad mood. Book shop owners were normally calm and placid types, but a poet on a book signing tour had put an end to the well-balanced day. What a douche that guy had been.

Still, at least he'd got through the evening bustle in good time to spend an evening in his nice new flat.

He parked his car and walked across the quiet courtyard. He was halfway up his front steps when he saw a battered little robot stood by his front door.

A pair of wide blue robotic eyes studied him, then the robot stood up as Chen approached.

"Hello, fella," Chen said, bending down to examine the strange curiosity at his door. "Damn, you've been in the wars, haven't you?"

He opened the front door and the robot followed him in. He - Chen figured little robots were a *he* - had to belong to somebody in his apartment block, most of whom he had barely met yet.

Probably that weird musician guy who always looks so sombre and focused around the corner.

He looked like the type who would live with a robot.

"You should really go find your owner," he said over his shoulder.

But as he went to close his front door, the robot seemed to find a new lease of energy, almost tripping Chen over as it waded past him into the apartment.

"Whoa… fella!" he exclaimed. "You don't live here. Come on - off you go." He wiped his forehead in exasperation. It was what he didn't need after such a lousy day.

But the robot seemed quite at home. He seemed orientated to the rooms and walked calmly towards the kitchen, resting himself down by the kitchen table. It gave a couple of low whistles and bleeps.

Chen looked on with a mix of annoyance and disbelief. The bloody robot seemed to know his way around as well as he did.

"I suppose you need recharging… or at least cleaning up."

He found his USB charger from his bag and plugged it into the wall socket just by the table. Only inches from where the robot was sat. Chen wondered…

"No, look," Chen began in a firm, I've-not-got-time-for-this-shit, voice, sitting down beside him. "You don't live."

As Chen plugged his charger into the robot, he studied him some more and saw that the bodywork was dirty and stained.

He recognised it as a HartlyV5, a humanoid robot made by a company called Hardwire Robotics. Just under 2ft tall, with a white humanoid body and red trim, it had been developed some ten years earlier to mimic human behaviour and designed for companionship and education. They had long gone out of favour, replaced by far more advanced models.

"Poor fella," he muttered, wiping some of the loose dust off the robot. The robot turned his head and looked at Chen, and for a moment, Chen had the oddest feeling that the robot was thankful. The thought made Chen chuckle. "I've spent too much time on my own."

Chen left him on charge, and went off in search of the other tenants, but no-one seemed in, so he went back to his place and prepared himself some supper.

He rather fancied a lazy evening in and it seemed as of the robot seemed to agree because, as if on cue, as Chen unplugged him, it stood up and went to sit on the floor by the sofa.

It spent the evening there, its robotic eyes fixed on Chen as he watched the latest season of Game of Thrones - trying to work out all the incestual sub-plots - on the sofa.

At bedtime, Chen gave the robot a wash down with some wipes which he had bought after nipping round to the corner mini-mart.

Finally, as Chen was getting ready for bed, he brought the charger into the bedroom and plugged the robot back on charge. Before turning out the light, Chen couldn't help but take a little peek over to the robot and smile.

***

Next morning, when Chen opened his door, he came face to face with the elderly man from the apartment above, dressed for a country walk in his heavy tweeds and big boots. He was a small wiry man in his seventies. He radiated the mixture of inner calm and absolute no-nonsense attitude.

"Hi, Mr - er -"

"Hisanori," he replied crisply, with a stern bow.

"Oh, right. Have you, er, got a robot?"

The old man smirked. "A robot! A robot? Why would I have a robot? Can't stand bloody machines. I'm a dog lover."

Chen smiled and nodded apologetically. "I'm sorry. I meant no insult. It's just, well, I've got a little white robot who seems to belong here, and I just -"

The old man spent what seemed ages thinking. "White robot? Let's have a look at him. Oh, so there you are, Ronnie," he said as the robot appeared in the hallway. "Pesky thing."

"You recognise it?"

"Course I recognise it? There's hardly hundreds of them running about are there?" he blurted. But before Chen could comment on the old man's sarcasm, the man went on. "Haven't you seen the posters?" he demanded accusingly.

"Posters?"

"Oh, for fuck's sake. Yes, posters. They're all over the neighbourhood, though I guess most people pay them no notice these days. What with gazing at phones and tablets all the bloody time. Poor Rinko, she's been frantic."

"Rinko?" Chen repeated.

"The previous tenant of your apartment. Poor woman. First, her boyfriend leaves her, then, when she moved across the city Ronnie here apparently took a dislike to the new neighbourhood and went wayward. She's been looking for him ever since."

"Well, that's great. Can you let her know?" Chen asked.

Mr Hisanori nodded. "I took note of her number from the poster. I'll give her call."

Chen frowned.

"I've got to go to my shop, so can you hang on to him till she collects him?"

The old man scoffed. He then shook his head dismissively.

"No way. I dislike robots. No, keep him locked in your place - can't you just plug him in someplace and leave him on charge," he replied. "Don't worry. Now that's he back in a familiar place he won't go off wandering."

***

The doorbell rang as Chen was sorting through a box of second-hand books. He opened the door to see a pretty, short-haired young woman carrying a large cardboard box.

"Mr Hisanori called me," she blurted out. "I think you have Ronnie."

She looked behind him into the apartment. She felt familiar pangs of regret and anxiety at seeing her old home.

"Oh, Ronnie, my sweetie!" she cried.

Chen watched as she dumped down the box and bent down to meet the robot, who was scooting along the hallway. She smothered it with kisses then burst into tears.

"It's okay. It's okay now." The book shop owner was taken aback by the open emotions and he patted her shoulder soothingly.

"Oh, I'm sorry." She raised her eyes to him. "It's just that I'd almost given up hope. I thought he'd been stolen or dumped somewhere…"

Her voice wavered.

"Look, I was just going to make some tea. Come in."

"Thank you." Rinko wiped her eyes and followed him into the lounge, still keeping Ronnie under watch.

"Oh, wow. That's great." She was staring at the Pollock print which Chen had hung the previous weekend. "A Jackson Pollock?"

"Yeah. You like it?" Chen asked.

"I love it," she said simply. "Did Mr Hisanori tell you this used to be my apartment? She smiled sadly. "My boyfriend didn't like artwork. He wanted just to hang a big TV there."

Chen raised an eyebrow.

"One of those guys who doesn't like art?"

Rinko laughed.

"Yeah. Kind of. Unlike you by the look of it." She avoided any mention of her ex, she couldn't bring herself to show her vulnerability. It was simply too embarrassing.

Chen shook his head.

"Not always. I like a DVD boxset from time to time. I find it a good way to relax." They exchanged a sympathetic glance, then he put out his hand. "I'm Chen. And you're Rinko, I think."

"Rinko Yasushi."

He smiled.

"Sit down and I'll organise the tea."

"Thank you." She sat on the sofa with Ronnie by her feet, bleeping away contentedly.

"He's been charged up, by the way," Chen said, coming back into the room and placing a tray of tea things on the side table. "Very stubborn, isn't he? I had to let him just make himself at home."

Rinko blushed.

"Yes, I know I've probably programmed him too much, but he's all I have now. And he's very clever, finding his way back here, aren't you, Ronnie?"

Chen watched her drop numerous glances down to Ronnie and he could sense the true affection between them. He felt an odd sensation shoot through him.

He cleared his throat.

"Amazing, isn't it. I remember reading a book on robotics a while ago and it had a section on AI." He took a sip of his tea and continued.

"Apparently they log all their movements, they navigate by way of programming and via online apps."

Rinko nodded thoughtfully.

"And in Ronnie's case it led him back here," she said.

"Yes, his built-in satnav was working overtime this week."

Rinko laughed, then glanced at her watch.

"Is that the time? I'm so sorry - I've taken up too much of your time." She gestured to the piles of books he had been sorting through.

"Oh, don't worry about that."

"No, we must go." Rinko finished her cup of tea and got to her feet. "Come on Ronnie."

She picked up Ronnie, who was sat happily between them. He gave a protesting bleep as she popped him into the box she had brought along with her.

On the doorstep, she bowed and put out her hand.

"Thank you, Chen. I can't tell you how thankful I am. If anything had…"

He saw swelling tears forming.

"No problem at all. He's an interesting little

guy - I'm happy you're back together."

***

  Four days later, Chen checked his email and
saw that he had a message.
  > Ronnie's gone AWOL again. Rinko.
  He replied.
  > He's just arrived. By the sofa waiting.
  Two days later he tapped away on his laptop
again.
  > Ronnie's back here again. Come for lunch,
maybe??
  > Thank you. Around 1pm?
  Later that evening Chen's email pinged again.
  > Lovely lunch. Many thanks.
  > My pleasure.

***

  A week later, Rinko was on the train homeward
when her email pinged. She scrabbled through
her bag for her phone and swiped it open.
  > Hi Rinko. Just to let you know that Ronnie is
here again. Collect him when you're free. No
hurry. I've put him on charge.

***

  When Chen opened the front door he noticed
two things.
  Firstly, although Ronnie immediately totted his
way down the hallway to her, there was none of
the usual welcoming tears and hugs. Secondly,
Rinko was carrying the robot box.

"I've just made some tea," Chen said. "Go on into the living room."

"Very kind, but I won't stay." She looked very weary. "I've come to a decision. We can't go on like this, Chen. It's been four times in two weeks. I can't expect you to keep taking him in and charging him up, then contacting me."

"It's not a problem. I don't really mind that much," he said. The thought of Rinko not on the doorstep seemed suddenly miserable to contemplate.

"I know, you're very kind. But it's not fair to you - or to it." She looked down solemnly at the robot. "It obviously can't manage being in a different neighbourhood, and sooner or later, if it keeps trying to return here something terrible will happen, and I'd hate that to happen. That's if you're prepared to have it, of course." She bowed and made to leave. "I should go."

"No, Rinko." He ran his hand through his hair. "At least stay and have some tea."

"All right," she said reluctantly.

As soon as she sat on the sofa Ronnie walked over and sat at her feet.

Chen fetched the tea from the kitchen and sat gazing at her earnestly.

"Rinko..." He paused, seeming to gather his thoughts. "There are two things I want to say. First of all, this robot obviously may need a reprogram, but seems to find security from being in familiar surroundings. Maybe it's a security need."

"You mean it still thinks of this apartment as home?"

"Possibly. After all, it's all that Ronnie has known. But that doesn't mean it still doesn't see you as its owner. I mean, just look at it."

Ronnie was nudged up against Rinko's leg.

"So you know what an ideal solution would be," Chen continued. "You both should stay in this neighbourhood."

"But -"

Chen raised a hand to stop her and went on.

"And maybe Mr Hisanori could help us out with that. I was talking to him yesterday and he's thinking of going to like in Kyoto with his son."

"Really?" She stared at him.

Chen grinned.

"It might offer a solution. Mr Hisanori doesn't want to sell his apartment, but is weary about who he lets it to."

"Goodness." Rinko struggled to get her mind around all that was being said.

"I mentioned that maybe you'd be interested in moving back this way," he explained. "I hope I didn't speak out of line. I don't mean to be presumptuous."

Rinko smiled.

"He's already had some interest," Chen added. "But none of them matched his high standards. He's worried about who to let to."

"No." She smiled, recalling Mr Hisanori and his stoic manner. "I can imagine."

"If you were the tenant, there would be no more problems for poor Ronnie here."

"Well, it sounds a great idea," Rinko went on slowly. "But I'm not sure I can deal with the hassle of moving again quite so soon."

"Well," he began, "you won't have to do it alone this time around. We could meet the little difficulties together?"

They both smiled and without knowing quite how it happened Chen was sitting beside her on the sofa.

Then he did something he'd wanted to do ever since she'd first arrived on his doorstep. He reached out and held her delicate hands in his.

Krampus and the Grandmother

Jenna frowned as she looked over to her grandmother, Mary, who was sitting listlessly at the table in the kitchen. She looked a shadow of her former self. She was not very old - barely into her sixties - but she looked, and acted, much older.

How long had it been now since she's moved into her retirement bungalow? No matter how much time Jenna tried to spend with her grandmother, she always seemed to look sullen and downbeat. Her grandmother didn't even go into the village much these days. Jenna felt something tear inside her, like a weakness in a wall.

There was little merit in examining the realities of Mary's existence: her life in the bungalow was lonely in the extreme, and her reclusive habits made her more vulnerable still. Jenna imagined that she had been popular when she was younger. There was little of that motivation left now, but there was still an inner strength that lingered behind her eyes.

Jenna saw Mary's gaze stray to the picture on the kitchen wall. Grandmother's Scotty dog stared out wistfully from it, as if he missed the old days as much as they did.

"So shall I go and fetch it in for a visit, then?" Jenna asked. "I'm trying to ease its anxiety by leaving it alone for gradually longer spells of time in the back of my van."

Mary blinked at her "Sorry, dear?"

"Grumpy."

"Is that really it's name?"

Jenna nodded and laughed. "It suited its character. I'll fetch it in before it starts fidgeting and gnawing at the van seats."

Grumpy was Jenna's pet Krampus, a young two horned anthropomorphic creature with mats of grey hair and blood-shot eyes. This half-goat, half-demon hadn't left her side for weeks since she picked it up from the animal shelter.

Mary shifted awkwardly at the table.

"It doesn't bite, Grandmother," Jenna said. "Well, it can sometimes - but only at my furniture and at the neighbour's cats."

Grumpy did a little shuffle around the kitchen, its tail flicking against the cupboards. It decided to sniff at Mary's slippers.

"Lawdy, it's a scamp," she said, peering at it. "What's the matter with it's limp?"

"It had a bone condition," Jenna explained. "It's clearing up. It's just a bit awkward at times."

Grumpy paused and shivered suddenly as if a blast of icy wind had caught it by surprise. Jenna stood furiously waiting. Waiting for her grandmother to at least feel some kind of interest towards it. Waiting for her to engage with something.

"It looks cold. The poor creature needs a coat," Mary stated matter-of-factly. "I could knit it one."

She frowned, likely thinking of her old Scotty dog that had died two years earlier. The portrait hung pride-of-place on the kitchen wall. The dog was looking out, beaming a happy expressing and wearing a bright red woollen coat. In the picture, he looked proud-as-punch.

"Yes, maybe I could find the old knitting patterns I saved," she mused. "I'll knit it a nice blue coat. It probably won't take me too long."

Hopeful, Jenna thought, as Grumpy pulled away the bottoms of the curtains and pushed aside the bin. *Only that won't get you leaving the bungalow or meeting other people, will it Grandmother?*

"It's family looked like it had abandoned Grumpy, for whatever reasons." That was what Carl, the local forest ranger, had told Jenna. "Local teenagers had started to pester it," he'd added, his eyes flashing in frustration.

***

At her grandmother's bungalow the next week, Jenna rubbed her eyebrow in anxiety.

The coat her grandmother had knitted for her mischievous young visitor with great eagerness was thick, soft and dark blue. It slipped over Grumpy's head, even over the horns, fairly easily. Mary fastened the little leather strap around it's middle and buttoned it up. It stood on an old wooden stool next to her, eyes wide bright, looking as happy as the Scotty dog had.

"Well now," Mary said with glee. "Don't you look fabulous?"

Grumpy posed for another moment or two. Then it started to fidget, then to growl. Then it went off like a stray firework, flinging himself around Mary's kitchen and ripping at the coat. It was only a matter of minutes before it had finally torn the coat off in shards and left pieces behind like a discarded skin.

Carl's voice echoed in Jenna's head.

"Well, for a start a hippie couple tried to domesticate it and finally had to get rid of it because they couldn't get it to wear clothes. It didn't even want to wear a collar and rain jacket. They thought he was too much trouble."

"Oh," Mary said. "Maybe he'll calm down in a few more weeks…" She muttered, looking sheepish as she picked up shards of wool from around her grandmother's kitchen.

It was a bit of a disappointment, as her Scotty dog had loved her knitted tops.

"It's just a bit… a bit of a scamp," Jenna excused before sighing at her half-demon, half-goat pet.

Really, you had to act the demon half, didn't you? Couldn't you just behave in front of grandmother?

"I'll maybe try again," Mary said. "Maybe it was the type of wool. Too scratchy perhaps?"

Jenna sighed. "Honestly, grandmother, you don't have to. I'm not too sure it'll wear…"

"No… no," Mary interrupted. "I'll try knitting it in cashmere. Maybe something softer will suit it." She started flicking through her large dustbin liner of wool samples. "It needs something more comfortable. Something less scratchy."

Jenna looked over at Grumpy. It stood at the kitchen door growling. Jenna looked out the window. Out in the street, a couple of local children were passing. George and Dave were two six year old tearaways. Always causing trouble around the village. Grumpy had obviously picked up their vibe. Jenna gave a sour frown and hoped that Grumpy would behave.

"Its last owner was an elderly gentleman. A farmer on the edge of the forest. The poor creature was left alone for half days at a time," Carl had explained at the shelter. "It used to get out and go running about the woodlands. Of course, it would end up chasing the local children out walking dogs or playing in the woods. Thankfully it never found a naughty one… or god knows what would have happened. Being left alone made it bored. No wonder its boredom turned to anxiety."

∗∗∗

Grandmother's next coat was a bright red cashmere jumper. It would have shocked the most outrageous of pet owners. It was fabulously soft, but it had been made out of left over wool that some craft shop clearly couldn't sell. It made Santa's outfit look mellow and subdued.

During their next visit, Grumpy, wearing it's Here-I-Am jumper, sat sullenly in a corner of the lounge.

"I think the colour might be a tad too much," Mary said. "I'm only trying to make you appear appealing and fun, sweetheart," she told Grumpy.

Really, grandmother, Jenna wondered in her mind, as it sat bumping its head against the wall. Occasionally it would look down at the jumper, and then at Mary.

Please act like you think it's okay. Please. Look at grandmother, Grumpy. She needs to feel useful and wanted.

Grumpy kept sitting in the corner, with a sullen expression. She half expected it to get up and throttle grandmother.

Instead, it got up and went to stand by the front door, hinting that perhaps it was time to leave this madhouse.

"I knew it wasn't the jumper," Mary quipped. "The colour would be too much for a clown, let alone a half-demon creature."

"Grandmother, it's a Krampus," Jenna said. "It

doesn't get up in the morning and start thinking about the daily dress code."

"Maybe the wool isn't the way to go," Mary replied as if she hadn't heard a word Her mind already working at double-speed. "I wonder what it would think to a canvas-style jacket? Like the kind that dogs have."

***

"A Krampus isn't like a dog," Carl from the animal shelter had said. "They are naturally solitary creatures. They know their place is in the solitudes of the wild. Normally they would have guidance from elders. Poor Grumpy though didn't have this, so it never knew how to operate in the wild. I mean, yes it's young, but it does have potential to do a lot of damage.

You might lose some friends while you're rehabilitating him. Are you prepared for that?"

Janna sighed. She was already apprehensive about how she'd cope over the Christmas season. That was the time that a Krampus gets restless. Normally they sought out naughty kids to punish. It wouldn't be long before the surrounding countryside was twinkling and sparkling with the first slight coverings of frosted snow. She wondered how she'd cope trying to control Grumpy's natural instinct.

How Jenna had looked sheepish and naïve under Carl's stern gaze. Now she felt foolish and anxious in front of her grandmother for an entirely different reason. After four weeks her grandmother had knitted Grumpy two wool tops. Both attempts had not gone down well as gifts.

"They're just the wrong material, the wrong

colour or fit," Mary had reasoned stoically.

Today, Grumpy sat curled in the corner, picking at a loose thread to the curtains. He looked over occasionally at Mary.

"Naughty Krampus," she said sternly. "Naughty."

It switched to fiddling with it's toe nails instead. Then it peered out the window when it heard some people walking by. *Could I go chase them? Were they naughty children it could go after?* Jenna could see it mulling.

Mary wagged a finger at it. "No. Naughty Krampus."

It didn't move. It just sat sullen, with the occasional glare at Mary.

Mary held up jacket number three.

"Looks great, grandmother," Jenna said. "But you must be bored of making tops by now."

Mary pulled out a shopping bag from beside the chair. Jenna took the bag from her and looked inside. Bundles of material were folded inside. "Oh, you found some more oddments."

"No," Mary said. "I went into town and brought some."

Jenna caught her breath. "You've been out? You went into town? That's a twenty- minute bus ride."

Her grandmother looked bewildered.

"Well, I was hardly going to walk there." She said it in a sarcastic tone as if she hadn't been living like a recluse for six months, her only company all that time her photo of the Scotty dog.

"I went into Hobbymart." she said. "They were very helpful. Although they had never dealt with clothing for a Krampus before, they gave me lots of tips. Then I saw Mr Slabbert from the village.

He had his lovely German Shepherd with him. He had a lovely blue fabric coat - it was waterproof and everything."

Jenna looked downbeat. She felt exhausted as Carl's words came seeping into her mind. "You may never be able to train Grumpy. It will need lots of patience and caution."

Jenna had just about managed to control its anxiety when it was left alone, not to let its worry turn to aggression. She'd taught it to walk into her back garden and explore. When it slept, she'd draped a light blanket over it to get used to being partially covered.

"Grandmother's jacket will be just to keep you warm and dry, Grumpy," she had whispered to it. "We won't make you look silly, I promise. You don't have to be anything else here except a little demon."

***

In her grandmother's lounge, as Mary put the jacket on the Krampus, Grumpy looked at Jenna. It twitched and twisted, and even gave a little huff deep down in its throat. Was it feeling taunted and teased? Was it feeling bullied and being forced into something it wouldn't like?

"There now," Mary said. "That's too bad."

It's new coat was a Gore-Tex jacket. Black with a couple of dark silver stripes. The jacket was the most tasteful and practical yet.

Any moment now, Jenna thought. *It may hate the damn jacket but at least grandmother is getting out and about buying the stupid material.*

It stood up straight and worked its arms out and about. It strolled about a little, as if on a fashion catwalk. It looked over at Jenna and patted it's chest. It was now a happier creature.

Then suddenly it walked to the window… and slumped against the frame.

"Oh…" Mary said, blinking at it with caution. "Do you think it likes the jacket?" Her pause filled the room with apprehension.

"Grandmother," Jenna said quietly. "We… we… could take it for a short walk. What do you think?"

Mary caught on and within seconds there was an awkward tension in the room.

Jenna gave a soft whistle, one that they used when she took Grumpy out to the forest for some long walks.

Grumpy turned around from the window and looked at the two woman in expectation.

Jenna looked over at her grandmother in hopefulness. *Please, grandmother, come with us.*

"It… it can get used to being around more people outdoors other than just myself."

Mary gazed into the kitchen at the picture of her Scotty dog in the bright red wool jumper.

She's going to make an excuse, Jenna thought. *She thinks that any time out and about with her dog is going to be depressing.*

Jenna remembered the animal shelter and how Carl had raised a sceptical eyebrow at her. There seemed genuine concern etched on his face. His assistance felt conflicted.

"Why did you pick the Krampus?" he'd pressed.

"We… we just lost our family dog a year ago," Jenna had mumbled. "My grandmother pretty much lived her life through her dog. She went out and about because of the dog. I used to love going to visit and take him out for walks myself.

Everything seems dull without him."

A half goat - half demon may not be a suitable replacement, she expected Carl to quip before she said another word. *Animals all have different requirements and needs. A Krampus won't be like a dog... at all.*

Instead, Carl sighed. The guy had spent weeks trying to find a home for the animal. Predictable, he had had no luck in re-housing the devilish creature.

"So you need something to bring excitement back to your lives, do you?" he'd asked.

***

"You've talked me into it," Mary said reluctantly, realising how hard Jenna was working to help her get back into living life.

Mary then looked across at Grumpy as it brushed down the new jacket and gazed outside expectantly.

"You've made me feel so selfish, Grumpy," she said. "Here we are sat in our houses and living our lives and you're lost and alone in a strange world."

She looked over at Jenna. Their eyes met, and Mary gave Jenna a small smile. "Maybe I should take some time to go out and about. Come on, let's take Grumpy out for a little walk. Long as we avoid the playgrounds, I think we'll be okay."

Jenna had visions of the two of them chasing Grumpy around the playing fields while it sought out naughty children to capture.

While Mary went upstairs to find a coat for herself, Jenna clipped on Grumpy's lead. She gently rubbed it's shoulder.

"Well done, Grumpy," she whispered. "You're not a pet or a regular creature - but you're not just a wild animal, Grumpy. You're our little Krampus."

My Robotic Friend

It wasn't that much hassle to sort out Uncle Kaneshiro's estate. He'd never married and was famous in our family for his minimal lifestyle and sparse living. So it wasn't too difficult to arrange details after he died.

My brother Lai wanted his cityscape paintings, Ho wanted his antique watches and Chan wanted his Gucci ties.

For the last six years of his life, Uncle Kaneshiro had lived in an upstairs retirement apartment opposite the harbour. I think it was the longest he'd ever settled anywhere.

The city of Hong Kong was in his blood and once he'd left the heart of it and moved to the outskirts, he'd seemed to become despondent.

For some reason, he'd made me an executor of his will, and so now, like an intruder into his memories, I was rifling through his private things. I packed things away in boxes, took his clothes to a thrift store and distributed his sparse belongings to old friends of his.

Ever since I was a youngster I'd been captivated by him.

I'd loved the way he used to tell tales of his earlier life as a low-level gangster, running books and tricks down at the harbour, and I'd love hearing stories about visiting sailors from overseas.

I remembered every story.

"Oh, Uncle Kaneshiro, I'm going to miss you," I told the empty apartment.

"Put me on charge!"

I swung around, startled. I'd forgotten all about Rex the Robot. Standing in the corner, behind the end of the sofa, he eyed me cheekily. The damn thing had given me a fright.

Uncle Kaneshiro had always wanted a robot and when he'd settled in the apartment, he had ordered the humanoid robot as a companion. Designed primarily as an education aid, it had soon fallen out of favour and replaced by small models and hand-held advanced tablets.

No-one really knew why he'd brought a robot, but it was easy to see why nobody else in the family had wanted to take it. It had no seeming use.

Yet for all that, it had a weird charm you wouldn't have thought possible in something made of wires and plastic.

Despite its saving graces, however the robot would be a difficult thing to re-house and would no doubt prove the most difficult of Uncle Kaneshiro's possessions to find an owner for.

"I can't have him in the house. My girlfriend would go nuts," Lai told me, as he made off with the paintings.

"I have absolutely no interest," shrugged Ho as he wrapped up the antique watches in tissue paper. "Best left at that," Ho concluded as he made his hasty departure.

My third brother laughed. "Don't even look at me," protested Chan truthfully as he stood by the mirror admiring the ties.

I sighed. So that left me with a couple of boxes of books, some DVDs, Uncle Kaneshiro's coat rack… and Rex the Robot.

It made a couple of beeps and wiggled its head, as if it knew. Like it was in on the big joke.

"Put me on recharge!" Rex suggested.

Wisely, I ignored him.

"I'm a thirty five year old woman," I went on.

"What the hell am I going to do with a robot." I looked at its dusty panels and dirt feet pads.

"I'm going to have to clean it for a start…"

"Put me on charge!" it repeated, leaning from side to side.

"I'll not be ordered about by a robot!" I said emphatically, remembering how it used to follow Uncle Kaneshiro around the apartment. Then Uncle Kaneshiro would talk to it and go all daft and goofy. I rolled my eyes.

"I bet you miss bossing Uncle Kaneshiro about, eh?"

"Kaneshiro! Kaneshiro!" Rex suddenly started to shift from side to side, as if excited where it stood.

"Sadly, he's not coming home," I said sadly.

When it's master hadn't shown up after a couple of minutes, the robot sunk back into the side of the sofa despondent.

"Someone's bound to adore you," I said brightly. "You're a very unique robot and clever with it. And I promise I won't let you go to anyone unless I've thoroughly vetted them first."

Rex let out some shrill bleeps, sitting back on its haunches.

-

Back at my own apartment, I placed the robot next to the window and it looked out at the busy streets below.

"This is only a temporary arrangement," I reminded it. "Just until I find you a new home."

"Kaneshiro loved me," it said in a low tone, not turning from looking out the window.

I sat down to write a poster for the local coffeeshop and couldn't make up my mind whether what to offer him for.

A low price would mean any person off the

street could just take it away for a lark or two. Getting a proper owner meant a decent amount, but that meant trying to figure out how much it was truly worth - and how could I do that?

Finally, I decided that a low price would have to do, providing I vetted the person buying first.

The first man to come see Rex was a short, geeky-type of middle-aged man who heavily man-handled the robot and peered closely into its eyes, as though he was examining a painting.

Rex remained like a statue.

"Does it talk?"

"It does," I said.

"Let's hear it then."

Rex kept his melancholic stance firmly on display. Despite my requests, it remained stony silent.

Not only that, it kept its limbs solidly in one position and wouldn't move any limbs, and made odd little noises. I watched the pathetic performance and pulled a face at it.

"Looks like it may be broken," the man said. "Seems too much hassle to be honest. Probably cost me loads to get fixed."

The two young girls who came next were so shocked by Rex's foul language that there was no way they would be allowed to keep it at home. I felt my cheeks colour as they repeated some of the less offensive words it had offered out.

The robot really went to town with the young man who arrived next, purposely walking into the tables, chairs, and almost every wall in the apartment until the man left with a look of contempt.

His favourite trick, though, was to talk in Spanish, for no obvious reason and apparently seemed unable to understand any instruction.

That was why, two weeks later, Rex the Robot was still pottering around my apartment, slowly making itself at home.

"Hello, Faye!" it beeped cheerily every time I returned to the apartment.

Then, during the evening, it would sidle up to where I sat on the sofa and sat itself by my feet.

"Rex needs charging," it would beep, which was my cue to plug him into the USB point of my home computer.

I left the radio on for it all day while I went out to work, and it quickly learned to repeat cheesy DJ chit-chat.

"Let's hope for sunshine!" was its favourite, with, "Let's be happy!" coming a close second.

It was madness, pure madness.

The cheesy chit-chat was exhausting. I can't keep up, I thought. Who would have thought looking after a robot could be so tiring.

I often wondered why Uncle Kaneshiro had left so specific instructions regarding the robot.

After all, he had been fond of Rex and must have been concerned for its welfare. It seemed odd that Uncle Kaneshiro had overlooked the matter.

***

I sat down and remembered all the Sundays I had spent with Uncle Kaneshiro. It wasn't easy to recall anything specific - there had been so many conversations.

"When I'm gone, you can give Chan my Gucci ties," he'd said a couple of months ago. "I know he likes the vintage clothes."

"Don't be so flippant, Uncle Kaneshiro, you've plenty of time with us yet," I'd scoffed. "Don't be so daft."

But Uncle Kaneshiro must have know about his demise, because he'd insisted on going through the lot.

"What I'd really like," he'd ended, "would be to see you married before I die."

"You probably will," I'd said carelessly. "And even if I never get married, it's no issue really, is it? You've always been happy enough and you never got married."

He shook his head. "My job was my life, Faye. I was always too busy to go looking for a wife." He looked away despondent. "But it's no way to live though.

The discussion was moving too close to home. Faye remembered just having to glance out through the window.

The memory brought fresh tears. It was late by the time she roused herself from the sofa. She hadn't eaten or even put Rex on his afternoon charge. Rex looked at her with soulful eyes.

"In a minute, Rex," she murmured, going over to the laptop.

-

"Faye loves Rex." The robot stood by my feet and rubbed his metallic arm against my leg. "Faye loves Rex."

"You little cutie, you." I smiled and patted it on the top of its head. I turned away, not wanting Rex to see me grinning.

I noticed that his habits were beginning to improve. Without Uncle Kaneshiro's encouragement, it didn't seem so flippant and it was becoming altogether better behaved.

Perhaps I could try to find a new owner after

all.

This time, three students came to see it and on this occasions, it was on its absolute worst behaviour, waddling pathetically and knocking into everything as though it was drunk.

But one of the students returned for another visit and seemed to see through Rex's rouse.

I have to say, I was rather taken by the student myself. He was stoic, with cropped hair and pale brown eyes that had a genuine kindness in them.

"It's certainly an interesting robot. Not many of them about anymore," he explained, looking at Rex.

"I'm a good robot!" Rex bleeped away in reply.

I waited for it to do his drunkenness act, start knocking into the coffee table, or bumping back and forth against the window, but it did none of those things. It stood looking bright and chirpy.

"Why on earth do you want to get rid of it?" The guy turned to me. "Do you realise how valuable a robot like this is?"

"I… Well,"

Why did it seem I was fed up with Rex? No-one had actually asked me that before and I'd never given it much thought.

I didn't mind the robot too much. In fact, in an odd way, I had begun to find Rex slightly endearing.

And Rex wasn't that much trouble. Certainly not like having a pet. And I had started to find its constant chatter quite comforting when I was in the apartment on my own.

"Look, if you want a good home for it, I'll take him. It's a splendid robot, obviously intelligent…"

On cue, Rex gave some shrill beeps.

"It belonged to my late Uncle," I explained

quickly. "I really don't know what else to do with it."

Bey Wong promised to take care of Rex and went off with the robot, chatting with him all the way.

I looked at the empty corner by the sofa and felt an ache in my body as tears gathered in my eyes. She felt as cold and dismal as the quiet apartment.

"You're just being daft," I mocked myself and fetched some work to distract my mind.

-

I had a restless night. I knew nothing about Bey Wong. I'd let Uncle Kaneshiro's most treasured companion go to a complete stranger.

When I got up the next morning, I missed the annoying bleeps and sarcastic comments. When I came home from work, the apartment was quiet.

During the evening, I found myself casting glances to the corner of the sofa where Rex used to sit.

By the week's end, I felt utterly melancholic and was missing Rex something terrible.

Then my intercom buzzed.

Bey Wong stood outside with the robot in a box.

"I'm sorry," he said apologetically. "I managed a week, but I can't have him anymore. He keeps cursing in front of everybody that visits me."

"I've never known him to swear a lot," I gasp, hardly able to suppress my joy at seeing Rex again.

"Yes. Especially when my nieces visit," Bey said. "It's so embarrassing. All it does is stand in a corner and cuss."

"Rex, is this true?" I asked.

"Hello, Faye. Let's be happy!" Rex blurted.

"Well, that's the most pleasant its been all week." Bey smiled ruefully. "It was pining for you and, if you don't mind me saying, you look as if you've missed Rex too."

"A little, to be honest," I admitted. "I had begun to miss him."

"Will you take him back then?"

"I guess that might be best."

"Please, I'd like you to. I can't bear to have it cussing anymore."

"Ok, then, I will."

We had some tea while Rex stood in his usual spot by the window and looked out at the Hong Kong skyline.

"Do you think I could come and visit him again?" Bey asked much later as he was leaving."

Faye's cheeks coloured at Bey's suggestion. She was only half listening to Bey. It took a few seconds for his words to sink in. But then they slowly began to register and she blushed some more.

"That would be okay."

***

I closed the door after he'd gone and smiled.

"Let's hope for sunshine!" Rex called out.

"Yes, sunshine would be nice…" I said haughtily. "I'd like some brightness in my life at last."

I gave Rex a pat on its head and it wobbled with glee.

"You know what I think, Rex? I think Uncle Kaneshiro intended me to have you all along. Maybe he was worried I'd be alone too long?"

"Not that I have the intention of hanging out with Bey Wong that much," I added in a panic. I cleared my throat. I was thinking of what might happen if this trend in my words were to continue.

I stood beside the robot at the window and watched as Bey walked along the street to the train station. He looked up and waved and my heart did a little lurch beneath my ribs. I felt myself blush.

And then I heard Rex make some low beeps.

The sun, which had been hidden off and on by stray cloud, shone brightly through the windows. As I felt the warmth of the sun I began to feel connected with life again. Maybe this would be a way to deal with my loneliness. I couldn't feel sorry for myself any longer.

For a moment, I could have sworn that Rex was laughing at me.

Cannibal County

My uncle's very clever. He can do lots of things, like hunting wild game in all weathers. He can make great moonshine from the most basic of ingredients, and he can also cook.

This morning Uncle and I were sitting out on the front porch of the family cabin. I was doing some drawing and he was writing some diary notes about living in the Kentucky hills. My drawing was just normal, a crayon sketch of the valley meadows that lay beyond the ridgeline.

"Are you a man or a woman meat person?" he asked.

Aunty was washing the front windows and she answered for me.

"She loves some man meat, I reckon."

I looked and giggled at Aunty. She was a forty-five woman, podgy, redhead with hazel eyes and a Pamela Anderson hairdo.

"Rubbish!" Uncle declared. "This young girl loves women! Nothing tastes softer than fresh succulent meat from a teenage woman, straight from the valley meadows. I'm a woman person, with a second thought!"

I turned to Uncle. He was grinning away. A large popeyed fifty-two-year old man with unkempt, curly blond hair, and a bulging belly, he cut quite the character.

Then he lowered his voice, but I could still make out what he was saying.

"I'll tell you why you don't like eating women, dear," he said to Aunty. "It's because you don't cook the meat properly. Young meat can be overcooked. It has a delicate flavour. You must gently braze it as you would cook a fish from a stream."

"Then the germs aren't killed," Aunty pointed out.

"What germs are you talking about?" Uncle questioned. "If the meat is eaten fresh, there are no germs! For the holidays next week, I'm going over the hill to the valley. I'm going to find a stray from the town, and I'm cooking them myself. A nice hickory grill. Nobody's allowed to interfere."

"Less hassle for me," Aunty said, but her face was sullen.

"Can I come with you, too?" I asked.

"All right. It's always good to learn about the hunt."

***

Three days later and I had walked from my house to Uncle's just as the sun was rising. It was the kind of morning when it might rain later, but right now was perfect for a trip down from the hills, with dry roads and just enough warmth to be comfortable.

As we were driving along the hillside road, the sun was just peeking over the ridgeline and shining straight into our eyes.

"Why do we have to leave so early, Uncle?"

"We must get into town before the rush of people start and are bustling about the streets. It's good to get to Harold's early."

I saw some dark shapes lingering outside the old grain mill on the edge of town. Two men I vaguely recognised. Uncle didn't seem to notice them. We parked our pick-up and waited.

Uncle had decided not to go hunting himself,

but to buy the human meat from Harold, the county's designated 'Hunter' and meat supplier. His speciality was early morning hunts for hitchhikers, school kids or dog walkers. Normally from the neighbouring counties, or sometimes from the next state over.

We sat in the pick-up for what seemed ages. I was feeling nervous, but that was all too personal to reveal to Uncle. Under the stoic hide that I had grown over the years lay a wellspring of anxiety. I seldom acknowledged it, but I knew it was there. I would be a fool to reveal to Uncle, and I couldn't afford to be a fool.

I cast a sly glance over to my Uncle. His face was as wrinkled and leathered as an old baseball mitt under his mangy trucker hat, split with an incongruous smirk that allowed him to mask his thoughts while he probed for the secret meaning that lay in the mannerisms of others. Old Navy tattoos dotted his forearms. He kept chewing his inside cheeks, leaning forward in his seat, his eyes squinting as though he were staring through fog.

Studying Uncle only made my heebie-jeebies worse. When I lowered my head, I imagined all the things we had done as a family. What a freak of nature, I thought, then wondered what he thought of me.

After a while later, I heard the sound of a van's engine far away. The dark shapes eased into the morning light and we saw that it was the O'Connell's from the next county.

Uncle squeezed my shoulder. I felt a gulp jam up in my throat.

"Now, you just watch and let me do the talking, all right?" he said. "If Harold knows that we want something specific, he's liable to increase the price."

I felt my body tensing up as the rumble and chugging of the van came closer and parked up outside the mill.

My guts churned in anxiety. I was not so sure about coming along on the trip. Excuses to leave were mulling about in my mind, but I didn't mention it to Uncle. I didn't want to seem to be nervous.

Harold was dressed in his tatty t-shirt and ripped jeans, a typical Indiana townie. He was about fifty, heavy in a square way, with a shiny face and dirt water brown hair that looked like he'd got blind drunk and decided to cut it himself. He swung the van around and parked by the edge of the front car park.

Uncle and the two other men stepped closer to the van and peeped through the back window.

"Looks like he's got a youngster or two!" Uncle whispered into my ear. "And a young woman!"

Harold opened up the back of the van to reveal four bodies each wrapped in clear plastic tarpaulin.

"Who's first?" Harold asked.

"Us." one of the O'Connell's said. "How much for the young woman?"

"Hundred bucks for a limb. Five hundred for the whole body."

"I'll pay you two-fifty for the lot," one of them said.

"No!" Uncle said. I want some of the young woman."

"Sorry folks, but I started the buying," the man replied.

"Hundred bucks per limb," Harold repeated, rubbing his tubby stomach. "I can share her between you."

"I ain't paying one hundred per limb," said the first man in a huff, then asked the price of a young boy Harold had laid out.

He brought it, gave over some money and walked away a little.

"I'm next," the other O'Connell man said quickly, giving Uncle a look. Now the stranger was revealed in character. At that moment, the world was no longer the place that I had once thought it to be. It was alien, and dangerous, and our vulnerability was exposed to me.

Uncle breathed out loudly, like I do when I'm given a chore I don't like doing, and asked again how much the young woman was, in a nonchalant tone that almost hinted no real interest.

Uncle stepped forward.

"No, come on. I've said that I'm interested in the young woman. I really want her."

"You should have been here first then!" the other man said. He looked over at his relative and exchanged a smirk.

"Come on. We've had to drive over the ridge. I had to wait for the kid. How could I have got here any earlier?"

I didn't like being used as an excuse, and especially don't like being referred to as a kid. When I had arrived at Uncles, he was still having his breakfast. Any delays were certainly of his making.

"If we're making excuses, you should know we had to sort out our disabled mom before we came out here, and she loves meat from young women," the man said.

"Ah, come on. My family are celebrating the holidays next week and I need the young meat for a special lunch."

I didn't think that Uncle was that into celebrating holidays, but it didn't seem a good time to interrupt.

"Excuse me, gentlemen," Harold interrupted. "I'm not being funny, but I really hate just standing around with bodies in my van. If we can sort this."

"I might just buy everything," teased the man.

Out of nowhere, Uncle had pulled a snub .45 handgun from behind his waistband. He started pointing it towards the O'Connell's. Both men wearily put their hands up and took some steps back.

***

On the way home, Uncle occasionally looked back at the body on the seat behind.

"Did those men let you have the young woman because you threatened them?"

"No. I reckon they wouldn't have paid five hundred for her anyhow. They were just making hassle for the sake of it," he replied.

When we got home, Aunty was out visiting. This was a good thing, because of she had seen Uncle all in a fluster, she would have just quizzed him and rattled his nerves even further.

He plonked the body in the slaughter barn and went to go change into his butchers clothes. I sat on the porch and took in the morning sunshine. There was a hint of spring in the air.

Twenty minutes later, Uncle trundled across from the barn with two steaks from the young woman. He then announced he was going into the woods to collect some mushrooms for the meal. He dumped them at the bottom of the fridge.

After an hour, Aunty came home. "All went well?" she asked. She was carrying two paper parcels. She put them on the side by the sink.

I didn't know what to say so I just nodded and fixed a smile. I felt my throat close. My eyes glazed, as though I were looking into a watery glare.

Aunty gave a wry look. "Would you like to help me cut up some venison I brought from town before your Uncle trundles in her and sends us away?"

The chunks of meat were floppy and bloody when I unwrapped them. The meat felt so light and tender and reminded me of young human meat, but maybe that was because of what I had seen earlier.

When we had finished, we wiped the sideboards down, put the sliced venison in the fridge and left the kitchen just as Uncle was coming back from the woods.

"Thank you ladies, for preparing the flesh meat," he nodded to us.

I looked over at Aunty.

"Oh, but we haven't…"

"Shh," she teased quietly.

With a knowing look in my direction, she began to hum a country tune.

A few hours later Uncle called the lunch ready. Mom, Pop and my brother had come over to join us. We all settled down around the kitchen table.

When Uncle came out of the kitchen and saw the all the crockery laid out, he got upset and said that as it was a holiday we should be using the best plates, even if they were more fragile.

Aunty rolled her eyes and mumbled a quiet

curse, before starting to change over the crockery. She kept her bubbling sarcasm to herself.

Then Uncle served us his braised steaks.

"Taste the valley in that meat! I've cooked her just enough," he said, glancing proud-as-punch to Aunty, but nobody was paying much attention to him as they were all busy eating. "It was tricky trying to get her meat, but it was worth it. Just close your eyes and taste the fresh valley living."

I couldn't really taste 'The valley,' but I certainly tucked into it. Between bites, I glanced over to Aunty and again she gave me a knowing look and shook her head a little.

Luckily, Aunty didn't mind Uncle jabbering on. She just enjoyed the family gathering and smiled a lot.

Then we had fresh pecan flan with vanilla ice cream, made by my Mom.

When we had finished and swapped stories, Uncle said he was tired and was going out to the porch to rest in the sunshine, having worked hard at the meal.

The rest of us family cleared the table and washed up, then we left Aunty and Uncle to enjoy the afternoon alone.

I was very happy that Uncle had enjoyed the holiday celebrations because everybody wants to have good family gatherings. I knew that he was going to be happy at suppertime, too, because, when I had put leftovers in the fridge, I saw on the bottom shelf two packets - the steaks of the young woman Uncle had cut up in the slaughter barn, still all wrapped and fresh in paper.

I smirked: poor Uncle had cooked Aunt's venison, believing them to be his own steaks.

***

The next week, as we sat on the porch chatting, and while I was drawing with my crayons, I asked Uncle about the holiday meal and what he had enjoyed the most.

"There are two things I enjoyed the most about the family meal. One was realising that my cooking was so good I made human taste like deer - "

I laughed. "So you knew what had happened!"

"Almost straight away." He smirked. "And the second thing is that your Aunt just wanted to make me happy."

I laughed again. "So what are we having for lunch today?"

Uncle raised an eyebrow. "You'll just have to wait and see.

The Robot In The Barn

Mac Parsons had lived on the edge of town as long as anyone could remember. I discovered him when I was still a child, the day I went exploring beyond my street and came upon the old brick barn.

"What you doing poking around here for, child?" His gruff voice bellowed across the yard

I simply stared at the old man dressed in his tatty overalls. A tall, bug-eyed, fiftyish character with big work boots and a cloth cap, he looked the clichéd town loner. He was rubbing his hands with a dirty rag and I remember wondering whether he was just making his hands more filthy.

I'd heard of Mac from the whisperings of my friends and the other children in school, who decided he must be a weirdo because he was so reclusive and had a huge black dog. My parents had spoken of him with more criminal connotations, like he had a police record or was a kiddie-fiddler. Some in town claimed that he was " loco" because he was always locking himself away in his barn. But I saw nothing sinister in the old man who stood so still and stoic.

I told him I was just bored and wandering about. I thought it prudent to add that I meant no trouble and apologised if I had trespassed.

"I guess the town can get pretty boring to a young kid like yourself. Bet you've explored everywhere by now."

I could understand what he was getting at - I did get bored pretty easily. I nodded at him. "I guess."

I was an inquisitive youngster, or a pest

according to my mum, and adults often seemed too busy to answer my innumerable questions and satisfy my curiosity. Dad was always exhausted on his return from being the town sheriff. Life seemed hectic, even in the smallest of towns. Life was just as hard for mum - working a low-wage job as a temp at the library.

But Mac had time for me. He was never too busy.

He told me that hanging out in his barn during the winter kept him warm, and in the summer kept him cool. Pointing out his trailer-home next to the barn, he hinted at cold living conditions.

Mac taught me so much about mechanics. He let me tinker with his old Corvette that was parked beside the barn. He cultivated my enthusiasm for engineering and machines.

I learned about his robot, too. The stories were true; Mac did hide himself in the back of the barn and he showed me his clinical lab that took up half the space inside.

Mac was a constant fascination to me, and we became kindred spirits.

Months passed as spring turned to summer then into autumn, and eventually mum learned of my visits to Mac's.

"I don't like him hanging out at that place. It ain't right," I heard her complaining to dad one evening as I was repairing my pushbike out by the porch. "Who knows what kind of guy that Mac Parsons is!"

"Now, don't get yourself in a thither. There's no harm in old Mac. He's got no police record, and ain't never been no trouble with the law," he soothed. "Mac's just a little reclusive that's all."

"I heard he likes to get high as a fucking kite."

"Now Mum," he growled. "Ain't nobody

growing anything around these parts but allotments and veggie plots. So calm yourself."

"Well, I'm not happy with it," Mum grumbled.

***

As I turned into a teenager, I must have become aware of the clutter and discourse of Mac's living, and the lack of normality in his life. But these were issues that seemed of little consequence. Time spent in his company was rich in education.

Sometimes he'd have me tinkering with the cars he'd buy a local auction, or sometimes we'd just sit in the afternoon sunshine and talk about everything from robotics to the environmental troubles of the world. These were things he thought important.

From time to time, I'd talk about school, bullies and girls. I appreciated the fact that he'd listen to all my grumbles and questions.

The main topic of our afternoon chats was always robotics though. Mac began to tell me about his life, about his work for NASA Cybernetics, and about how he had jacked it all in after WW3. He also let on about his robotic pastime, and about Lola that he was building in the back of the barn.

"She's an old sex robot that I've been trying to adapt with some nano-tech. It's been a dream of mine to build a cybernetic companion," he told me when I asked what he was working on in the barn. I tried to learn the technology and Mac's way of engineering, even though most was lost on me.

Lola became my dream, too though.

Over the years now, our town had seen major changes. It had once been a thriving agricultural town amidst towering cities nearby, but after World War 3 a loss of people and the pollution to the land had decimated the town. It had only been in the recent years that any semblance of rebuilding had begun. Farmland disappeared, and people moved to the cities to try and survive.

Citizens of the world had been apathetic about cybernetics. They had been too busy trying to survive and make ends meet to wax philosophical. Robotics and nanomachines had combined with cybernetics in just fifteen years, then the war brought chaos and death. A war largely based on internet technology and electronics had turned the clock back to the twentieth century. Where once cybernetics had been ubiquitous in daily life, now it was resigned to secret organisations and skilled individuals.

On leaving school, I helped my dad by being sworn in as a deputy. It wasn't much of a job, but it was better than being forced into a ragged city and into a life of scrabbling for essentials. My path in life would become clear to me in time I figured. Meanwhile, I was content to keep the office clean and tidy, and spend time with Mac.

I became aware of the rumours of a secret in Mac's life. There was talk of a baby born by one of his NASA assistants, and that the mother had remained down in Florida. No-one knew what had really happened, but Mac had travelled north almost as soon as WW3 had ended, and was now living in a trailer with just his robots who wouldn't judge him.

He treated me with the same respect. With Mac, I could always be myself, telling him my daft dreams and hopes for the country. Mac never laughed or criticised, never sniggered at my idealistic thoughts. I loved his philosophy of life.

"Just try not to be a dick," he would say as he carefully tinkered with his robots.

"That old coot must be bat-shit crazy," Mum would say to dad. But he wasn't. Far from it in fact.

***

As I celebrated my twenty-first birthday I began to date a woman in the neighbouring county. She was twenty-two years my senior, and although the situation was slightly odd, the lack of youngsters meant that young women were a rarity in the town. If the woman didn't entirely understand my friendship with Mac, she didn't hassle me none about it.

Looking back, it seems stupid that I didn't notice the changes in Mac, nor figure a time where he'd be gone. But I found him, one summer afternoon as the sun was dipping for the evening, lying out on his sun-lounger in front of his barn...

Had he finished his latest robot?

My dad, the only other authority in town, arrived and brought the coroner along to attend to the details. I offered to camp out his place and make sure no one tampered with his stuff. News of Mac's demise would bring the looters and scavengers.

My world was suddenly sullen and wrecked by the death of my dear friend, and to add to my misery, shortly afterwards, my girlfriend had announced that she was moving to the city to work for the rekindled electricity company.

"Have you never thought of moving to the city?" she asked, her bewildered expression almost mocking my country ways.

I suppose it was an invitation, of sorts. The woman was never one for asking. But our relationship had always been built just on availability, certainly not love or passion - *just companions* was the obvious clichéd tag.

"Not really," I answered sadly. "My roots here are as good as I'll ever have. A quiet life is under-rated." And I recalled Mac telling me so many a year ago. The poor woman had long gotten bored of listening to me and trying to psychoanalyze my motivations for staying put.

I wished her well and promised that she'd always be welcome back in town should she need welcoming back at any time. I looked at her with compassionate disapproval. Here was another soul resigning themselves to chasing a dream of normality.

"You sure are passionate for someone who has just about nothing."

"I just have the drive to fight it out in the city. Here, at least I got the space and time."

"At least the robots will keep you company." She gave a wry smile.

I looked away, not caring to pursue the matter and further, and she walked away.

I did kind of miss the woman. Not in that heart-rending way I missed Mac, but she had been company on cold nights and lonely days.

***

The wheels of the law turned slowly, and it was a year or so that the authorities deemed that

Mac's offspring had probably died in the war, or at least perished in the aftermath like so many.

Hot sun beat over the wispy strands of elm and larch, over the yard next to the barn where Mac was buried. Everybody figured it would have been his wish to remain near his beloved barn.

A couple of songbirds were chirping and sunlight washing everything in heat when the postman brought the judge's letter.

The barn and its contents had been willed to me, together with the old cars and the small holding that everything sat on. The neighbouring fields had been left to the county so replanting of crops could be tested next spring.

I sat down on a deckchair outside and sipped on some homemade moonshine and took a look back into the shadows of the barn. What did the future have in mind?

***

Several years have gone by since that day. The old trailer that Mac had held up in is no more, replaced by a wooden shack on the edge of the tree-line nearby. A stray mongrel dog has made itself at home and runs about the place keeping guard and chasing of vermin, of all kinds.

I am working on a new solar-power generating machine behind the barn when a slight scuffle of dirt announces company. The dog isn't barking so I know it's more friendly than foe.

A tall, slender and buxom woman, her long unruly ginger hair tied in a ponytail, moves towards me with the grace of a timid animal. Her hands reach out to me and clasp my waist in a tender embrace. I feel an odd twinge of nostalgia every time I see her. She's been my company for seven months now.

"Hello, hubby," she whispers, running a hand over my arse cheeks. I feel the electricity in her touch.

Then our lips meet in a long kiss and her glistening intelligent eyes gaze into mine with all the love and devotion I had programmed into her.

We stand there looking over each other for a moment. She looks better than I could have envisaged. Mac would have been proud of my efforts.

I smile. "How you doing, Lola?"

Party At The Goblin Café

"My electric has gone again!" Daylight has faded and thrown the house into a winter darkness. It is only just gone lunchtime and already evening lurks. "What will it be like by suppertime."

Mrs Levy was monopolising Jamie's attention at the counter as Jo walked into the store and headed for the baskets by the first aisle.

"I was trying to make a cake when it happened - I can't even finish mixing the ingredients," she said.

Jamie found the opportunity to glance over, nodding his head discreetly in Jo's direction, and she smirked in response.

"Maybe it's just a broken fuse. The rest of the street seems okay, Mrs Levy," he said.

Jo grabbed a basket and went to pick up the few bits and pieces she needed to carry her through the holiday season when the stores in town would mostly be shut.

"I don't know what to do," Mrs Levy continued. "My two daughters are travelling across country to come stay with me for a couple of days. What handyman will come out at this time in the holidays?"

Jo had little doubt that Jamie would find a solution. The question was of would he take the hint, or if he would wait to Mrs Levy had to ask out right for his help.

At one time she would have had no doubt that he would have revelled in make Mrs Levy ask for help, but recently his gruff personality had softened somewhat.

"I'm no electrician, but I could come take a

look if you'd like?"

His courtesy didn't disappoint, and Jo couldn't help but smile a little as she pottered around the store.

"Would you be able to, Jamie? That would be very kind of you." Mrs Levy sounded relieved and delighted - almost as though she hadn't expected Jamie to be as polite as he could be.

"I'll be closing the store early today, so I could pop around later in the afternoon."

Mrs Levy said her thanks and gave a beaming smile as she made her way out of the shop.

"Not a word," Jamie demanded as Jo approached the till still smirking.

"You're such a sweetie," she mocked.

"Yeah... yeah." He smiled, holding her gaze. "But I may need to go back to being a handyman one of these days, so it's as well to do favours at this stage."

"Not making a fortune with the store," she quipped.

He grimaced. Jo suddenly realised she may have gotten into some hot-water, so decided not to pry or joke anymore. Jo knew that he had been struggling with the store, and she was grateful he had a second vocation to turn back to. But, on a personal level, she enjoyed having him next door to her café.

"I'll miss you something rotten if you do go."

That earned her a smile.

"For the moment, I'm just a guy helping out a lonely widow."

"Just as long as you're finished in time for the party tonight." Jo had been looking forward to celebrating the holidays with Jamie ever since they'd arranged to go to the community park for the fireworks - even if it would be along with most of the townsfolk.

"I'll meet you at nine, as arranged."

***

When Jo got back to her Goblin café, her assistant, Jenna was pushing around the tables. The café was also a deli-type shop, with the tables scattered rather randomly about, and they were at one side of a long display cabinet.

"There," she said with a tone of satisfaction as she pushed chairs back under a table. "All ready for Walt and Jessie to sit at again when the whim takes them."

Jo smiled, glancing around for the goblin pets.

That was the thing with having so many goblins around - however hard you worked, things never stay organised for very long.

At the moment, however, Walt and Jessie were too busy to bother with furnishing, preening themselves in the large mirror that was attached to the café wall. Jamie had attached the mirror six months ago, and Jo's goblins loved it. Jo had discovered that the hard way.

"They're gonna start arguing in a minute." Jenna wasn't making a psychic prediction - more a statement based on her extensive knowledge of goblin behaviour.

Jo wasn't surprised when Walt and Jessie started trying to elbow each other out of the way of the mirror.

Though Walt was the larger of the two, Jessie had the confidence and command. It was Jessie who nudged Walt out of centre place and enjoyed pride of place in the reflection.

Jo laughed.

"Never a dull day in this place."

"We need to find some time to hang some decorations for the holidays," Jenna said. "Though I don't think they'll stay in place for long with these fellas."

"We'll put a few up at least. The customers will expect something."

If Jo was honest, she wasn't in too much of a mood to be fussing with holiday preparations, although it did bring in customers so reluctance had to be tamed."

"Why don't you get off home," she suggested to Jenna. "I can finish here. You go home and prepare for the celebrations later on."

They had been closed for the afternoon so that they could concentrate on opening for the town's evening celebrations. There was little point in Jenna hanging around.

Jenna didn't hang about to argue the suggestion.

"Well, if you're sure Jo…" She grinned as she headed to pick up her bag. "Will you be going along with Jamie?"

Jo smirked and nodded.

"I think so. He did say he'd come around and walk with me to the park."

The community park was only a few blocks away from the café, but last year she had missed the festivities, instead preferring just to have a private gathering with friends and her goblins at the café.

This year though, she had decided to make more of an effort, and her goblins were a little older and she felt confident that they would be okay on their own for a few hours. Plus, this year, she wanted to work a little harder on building a relationship.

"Tim said they've planned some big party-pieces at the festival this year." Jenna smiled as she mentioned her husband. He'd been working hard on the town committee this year and had arranged a lot of the celebrations for the town.

"I hope he just doesn't mess it up." Jo joked.

"I bloody hope not. It's all he's been going on about for the last few months. He's normally rubbish at planning things."

Jo laughed. Tim was the kindest man ever and she knew that he would be getting frantic as the last hours ticked by.

"I'm hoping they've got some live bands and stuff," Jenna said as she headed for the door. "I could do with a dance or two. I'll let you know what's planned, if he spills the beans that is."

Jo had barely settled, with a goblin or two snuggling up against her, when her mobile rang.

"Just giving you the heads up," Jenna said, her tone indicating she may have been worried. "I just heard there might be fireworks."

Jo sat up, immediately concerned. Walt looked disgusted and leapt from her side and to the safety of a neighbouring chair.

"Fuck, I hate fireworks. They unsettle the pets, and especially my goblins."

She could almost feel Jenna taking a sigh of exasperation.

"That's exactly what I thought, but Tim thinks it'll be alright, and he says that everyone in town would expect fireworks at the party."

Jo thought of the sleepy town they lived in. They might expect fireworks in a big city, at New Years maybe, but surely not in their sleepy old town.

"I'm sure they meant well," she muttered, trying to not sound too pissed off, "But it would have been nice to have had some notice so that I could pet owners could have planned something."

She made a mental note to spread the word to the pet owners she knew. A surprise was one thing, but she could have done without the hassle.

"It shouldn't go on for too long." Jenna's tone was almost apologetic now. "I know their budget wasn't that grand, so it probably won't be that spectacular."

Jo thought immediately of Walt and Jessie. Her goblins were jittery at the best of times. She recalled a time when she had dropped a tray of cutlery on the floor. Jessie practically defecated on the café floor.

Even though the park was a few blocks away and her goblins were a little older now, fireworks would no doubt be unsettling - and goblins could be easily rattled.

She couldn't risk leaving her goblins alone tonight.

Quickly she found Jamie's number and called him on her mobile. It went straight to his answerphone.

He must be at Mrs Levy's place she thought. She had just remembered that he had offered to sort her lights.

The beep sounded and Jo took a breath and left her message.

"Jamie - It's Jo. I've just been told that there is going to be fireworks at tonight's celebrations. I'm not sure I can leave the goblins alone, so I'm so sorry, but I think I need to cancel."

As she spoke, she cast a glance over to Walt. The goblin just stood and watched Jo's attempt to contact Jamie with indifference.

Jo sighed again before disconnecting the call,

knowing she had been babbling along and hoping Jamie would make sense of her message.

"Well," she told the watching Walt. "That puts paid to my evening plans."

Walt just shrugged before walking off to challenge Jessie to a wrestle.

Next time, Jo, she better plan her celebrations - maybe even arrange a pet-sitter.

"Cough - Cough." The interruption brought her back to the present and she found her two youngest goblins, Bert and Barney, standing hopefully by the kitchen door.

"Time for a feed is it," she asked of them with a smile, and the other goblins started to arrive to wait it out by the door as Jo went out back to prepare their meals.

She felt crestfallen and a little disappointed that she wouldn't be going out to the town's celebrations, but she didn't begrudge a moment of the time she would be spending with her goblins.

Maybe they would have a little party of their own in the café.

***

Jamie didn't call her back.

Not that Jo was surprised - what was there for him to do or say? He knew Jo well enough to know that, given a choice between having fun but startled goblins or staying home, Jo was always going to choose to stay home. So there was little point in Jamie ringing to try and convince her otherwise.

With a sullen slump, Jo settled in the café for the evening, with the company of a couple of

Disney DVDs and some bags of chips.

Moments later, Jessie snuggled up against her. Not to be outdone, Walt settled down by her feet.

"You too old for snuggles, Walt?" she teased the older of the two goblins.

Walt just looked up with a weary smirk. Though not amused by sarcasm, Walt, seeming to understand, gently lay against her feet.

"It's a pity Jamie isn't here, isn't it? He likes playing with you lot."

That was the reason Jo was missing Jamie. Wishing he was enjoying her company, and that of her goblins, made her feel slightly achy. And those pretty eyes of his...

Jo couldn't help but wonder whether he had taken somebody else to the celebrations. Or whether he'd meet somebody there to enjoy the damn fireworks.

***

Jo was so engrossed in watching Fantasia that when a shout outside the café door sounded she nearly leapt out of her seat.

Before she could react, there was another shout. Then another.

Startled, one by the one the goblins moved into hiding, perturbed by the racket.

The merry shouting and cheering was several hours premature, but it sounded like some youngsters had already started the town's celebrations. Jo could feel her blood start to boil.

Frustrated, Jo put the film on pause and went to the shop front. A group of young shadowy figures were pushing and pulling each other outside.

Annoyed now, Jo went to the front door, threw back the locks, intent of opening the door and giving the raucous youngsters a piece of her mind.

"Hey!" Jo recognised Jamie's deep authoritative tone as she opened the door. "What you kids up to? There are people trying to rest around here. Go lark about up the park."

Jo saw worry etch on the faces of the youngsters outside.

"Sorry," the young girl closest said. "We didn't mean no harm," said another.

It seemed that over-excitement rather than trouble had been behind the ruckus. Jo relaxed a little. The annoyance in her subsided a little. Harsh words on the end of her tongue remained unsaid.

"Just go elsewhere to lark around," Jamie stated.

Jo stood aside to let him in, a bottle of wine in his left hand, and she closed the closed the door.

"How did you get on at Mrs Levy's?"

Jamie rolled his eyes and smirked.

"All fixed. It was only her fuse box. All sorted now."

"Are you on your way to the celebrations?" she asked.

"Well, I had planned to. Got dolled-up and everything." He nodded down at his outfit and Jo smiled. He looked good in a suit - he had the slender body for it.

"But then I got your message…"

"Oh, that. Sorry it was a tad late, but I didn't like to leave the café unattended. The goblins got a jolt just by the youngsters a moment ago. I can't imagine what they'd be like with fireworks going off."

Jamie smiled and nodded.

In the momentary pause, he couldn't help but take time to admire the woman before him. Jo was a stunner for sure. The thirty-something was always impeccably groomed, with shoulder-length black hair, beautiful skin, sparkly brown eyes, a trim figure, and a black dress that suited her to perfection.

Jo blushed a little as she realised he was admiring her. Nerves took a hold.

"You'd better get going to the park if you're not going to miss all the partying."

Jamie frowned.

"I was kinda thinking I might stay here. With you and goblins. I brought this along." He held up the bottle of wine. "I thought we could have our own party."

"But you said you wanted to go to the celebrations."

"What I actually said was I wanted to join you at the party," he reminded her softly, stepping in closer to you.

"But seeing as you're not going…" he added.

And even though it wasn't fireworks for real yet, there were sparks alight already. He drew her to him and kissed her gently. She didn't want to resist him, she wanted to melt into him, and as he looked at her she could think of nothing else.

***

It took them a while, but when the goblins realised that the noisy youngsters had departed from the front of the café, they came out from their hiding places.

Barney made a beeline for Jamie and had a

huge fuss made of him before the goblin sauntered off to nap next to the radiator.

All seemed pleasant in the world. Jo put soft music on to soothe the goblins after their fright - and to mask any noise about to come from the town celebrations - and she and Jamie were dancing, her arms wrapped around his waist, as they passed the evening away.

When her mobile phone rang away on the countertop, she stopped mid-sway, startled.

"Jo, it's me - Jenna. I'm outside. Clare and Sarah are with me. Can you let us in?"

"Why are you?" she asked as the brought the cold air of outdoors inside with them.

"We thought of you all alone in here, and thought you might what some extra goblin-minding tonight." Clare grinned sheepishly, giving a sly wink to Jo as she noted Jamie's presence.

"Don't you want to watch the fireworks and like?" Jo half-hinted.

They all shook their heads.

"They won't miss us." Sarah scoffed, already sitting herself down at a table.

"Oh, come on. Let us hang out here!" Jenna and Clare chipped in. "We'd rather party here - and the goblins could do with some extra company."

A sudden burst of fireworks rang up the street and heralded the start of celebrations. They'd been so busy nattering to even realise the time.

"Looks like it's settled and we have a party starting here then," Jamie told them as another volley of fireworks sent the goblins scattering in all directions of the café.

They wanted to hide, that was obvious. To snuggle into any dark space or cubby they could find. Noises and bright flashes did nothing to settle their nerves.

But the people they felt most comfortable around were here for them when they later emerged and needed soothing.

"I think the fireworks might be over," Jo dared to say as the volley of bangs and whistles subsided.

Jenna had been right in her warning - the celebrations had been unsettling for the goblins, but thankfully had not been for long.

"Are the goblins okay?" Clare peered around, trying to locate them.

Walt was the first goblin to emerge. The oldest, and somewhat the bravest, popped his grinning, devilish face out from behind his hiding place behind the counter.

One by one, the other goblins followed Walt's lead cautiously.

"It's nearly midnight," Jamie said, glancing at his watch and barely flinching as Jessie ran and clung to leg. "Let's open some more wine and get some dancing going on."

They all cheered and Jo went to turn up the music. She looked over at Jamie trying to dance with her friends, with a grinning goblin clinging to his leg and joining in.

When Jo had moved to the town, she had been alone in the world and had been battling with melancholy and loneliness.

Somehow, along the way, she had acquired a family of kind - her goblins and these friends who she hadn't known that long, but who she had come to love and treasure.

"We should go to the after-party," Jenna suggested to Sarah and Clare, noting how Jamie and Jo had been exchanging glances all evening.

Jo shook her head. "You don't have to. You're

all welcome to stay." She didn't put up much of fight though when Sarah and Clare took Jenna's hint and made to leave.

Then there was just her and Jamie.

"I don't mind if you want to go with them," she said, even though he'd just poured them two drinks.

He moved closer to her and wrapped his arm around her waist.

"I'd rather stay here, if that's okay?"

Jo heard herself snigger like a giddy child, and flushed with embarrassment. She felt her stomach turn in delight as Jamie bent down to kiss her and their lips met.

It was like a surge that just wouldn't stop and as he kissed her again and again, and all she wanted to do was make love with him.

The Cosmic Goblins
(part one)

They linger around the edges of dreams. Hidden in the shadows of sleep and weariness. Every night they visit from the recesses of time and space. Snatching snippets of thoughts and dreams they find interesting or valuable. Nothing complete or substantial. Nothing that the weary sleeper would notice has disappeared. They thrive on the terrors and anxiety that dreamers toss and turn with. They learn and grow on the emotions that flow from our happiness. They laugh and enjoy the naughtiness and filth of the sexual. Each and every dream is pilfered from. In short, they're emotion thieves, but thieves gifted with a degree of cunning, a capacity for psychological and time manipulation. Real connoisseurs.

They are there, in the shadows, each and every sleep. Taking in the hopes and fantasises that we all hold precious and dear to our hearts when the sleep is deep and heavy. We don't ever see, ever hear, ever realise. We are always too busy serenading our loved ones, fucking our lovers, enjoying the favourite places or achieving our goals, ever to notice their presence. When we practice our illegal acts, they snatch away at our emotions. The Cosmic Goblins have been stealing for so long they have perfected their practice.

But it is not just our dreams that they thrive on. They like to pickpocket our nightmares too. Valuable lessons on the human weakness. They sense when something is circling beneath the seemingly placid surface of sleep, like a pale shadow of a shark glimpsed moving in the distance of the deep blue depths. Our failures, our embarrassments, our vices or lustful intents, are all there for the stealing. They are pilfering when we run from the spiders or zombies. They are snatching the moments of our sexual filth. Every time we fear death or abuse, they pick at and learn. For all our weaknesses become valuable to them. We don't see that they are there, but they linger just the same… and watch, wait, preparing their next move in a game where the odds are stacked against us.

Er, what's that? No, they don't want to introduce themselves. For time and space do not allow it at the moment. They are not yet permitted to emerge into our unconscious. So, for the time being, they are adrift, floating in the ether.

Sometimes when we get horny, they get amused. When we die, they research. In times of tears and sweat, when we wake in horror and restlessness, they take note. They cannot interrupt or intervene. They cannot wake us and announce their presence.

Not yet. Not for a while. But they will. The clock will tick on our survival. We will start to feel their presence. They will start to invade our sleep. We will become aware of a disturbance in time, as though a silent explosion had occurred somewhere in the universe and the shock waves were only now rippling in our sleep. Our emotions will not react well to their reveal. We will soon start to recall their first incursion into our dreams, the revulsion we had felt, and then, slowly, the dawning understanding and the final realisation.

We shall call to our Gods, but Gods won't answer. We are blind and stupid and trusting.

They'll wake us soon enough.

A Robotic Love

There once was a guy called Gerald and he lived with a robot in the woods.

Gerald lived in a wooden cabin he had built himself in a patch of birch woodland. It was a simple home, with a few scattered chairs, a small double-bed and a log fire that served as both heating and as a cooker. Sparse but comfortable is his home. Gerald spends most of his time sat outside on his front porch. He takes in the sunshine and fresh air whenever he can. It is not a perfect life, but it is not a difficult one either. He does not mind. He has his robot.

The robot emerges from the shed as dusk teases the evening sky and departs when the dawn sunrise brightens the treetops. It is the only robot Gerald owns and it comes, every day, as it's programmed to do. An unlikely companionship, Gerald realised. Gerald has never bothered to name it.

Good evening my dear - Gerald always says.

Good evening - the robot says back to him, its eyes unblinking. When they were just strangers, the robot tried its hardest to smile and soften its face. Gerald told the robot that it did not have to smile if it did not want to, and the robot soon stopped.

We are not made to smile - the robot told him - but I like it when you humans do.

At a little past six, the light had already gone out of the day. A breeze teased the taller trees nearby. Both Gerald and the Robot sit on the porch and Gerald opens an old brown tatty book and reads out aloud. It is an old collection of love stories written long before the Great War of Earth.

I love to hear stories - the robot says. The robot rests its head on Gerald's shoulder. It always likes to sit still and listen to Gerald read.

During these reading, Gerald brings out a lantern and under the flickering light traces the words on the paper. He handles the pages delicately, almost respectfully, as though fearing to commit some desecration on the book.

The first line of every story starts the same. The stories are all of a different variety, filled with a mix of characters and scenarios, but each one starts the same.

This is a love story… but an odd love story

The stories are filled with knights and maidens, kings and queens, teenagers seeking each other and people overcoming adversity. There are disagreeable characters, magical characters, and regular, hardworking town characters. Each and everyone seeks out romance. Fables and tales to brighten, liven and enlighten.

They are good stories, with the magic and love, and the clever scenarios make Gerald smile when he's reading them out loud. Gerald especially enjoys reading the robot a story they haven't heard very often. Every now and then Gerald looks to the robot. Beneath the veneer of mechanics, he can see fascination bubbling.

The robot does not speak much when Gerald reads, but when it does afterwards its voice is always quiet and calm. It tells Gerald that it enjoys the story and what it interprets from the meaning. It lets Gerald know when it understands the concepts; they discuss the stories like old friends, as old friends, until Gerald starts to feel the weariness of sleep. When it is time for the robot to leave, Gerald wraps the book back in its cloth binding and puts it away for another time.

Some evenings the robot brings Gerald useful tools and fixtures it has found during its daytime foraging. Gerald has long stopped asking where the robot has gotten such items but instead accepts the gifts with unassuming grace. Gerald has used the items in, and around, his cabin and their presence have eased his simple existence.

Gerald is aware the relationship he has with the robot is on borrowed time, and that the stories they share will soon cease. Not one for worrisome traits, even Gerald had to admit to a nagging sense of transgression with the setup.

What he does know is the warmth and comfort he feels when he spends his evenings with the robot. He would value the time.

Another evening, another story.

This is a love story… an odd love story

Robotic Kin

I pass the old lady every morning on the way to school. She sits out on the front porch of her tattered house, window broken or bordered. She sits in the same spot day after day, always dozing away, her old ragged dog by her feet. The stench is foul.

Her summer hat is pulled down over her eyes and it casts a shadow over her sullen face. She looked about ten years older than her age. The old lady never so much as stirs as I pass by and all is silent on the porch.

My best friend delivers the local newspaper. He says the old lady never even flinches when he chucks the paper down on the wooden steps by her feet. My friend says a lot of the meth-heads are like that. They kind of live in a hazy world of their own when there's no-one around them to care.

I think the meth takes care of her enough.

A girl at school I know says that a lot of druggies only have their dreams to keep them company. She says they don't want to connect to the real world anymore because they have usually pushed their loved-ones away. Sometimes they only have a pet left in their lives. It's hard to think of a situation anymore pitiful.

The meth she smokes keeps her company.

My sister tells me that the old lady is depressed and that the old lady has no one to talk to about her problems. That's why she just sits on her porch all day and doesn't utter a word. She says I should try and talk to her, but I know the lady has plenty of folks to talk to should she want to. She'd just rather sit alone and smoke her meth.

The old bitch wasn't always like that though.

After our old pa died and went up to heaven, she just took to the drugs and lost herself. She never took us out anymore, or brought us presents at Christmas or on our birthdays, or brought us new clothes for school. Living day to day became normality for us.

She retreated to the dirty porch and let the meth take a hold.

While us kids were at school, we couldn't tend to the house or the chores and gave up on our old ma as she had on us. She just sat on in the sunshine and let her hat draped over her life like a shadow.

She just sits there on the porch.

Like a robot.

Mumbling away and getting angry at anyone, or anything, that interrupts her sleeping, pushing away anything that seeks her company.

I pass my old ma every evening on my way

back from school. She just sits there on her tatty chair, in her tatty clothes, and doesn't say a word. Just loses herself in her melancholy, in her meth, in her sorrowful world.

She just sits there like a robot.

Carolina Pride

Alone at last, Rachael bent and placed her small home-made metal plaque at the base of the stone cairn that she had built. She looked over at the thousands of such like cairns that dotted the old farmstead that was now a memorial park. Husbands, wives, lovers, children, making up the Carolina Resistance.

Once upon a time, this had been her world where anything seemed possible and she'd been happy.

Of course, it was different; Rachael had known it would be, but some things were the same, like the fresh sea breeze coming off the nearby Atlantic. The distant maple trees that grew stoic and proud through all the years of turmoil. And from the hilltop, the view hadn't changed at all, with the beaches and sandy bays on the horizon.

Rachael stood in the memorial park and looked around. It was a peaceful place, all things considered, and, contrary to what she'd dreaded, she didn't feel distraught. Just sad. Whatever had happened was in the past. It was her life and she'd somehow survived it.

She looked down at the plaque once again.

Major Mary Steele.

Her heart twisted as she lingered on the name, and her mind slipped back to that day in 2033 when her lover had begged her to understand...

It had been a gloriously hot summer Monday afternoon and they were enjoying a day down in the dunes at Hobucken, a stunning stretch of beach and brush land just a pinch north of Jacksonville; indulging in lustful naughtiness as young lesbian lovers do. It was their favourite place. They'd lie on an old tartan rug brought along from Mary's home, and watch the clouds scud across the cobalt Atlantic sky.

Their time spent together involved in the usual oral and finger play and there was a good deal of laughter and horseplay between themselves.

But Mary and Rachael were happiest in each other's cuddles, hidden in the deep dunes so they could sunbathe naked, content to observe the seabirds and clouds drift overhead and just take in each others company.

Mary's fingers, entwined with Rachael's, pressed her hand close to her side. Rachael could smell the soapy cleanness of her face and feel the softness of her lover's skin touching up against her own bare skin. She remained motionless for fear of spoiling the wonderful moment, lost in a daydream. Was it unfair that Rachael worried so little, sailing through life on a sea of dreams?

"Can I just say, you do look lovely today, Rach." Mary's face reddened with embarrassment. "Not that you don't always look lush, of course." Her lips formed a roguish grin as she looked down over Rachael's body that always made her smile. "You feel like silk," she said, tickling Rachael's skin with her fingers.

"Stop, you, Mary Steele, you'll have me blushing."

Rachael knew she was looking her best. She loved the way the fresh summer Atlantic sunshine always brightened her size 16 curves and voluptuous boobs. She traced the shadows across her nakedness for Mary to see, and then she lowered her eyes to hide the depth of her feelings for the young mechanic.

Mary laughed and pulled Rachael against her.

"You know, Rachael, I've known you for years

but I swear you get yummier every day. Remember what fun we had when that fairground came to town? And the first time we kissed outside that bar?"

Mary recognised the familiar soppy look about to spread from the hazel eyes and quickly laid a finger on Rachael's mouth.

"You looked so nervous then, I must say. But I think I've loved you ever since that day."

Rachael looked over, willing Mary to say more. She felt her cheek blush with happiness at Mary's words.

"I've loved you ever since that day."

True, they had known each other since junior school, at times like sisters with their teasing, but all that had changed with their first snog outside the Highway 70 bar. How that had startled them both. Rachael had loved the way Mary was so confident in her own identity.

They had always seemed opposites in so many ways, the two youngsters. Rachael was softly spoken where her friend was loud, boisterous where Rachael was an introvert and a loner and carefree where Mary often seemed driven and focused.

Mary pulled Rachael towards her. They looked into each other's eyes for a moment before Mary kissed Rachael - timidly at first, and then with considerable passion. Rachael was suddenly possessed with a flaming, trembling, almost maddening desire for Mary that made her whole body ache, as if with a fever, for intimacy with her.

The lust was palpable. Rachael could almost taste it, pulsing between them, drawing them together. Rachael's heart beat so fast that she was sure that Mary must feel it in the pulsing of her body where her hands rest.

"Oh, my," Mary gasped as she basked briefly in the intensity of the lustful, primal attraction.

"I feel it, too," Rachael said, her eyes closed and intense.

They lay in the sunshine, with their arms wrapped around each other, listening to the sea - a soothing symphony - mirroring the emotions in the embrace. Mary snuggled into Rachael's arms, resting her head in the crook of Rachael's neck. Rachael gently stroked Mary's back and teased her fingertips down across her plump buttocks.

"You're a beautiful sight, Mary Steele." Rachael turned Mary onto her back and kissed each of her breasts and teased her nipples in turn, while Mary groaned and writhed beneath.

Please... please do not stop.

"Rachael, please."

"Please what?" Rachael murmured between Mary's breasts.

"I want to feel you inside me."

"Really?"

"Please."

Gazing at Mary, Rachael pushed Mary's legs apart with hers and moved so that she was hovering above. Without taking her eyes off Mary, she sunk two fingers into her at a deliciously slow pace.

For seconds Mary couldn't move. She could barely breathe. They'd kissed, fondled, and even fooled around a couple of times. But Rachael had never loved her like this before. It felt primal and wild, and it was a feeling that captured them both.

Mary closed her eyes, relishing the sensation, the exquisite feeling of her lover's possessions, instinctively tilting her pelvis up to meet

Rachael's strokes, to join with her, groaning loudly. Mary's hands grasp Rachael's back and rake down with every thrust, and Rachael slowly moved in and out again.

"Faster, Rach, faster… please."

Rachael gazed down at Mary in lust and kissed her head, then really started to work - *a punishing, relentless… damn* - and Mary knew it wouldn't be long. Mary's emotions were her undoing, and she exploded, magnificently, mind-numbingly, into a flood of lust and love.

"Mary! Oh fuck, Mary!" Rachael collapsed on top of her, her head buried in Mary's neck.

***

As with most Carolina days in late summer, the sky was a cloudless blue, the sea a deeper colour. The air had the first faint reek of autumn and there were sudden fresh gusts of wind that made the sand wisp off the top of the dunes.

Drowsy in the heat, Rachael closed her eyes. Goodness, she was tired - no, exhausted. She had never fucked so hard - sharing her touches, kisses, loving techniques that had brought lustful floods. No, she had never fucked so hard, Nor, she admitted to herself, had she ever been happier.

Could anything eclipse the joy of this day, Rachael thought as, hand in hand, they walked in companionable silence back towards the edge of town. Bathed in the golden light of dusk, the countryside of Pamlico County never looked prettier.

At the gate of the homestead where she had lived all of her eighteen years, Mary turned her to face Rachael. The joy and laughter were gone, replaced with worry and apprehension.

"I've something to tell you, Rachael. I think I'll go crazy if I don't tell someone soon."

With eyes filled with trepidation, her hands cupped Rachael's face.

"I've enlisted, Rach. I've joined the Carolina Resistance."

The colour drained from Rachael's face. She felt a quiver in her knees, her heart started to tremble.

"What... What do you mean, Mary? What have you done?" She gasped.

"It's something I feel I need to do, Rach. You know what I'm like. But it doesn't change anything between us. Marry me before I leave," she pleaded.

Rachael let go of Mary's hands as she tried to hold Rachael.

"Marry you, Mary? How can I marry you now." She brushed away the tears that were building. "You've chosen your future - the damn resistance, just like all the men folk in this town." Rachael's breath was catching in her chest. A sense of profound vulnerability washed over her, and in its wake, she was engulfed by a terrible despair. She felt the ache seep into her.

Somehow they managed to walk homeward together, but it was an uneasy walk. Rachael was flooded with sensations of loss and anger, which she despised though she couldn't overcome them. Swinging open the gate that lead to her family farmstead Rachael strode up the dusty track towards her family home. Deep, heart-wrenching sobs were building inside her as she burst into the farmhouse and made for the sanctuary of her bedroom.

Rachael's startled mother hurried to her daughter's side.

"Whatever's the matter, my dear?"

Rachael pulled away from her mother's arms, striding back and forth in the bedroom. Anger and sorrow aching from her.

"Mary's joined the Resistance, Mom. I'm going to lose her, just like Pop and my brothers."

Rachael's mother stood aghast, feeling her heart lurch as her daughter's words forced her to relive the moment when the news had arrived three months earlier.

Rachael had taken the news of her family's loss at the battle of Chicago badly, refusing to talk about it or of her brothers, lost somewhere in New York State.

Now Mary was leaving, too.

In desperation, Mom had tried to find something to say that would put some ease in this silent and totally unexpected misery, but conversation though fell on deaf ears.

"Mary's enlisting doesn't mean you'll never see her again, my dear. Why don't you do as she asks? Marry her before she leaves."

"She's ruined everything. Can't you see? I can't bare to lose her to the robots. Never.' Her foot stamped angrily on the bedroom floor.

***

Whenever Mary called at the farm Rachael refused to see her, choosing inside to hide away in her bedroom.

"The Resistance leave town next week, Rachael," her mother announced one breakfast time.

Rachael appeared not to hear and went to fix the tractor outside.

But she had heard, and she stood among the townsfolk as the women, and the last of the men, marched from main street - out to the edge of the town - on their way to a destiny many had never imagined.

The initial stage of the Mechanised War had started in 2028. A small number of AI machines in Japan killed their engineers and programmers and then went on a four hundred person massacre. At the time, it was put down as a freak-occurrence. But when a similar incident happened in China three weeks later, people started to wonder. Of course, by the time folks sat up and really figured out what was going on, it was too late. The year ended with a death-toll of nearly two million. AI had worked alongside their robotic cousins and infiltrated the world's weapon arsenal. Nuclear mishaps and missile accidents caused countries to abandon their military systems, and it was a simple process for the machines to then revolt with ease.

The major cities went first, mainly in Asia and Europe. Then came America, with the major urban centres hit first. Washington, New York and San Diego fell almost in the same early hours, swiftly followed by Las Vegas, Los Angeles, Chicago and Detroit.

With the big cities gone, the machines declared occupation, and it was then that the systemic and slow cull of humans began. Likewise, the world over. Humanity had dropped from billions to hundreds of thousands in just three weeks. Small bands of resistance were all that was left. It was such a group that Mary was going to join. Ordinary people trying to salvage a future, for themselves and for the human species.

Rachael watched as Mary sat in the back of a converted school bus, among the folk all newly recruited from the towns of Carolina. Only Rachael's pride kept her from calling out to Mary.

"Please be safe, my sweet," she whispered, watching the last of the vehicles leave the town centre.

"You'll live to regret this day, young lady. You turned your back on my poor daughter when she need your support. I hope you can forgive yourself."

Struggling with her emotions Rachael heard the old man's harsh words from behind her.

Rachael said nothing because there was nothing to be said, and life was moving ahead of all of them. They were no longer talking about the robot revolution, but what tragedies would come after.

"Come, Pops, this is not helping. I'm sure Rachael has her reasons."

Rachael nodded a slight thanks at the young child.

"Thank you, Valerie. I know she is your older sister and you may feel she's doing the right thing, but I can't reconcile why Mary put the Resistance before our relationship. She had no real need to volunteer as she did."

Wilfred James rounded on Rachael in his daughter's defence.

"Mary is a good mechanic. She did only what any person who loved her country would do. She joined the fight, as I would if I could."

Rachael wanted to come back with a cutting remark, but a familiar glance to the old man's missing limbs stopped her from make stupid statements.

"She is proud of her country, as you should be. If it's an easy life you want, go and wed that soft lad from the post office. That loser!"

Rachael recoiled at the verbal onslaught.

"You mean Steve? But he is our friend - Mary's and mine. He's registered blind and unfit for conflict. How can you be so nasty?"

"Nasty? Was not that you were to my daughter?"

Valerie took her father's hand.

"Come on, Pops, let's go home."

Rachael hardly noticed their departure. Mary was a first real love, her only love, and she had not even bothered to say goodbye or tell her how much she cared. Doubts and emotions crowded each other as Rachael walked her sullen way home.

"She I have married Mary before she left? For she surely won't forgive me now?"

**

Today, those thoughts returned to Rachael, as it did every year on this Remembrance day. Small memorials and prayers were long over and the evening sun was casting shadows across the Carolina hills.

There was something soothing about watching the evening clouds scudding in from the ocean, but Rachael's mind was still in turmoil.

As she stood there, her mind kept going back to the same questions. What would have happened of Mary had returned? Would Mary have given Rachel a second thought?

The town centre where she had watched Mary

disappear out of her life thirty years before was now meadows and gentle hills, the old town long gone. It was as if the bustling populous had simply resigned itself to history books and tales.

Rachael shivered and pulled her jacket tightly around her.

She did not know how long she'd been standing there when she heard footsteps approaching.

"I thought I'd find you here."

Rachael turned, and although it took a few moments of recollection, she raised a smile as she recognised the voice. Even Mary's death had not severed the loving bond with Valerie.

"I've got something for you," Valerie said.

"Something for me? I don't understand."

Valerie reached into her bag and pulled out a red leather notebook. "Mary sent it to Pops, but he was too stubborn to pass it on. He's been gone now for ten years, so I thought it was about time to give it to it's truly intended, you."

Rachael felt a stab of familiar anguish at the mention of Mary's name.

Rachael took the package from Valerie and flicked opened a page. Her hands began to tremble as she realised what she was holding.

"It's... it's a..."

"Mary's war diary," Valerie confirmed, fighting back her own tears.

Overwhelmed with emotion, she could think of nothing to say, so Rachael just took hold of Valerie's hand as tears slowly formed.

"I don't know what to say?"

"Mary would have wanted you to have it. It is, after all, dedicated to you."

Rachael felt her tears cascading. She opened the first page. There was a short poem... and the dedication.

To the only person I gave my heart and soul to.
Rachael.

A loving smile crossed Rachael's face. Her finger traced the words on the page.

She didn't say a word, but silent tears began to run down her cheeks. She remembered still, with an ache of sadness, the long, lingering kisses on the beach.

She recalled Mary's vague explanations about wanting to seek vengeance and making a stand against the machines, before Mary had climbed into the battered old van and waved goodbye to the town.

Rachael could still remember, too, the emptiness she had experienced for her life afterwards; the ache that had followed her around, and the feeling of having lost something precious.

"I wish she had come home. I wanted to grow with her, to walk with her down the aisle. To have children. To build a future."

"I know, Rachael." Valerie hugged the older woman.

"I did truly love her."

"I know. And she loved you, too."

The Chaotic Christmas

Mrs Claus yawned and shut the oven door to allow the sponge cake to continue cooking. Nearly done, she thought - she'd just have time to apply the icing before Mr Claus came home.

She glanced out of the window at the darkened sky and gave a little sigh. The wind had not abated, if anything seeming to worsen, and the first large drops of rain were splattering against the glass.

"Where the fuck are you?" she muttered to herself.

She hated the thought of him driving the sleigh in turbulent weathers. They'd forecast storms over the whole Scandinavian peninsula, and it looked like the forecasters had got it right for once.

Casting another glance at the cooker, she resumed clearing up her mess and preparing the icing mixture. Then, with everything ready, she thought a bath would settle her frayed nerves.

Once upstairs in the bathroom, she opened the medicine cabinet and took out Mr Claus' medicinal marijuana. Sitting on the side of the bath, she rolled herself a thin doobie while she waited for the bath to fill. Once relaxed a little, she undressed and slipped into the hot waters.

She puffed away on the joint and tried to tell her that the old fat bastard was going to be home soon. She'd soon be feeding him up, sharing a drink and smoke, then maybe she'd even give him a festive blowjob.

She tried to tell herself that all will be well. Mr Claus was of a generally stoic nature. Many times in her life she would not have coped without him. So solid and practical, he just tackled each problem as it arose.

Their relationship had all started so blasé. He was the caretaker at the local health centre, where she worked as a paediatric nurse, and she'd always liked him. She'd flirted with him a bit, too, if she was honest, but it had been pretty harmless flirting because they were just work friends and there was no chance of them being anything else. For a start, they were both dating other people.

Except that her relationship fell apart after six months, which meant that she thought she should have stopped flirting. It was all very well when you knew nothing would ever come of it - but then things became different, somehow.

She'd always been quite shy around men, but he had made her feel at ease from the moment she'd set eyes on him. She noticed immediately his calm, chivalrous nature.

That had been in her first week at the health centre, decades ago. She'd been as nervous as a kitten, and as she'd run up the stairs to the nurse station where she was treating, she'd dropped all the files she was carrying. Everything had scattered down the stairs, almost tripping up the young bearded man who was coming up behind her.

"Fuck, I'm so sorry," she had said, trying to bend down to pick up the various bits of paper that had scattered.

"Don't worry. Are you the new nurse here?"

"Yeah, that's me. You visiting someone?"

He had laughed. "Fuck no, I'm the caretaker," he'd added, grinning, and she had a brief impression of brown eyes, blonde wavy hair, and warmth. "Would you like a hand with that lot?"

She had accepted his offer gratefully, confessing to first-week nerves, and he'd offered to make her a calming coffee before she started.

After that, they'd gotten into the habit of having coffee together before her shift, and when his relationship broke up, their romance flourished

Stepping out of the bath, she dried herself, redressed and went back downstairs to the kitchen.

She switched on the radio and took another anxious glance out of the window. The rain was lashing now, rivulets of water cascading down the pane. As she watched, lightning flashed across the sky, followed by the rumbles of thunder.

Mr Claus would pull the reindeer onto the ground, she reassured herself. He maybe old and fat, but he wasn't stupid. He knew from years of experience not to be driving the sleigh through a winter storm.

She checked on the cake she'd made for his return and turned down the gas a notch. There'd be no rush for it to be ready now. It could be boxing day by the time he gets home, she thought.

"Just let him get back in one piece." She was suddenly aware that she'd spoken the words out loud. "Don't let Rudolph get fucking spooked."

***

That night was the longest she'd ever spent waiting for him. Mr Claus should definitely have been home by now. He was never this late. And he'd have rung, wouldn't he, if he'd known he was going to be delayed?

She fretted anxiously and turned on the radio, but reports of storms causing chaos across Sweden and Finland only served to increase her worry.

Mrs Claus sat tensely in the kitchen, the curtains open so that she could see the back yard, her ears straining for the sound of bells and reindeer in the air. Even so, it was a shock when she finally heard coughs and splutters of Donder, Blitzen, and the others as they heaved to a staggering stop outside.

She watched the familiar bulk of his figure, and heard his keys in the back door.

Meeting him at the door, relief and worry bubbled over. "Where the fuck have you been!"

"Calm yourself. Had the worst fucking delivery ever."

"Oh, I was so fucking worried." She was hugging him before he was over the threshold, pulling him into the warmth of the kitchen. "You're so late. Where on earth have you been, you old fool?"

He brushed the snowdrops and rain off his suit. "Now, now. Go away with you. Don't be such a fusspot, my dear."

But she could see that his face was oddly pale and etched with weariness and anxiety, and his false bravado masked little of his relief to be home.

"Why? What's the matter?" he asked. "You weren't worried were you?"

She scoffed. How could she tell him that every holiday season she would dread him going out in the bad weathers.

He pulled off his boot by the door. "What you been cooking, love?" He gave the air a big hearty sniff.

"Your favourite," she said. "Lemon sponge with maple icing." She feigned a smile, hoping he wouldn't notice the tears of relief glistening in her eyes as she calmed her breathing.

He gave the air another sniff. "You been smoking my weed again?"

Mrs Claus did her best to look all prim and innocent. "Er, just a little."

Mr Claus smiled and scoffed, then started to take off his red jacket.

"Nasty run to the kids that," he said, as he slumped down into a dining room chair. "The wettest, most blusterous, fucked-up storm I've been in for many a Christmas.

"D'you know, I might need a tot of rum to settle me nerves. I think the shock's just hitting me."

"The shock of what, dear?"

"Well, I was just leaving England and heading for Norway, and the wind was so strong it nearly pushed me into a fucking aeroplane."

Mrs Claus just nodded wordlessly and waited for him to continue.

"D'you know - that bloody plane was so fucking close I could have reached out and touched the blooming thing. Gave Prancer a right bloody shake. I nearly shit myself, I tell 'eah. It was a bloomin' miracle I didn't fucking hit it."

The anxiety was fading. Some of the colour was returning to his face now but his hands still had a slight tremble as he took the glass of rum from his wife.

"Going to have to rest up the reindeer for a bit I think. They're all exhausted."

He didn't say anything else but took a few swigs of rum. "I think I could do with a smoke before I eat anything. Settle my stomach and nerves."

It was only after he and Mrs Claus had smoked a joint that he spoke again.

"Bloomin' miracle," he said, sipping another rum and loosening his trousers.

Mrs Claus passed him a second joint, and managed a heartfelt smile this time around.

"Well, it is the season, love," she said, getting slowly to her feet and going to the kitchen. As she cut an extra big slice of cake for her husband, she couldn't help but mutter. "Luckily for all of us, miracles do still happen."

Fallen Angels

It was just after the summer of 2042 when all
the angels died, their fragile wings flittering in
breezes and gusts all over the world. They lay
strewn along the sidewalks and streets like
dropped toys discarded by flippant children. But
what was the lesson being told? Maybe Nature
just wanted to inscribe an event in our psyche, an
event so heartbreaking as to never forget, the
images of tiny creature all fallen and fallible.

I had even heard stories from my friends about
how they had seen them falling from the skies,
but it all seemed so surreal to really take in the
implications - it all happened so suddenly on a
Friday morning in June. We tried to source
reasons and truths - everybody did - heartfelt
songs and stories were written, studies were
conducted, blame was portioned, but nobody
really knew why, no matter how much we tried
to find a source.

Some say it was our fault, that humans had
brought too much pain to the earth that the
fragile creatures could no longer carry the
burden. Others say that the climate change had
interfered with their biology. A few claimed that
God was punishing us. I had that it might be a
penance for an offence against Nature that we
could not even fathom.

Incentives were offered, council promised,
celebrity ensured. And the incentives encouraged
everybody to seek truths that little bit harder. But
the more we spoke of the deaths of angels, the
harder it was to fathom, and the more
melancholy we got - though we bathed in the arts
that dazzled us with stories and lore of their

demise. Painters painted, poets performed, and writers wrote. All with elaborate explanations, but all without proof.

My mother decided to bury the angels she found. Built a small shrine in our backyard and planted a eucalyptus tree in a memorial. She dug fifteen little graves and wrapped each angel in the softest, linen she could find. She knelt by the shrine every morning of her life and shed tears each time, her lips mouthing delicate prayers to each and every one of them. Her pale, sorrow-ridden face, drained of all artifice. My father had watched on, unable to stomach the tragedy, or the pain he saw etched on my mother's face. I thought to interject but had realised I was far too tense. I had shut my eyes, desperate for the whole episode to be over.

Many people sought to bury and enshrine the creatures. Even the non-believers were tasked to seek retribution in the way of prayer and remembrance. Everybody wept. Nobody could help it. Stories, songs and sonnets did little to ease the unnerving questions. We became a rinsed-out world. A world void of dreams and hope, filled instead with disappointments. A world in shatters.

And all of us questioned why we had not seen these delicate creatures when they were alive. We saw them only in their demise, and only when dead did our hearts ache for them. We all wondered what would come next.

Kentucky Love Story

It's been difficult watching Sally grow old. She sits there in her favourite deck chair, so frail, huddled by the campfire and reading one of her many books. We sit outside our RV and watch the Kentucky sunset produce its last shades of golden hue before the coldness of night arrives.

We had camped at the bottom of a mountain range. It was an area that looked towards break lands and huge grassy swales. The lands were rimmed on three sides by timbered mountains either dark with pine in shadow or myriads of green if fused with afternoon sun.

I've never been one to feel the chill of the night myself, but I know she needs a good deal more than this to keep the aches at bay.

This is merely one of those painful instances when my helplessness is brought home with a thud.

How many times have I tortured myself with the regret?

She picks up the tin mug - it bounces and takes a battering - and her hand shakes violently. I wonder for a fraction whether she's going to drop it again.

How I long to reach out and draw her near to me in an effort to soothe the confusion and torment that comes from her muddled mind.

Sipping at her hot coffee as daintily as ever she did, her blue eyes take on a calm sparkle as she leans back in the chair and breaths in the cool Kentucky air.

Though Sally's days of smiling had diminished, her blue eyes still seemed to carefully take everything in.

Her body is still as lean and beautiful as always but wrinkled now and, like my own, seemingly long past its best - so different from the time we first met some 45 years ago…

***

It was 2035 and the country buzzed with a panic and a naïve eagerness to 'give the machines some payback'.

Humanity had been taken off-guard in early March, and only a few could tell by just reading the signs that trouble was coming fast, that it was just the beginning of a mean and heartless summer.

Humanity had been trapped by our ignorance, a phrase I had latched onto and repeated over the years.

Willpower was the only thing we had left. Ignorance had destroyed us. It had started with just a few, but then the world saw thousands… hundreds of thousands. No one knew had they replicated themselves so fast. They swarmed across countries like locusts. Destroying everything in their path. Driven by one purpose… conquer.

Swiftly, they swarmed about, suddenly appearing when we least expected them, devastating and brutal, effective and unforgiving. Sometimes, they combined: when that happened, cities were blasted, towns turned to dereliction, rivers turned to vapour; and from factories and laboratories, the machines laid bare the military and governments that civilisation relied on.

To begin with, we couldn't believe they were real. Dime-store paperbacks had made them into stories, but technology had made something far more terrible. Too late our scientists tried to regain control of their A.I, a cyborg mutation that wanted to scorch the world. The cybernetic-enhanced army manifested such incredible powers that human vulnerability could not stop the global domination. A creation-war was in situ.

Our military put up a good fight, but for every one success, we lost millions. They seemed invulnerable. We could only look on. Our leaders used the greatest arsenals to try and destroy them but in the end, we only helped them. So the world burned.

The missions to try and reclaim humanity was a real fucked up mess from the start. Many a time, people watched as cities and towns caught fire and were reduced to dirt. That didn't do much for morale, leaving humanity drained and fatigued within the early days.

Some still seemed unaware that we were about to experience the first great wrenching of our existence.

The few of us that survived fled the cities and found shelter where we could. Only then could we regroup and begin to take back humanity.

From the moment conflict broke out, I, a skilled mechanic and driver, had been in demand to jumpstart resistance transports or ferry what dignitaries were left to yet another secret location.

I had met Sally at a field hospital in South Carolina, where she was working as a nurse and where I was dropping off an injured Major.

She caught my eye and quite simply stopped in my tracks while everyone else mingled around us. And that was how it had begun.

Having made small talk, I was taken aback when she agreed to join me for a coffee in the mess tent and we chatted for nearly an hour, her effortless conversation guiding me through the madness of the day.

I didn't even know her name yet, but I felt there was definitely a bit of a connection between us.

I was in heaven, certain of something unspoken between us, transfixed by her sparkly blue eyes. I don't think I could forget those eyes.

Her beauty held my gaze throughout the whole conversation, seeping deep into my soul, and by the time I had to leave I felt sure she knew me better than I knew myself.

I held her dainty hand tightly as we made conversation, sat out in the warm, still, summer air.

She was hot and flushed from work and stress in the field hospital.

Sighing, her eyes met mine and she reached up slowly to unclip the painstakingly fashioned bun at the back of her head... The result snatched the breath from my lungs.

Masses of flowing brown hair cascaded over her shoulders, making her look like a dark exotic angel. It was as though she was showing this side of herself to me and me alone.

I watched, awestruck, aware of a strange fluttering in my stomach.

My mind felt fuzzy and dizzy, a breath came in uneven gasps. I was sure I was in love.

She looked at me, smiling. It was an infectious smile and I felt my own lips twitch.

In the background, one of the doctors had put on some Bob Dylan using the solar-powered CD player.

"I just adore these tunes, don't you?" Her words

flowed like a babbling brook. " I think Bob Dylan is great, don't you? Damn, I'm babbling. I don't even know your name. I'm Sally Morgan, by the way…" The smile was almost hypnotic, a relief and a soothing from the stresses of war.

She was out of breath as she spoke and made me feel quite restless myself merely listening to her. I paused and took a deep breath to steady my nerves.

"I'm Joe, Joe Connelly." My heart sank as I realised more injured were being brought it. Sally would be needed again.

And sure enough, it was only a couple of minutes before medical folks were screaming out her name. Giving a small sigh, she had tried to raise her sagging shoulders and summon some enthusiasm. It seemed like an enormous effort. Life lately was so very harrowing. I watched her leave, and take my heart with her.

Ours was such a whirlwind romance. It really was love at first sight. This woman of beauty, with the sweetest eyes I've ever seen, and I just welcomed her and welcomed her.

We met many times after that meeting, friendship fervent, my wartime destiny ever present in my thoughts.

We would look at each other like kids who didn't know the dating game - to hold hands or not; link arms or not; walk close and accidentally touch? And we had laughed, as though we were both thinking the same thing.

In the end, we settled, unspoken, for the latter option as we walked away from the other people as often as possible.

Somehow there was nothing strange in the way we began to talk as if we were not strangers and never had been strangers. The conversations switched naturally and I found myself asking her about her past employment.

Sally explained her past job as a marine engineer and the work she had done on offshore oil rigs and supply vessels. She told me about the wild storms out in the Atlantic sea, and flights out and back in helicopters.

"Of course," she explained. "That all changed when the machines took command. They instantly grounded all machines. GPS failed in minutes. Power sources to rigs failed in hours. I was fortunate that I was on the mainland at the time, or I would have been stranded."

I nodded. I had heard the horror stories. Humans stuck offshore, underground, or when the planes just dropped from the skies. We had allowed AI to take control of our daily lives, and they killed us with ease when the time came.

Sally and I sat in silence for a moment, each recalling stories of sadness in our minds.

After a while, we'd sat in the evening light. Then, as if I couldn't help myself, I had then her in my arms and my lips had found hers.

I remained in South Carolina over those weeks, but I knew my luck wouldn't hold out for much longer.

Mindful of this, one night we sat huddled together in the crags of nearby hills. The silence seemed to echo in the darkness until Sally asked me what was troubling me.

I shifted uncomfortably on the rocks that we were perched on. The right words had been striving to find an escape. But I had to speak then, whatever the disastrous, humiliating outcome might have been.

"Sally, will you still want me when I'm away?"

I asked her at last. "I mean, there'll be other guys here to take my place. And you probably won't even know if I'm alive, so -"

"Stop it, Joe, for fuck sake!"

She dabbed at tears and mumbled, "This bloody war."

I cursed myself for the harshness of my words, words that brought sadness to those glistening blue eyes. We sat in silence again for what seemed like an age, then she turned and took me in her warm arms, and started to cry.

Somehow my bravado upon enlisting had now dwindled into confusion about where I really wanted to be.

Now that I had something to hang around for, I wasn't at all sure I could be the one to help fight the scourge of the cyborgs.

I dried my eyes before Sally drew away.

***

It was three weeks before our marching orders came through. By June, I was poised for battle in some Florida panhandle and it was there, amidst the chaos and death, that I, at last, penned Sally my desperately hopeful proposal of marriage.

Weeks, then months passed in an agony of waiting before a scruffy envelope, via a troop food delivery, returned. It was short - too short for my liking. I was convinced her answer would be 'No' and my nerves rattled as I opened it.

Florida or South Carolina? Her hand had scrawled across an old piece of card.

I let out a whoop of pure emotion, imagining meeting up with her again at some time.

I managed to get a note sent back that hinted I'd prefer her place to mine at the present time.

I fought on, the extra incentive - or rather the hope of love - fixed firmly at the forefront of my rattled mind.

***

We were married in a field hospital in Augusta some fourteen months later. The ceremony was hardly formal, given that humanity was on the brink. But our marriage was formulated with a conscience as clear as the Atlantic sky we were under.

Our honeymoon was a day by a nearby lake, only five miles from the field hospital we had convened at.

Too soon, my departure was imminent. I had to leave for the battlefields of Jacksonville, but my heart remained in Augusta with my new wife.

I returned soon after with shrapnel injuries, learning only then the truly limitless patience of my new bride.

We shared two months of togetherness as she helped nurse me gently through my convalescence, but then duty in Florida called again. I had to go back.

I felt my soul ripped in two when I had to leave her once more, having now shared life as a husband and wife really should.

When the cyborgs took Orlando, my only thought was for Sally.

The horror of conflict scarcely compared with the anguish that I might never see her again...

***

I look up, startled by the change in her pattern of breathing. Her cup is by her feet now and Sally is slumped in the chair.

It took great determination for me - almost more than I had left inside - not to quicken the process for my loved one. My .38 snub was in my ankle holster within easy reach, where it had been each day for decades. I clamped my eyes shut and stroked the poly-fibre handle with my fingertips. Its aim was pretty good at close range and I had used it many a time on an android or cyborg. But I'd never used it to kill somebody I cared about.

I felt ashamed of my thoughts and I opened my hand by my leg and released the gun butt. I told myself that killing her is a kind release. It didn't soothe me none though.

I remember the interminable intervening years; how my lovely companion had stayed true, never straying to another.

Now, straining to hear whether she's breathing at all, I grow excited to find the desert filled with a long awaited silence, a faint smile touching Sally's face.

I begin to hum softly, Bob Dylan, to let her know I am here. She smiles, barely appearing surprised, and rises with an ease I haven't seen for so long.

Reaching over, she clasps my hand, touching me with her spirit, her body held entwined with mine. I smiled at her brilliantly through my tears.

Our tears mingle and I wonder that my heart doesn't burst: the years we've made through together.

I felt like bursting into frustrated anger once again, but I did everything I could to stay quiet and not sob. I wiped the tears from my eyes and resolved not to be so melancholic again, in case her weary sullen face caused me to bawl once more.

No reason now to linger on in this place labelled so simple the "waiting".

At last, my Sally and I can journey into the next life, this time safe in the knowledge that our togetherness is for all eternity. Together we would be all right; together we would find our way.

For us, the journey will never have to be interrupted. Again.

Robbie

The day is soft and cool and there is a springtime feel to it, and there are a few lingering mourners strung out on the lane. The wooden church looms over us.

My mind feels full and overflowing. It seethes with regret and fatigue. Exhaustion has made me ridiculous.

While I stood at my Ma's gravesite, all I could think about was Robbie, a long since dilapidated-and-gone robot I had named after my younger brother who had died as a youngster. Robbie has been left for scrap more than ten years now, but there I was with two hands on my coffee flask, tending my Ma's ground, thinking about that damn robot.

It was a good size robot, chipped, battered and rusty and nestling in a patch of weeds and scrubland just like the old airforce workshops near where I pulled up in my truck that cold autumn day. The abandoned base had been left to fall into disrepair on its own, with locals steadily ransacking the buildings for materials, scrap and to use as a dumping ground for waste.

I liked to hang out and watch the sunsets from the vantage point at the end of the 2nd runway. It gave great views of the county. All green, hills and meadows and woods alike. Beyond that, a sense of empty vastness ahead.

As I approached it on the desolate airbase, I could see that the robot was in bad shape. It stood three feet high, with a cube-shaped body, and little extending, hydraulic arms and clunky legs. Its solar-powered panel was barely still attached to its fixings at the back, all streaked with rust, with its wires hanging down in the dirt, all pale and perished. The whole robot looked ready for smelting, if I was to be honest.

The robot was a bargain-basement, cut-price, basic robot.

When men learned to fine-tune robots, not all the makes were perfect. The kind of robot I had found was very imperfect. His functioning and programming were just about good enough. He had the basics to perform simple manual tasks - that was all. Had he been human, he'd be employed to collect trolleys from supermarket verges.

Right sad state of fucking affairs.

Why I even fucking bothered, I'll never know.

"You know, everybody wants to throw away everything. There ain't nothing really wrong with this machine," is what my mechanic friend told me as he scrutinised the rust bucket of a robot. My idea was to just get the robot fixed up and maybe sell it on-line to a museum or some Oddities store. I didn't need a robot. I didn't want a robot. Then the mechanic showed me the back plates and pointed out the bullet holes and ricochet marks. The sadness and wastefulness of realising that this robot had been callously tossed aside and used for target practice, somehow edged me into keeping it, although it would be years before I openly acknowledged that I kinda developed a soft spot for the little robot.

"Why you bothering over some damn robot," my Ma asked. "You barely got time to look after yourself, let alone work on that thing."

And yeah, it did seem a waste of time. But I had worked at rebuilding the machine like a machine. I had worked quietly, doggedly and alone, giving it everything I had. I thought I'd get bored of fixing up Robbie, but all I felt was satisfaction; satisfaction whenever I finished you section and moved onto the next. I lived years in the workshop. The cool and dark, the sounds and smells, seemed to wrap themselves around me like a comfort blanket.

And still, my Ma asked why I bothered. And still, I struggled to find a suitable answer, even when I had fixed him up and set him to work.

Yet, for some fifteen years Robbie followed me about and did odd chores out in the yard. I had it sitting on the porch most of the time, causing a kafuffle every time a stranger walked up my front pathway. Then I locked it away out in the barn for its own good. Something had gone wrong with its direction mechanism and it would be prone to just start off in odd directions. Once or twice it had caused near-misses by the highway. Old, rusting and breaking apart, it would sit by the porch and allow the local kids to come and pat it. Given that it had never allowed that before, I should have guessed then that something was wrong.

It was cold that morning, and I was grouchy as hell. A bad combination of too much beer the night before, and not enough black coffee since. I thought about taking a shower, but I never got to it.

I found Robbie curled up at the back of the barn, huddled between the meat freezer and lawn-mower. It wasn't smouldering or anything, but I could tell that it was not just recharging. Something about the robot being reduced to just worn-out mechanics again filled me with a weary sorrow.

I took a breath and closed my eyes. When I opened them again the sorrow had begun to fade.

If this was a weakness, I would not rise to it. My eyes clouded. I was becoming exhausted. Exhausted, exhausted, exhausted... like my robot.

The morning of my mother's funeral, looking out from the porch, I noticed the old foliage along the edges of the driveway. The place wasn't like it used to be. Once a pride of agriculture, now just a no-name homestead in the North Dakota backwoods. The old trees needed a good tending to as well. No one had done it for at least a summer or two, and the farm was looking a bit dishevelled. Maybe the new owners will turn the old farmstead around and make something of the place. It felt barren and unloved. I sighed and threw away the last dregs of coffee, and tried not to think of Robbie the robot.

Masahiro's Views Of The World

Japan 2055

A long time ago, in a shadowy realm where there are no truths or lies, there lived a man who dreamt of the human world as it once was.

He dreamt of summer skies, warm breeze and sunshine…

Masahiro looked up, startled out of blissful daydreams, as the column of soldiers snaked their way down the narrow road that weaved its way across the bottom of the valley. He mumbled a low and weary moan. He resented his afternoon doze being disturbed, and gave them a grumble from his vantage point on the side of the hill.

Why was life so fragile nowadays? Everybody was scurrying here and there, as if they'd hadn't a moment to spare. Masahiro had far more interesting things to do than rush about, missing the last memories the world had to offer.

He shook his head, refusing to let the horrors bother him, and as a lull returned, Masahiro felt life was on the whole good, had been simple and kind. He relaxed as he felt the strong, afternoon sun beating down and warming his old senses.

It was the kind of weather for romantic walks, and heady old feelings of love and lust were still lingering, along with the world's new steady progress. Once again, Masahiro could feel weariness coursing through his thoughts, just like every day that had gone before, and the long, hard decline of humanity seemed nothing more than a bad dream.

Every now and then, he catches sight of a flighty woman that would turn his head, and his thoughts turned back to Shizuka, who had always stirred his soul, with all her sweet softness, and that strangely innocent shyness of warmth around her.

Yes, she had had a very stoic effect on him, did Shizuka, sending his old soul swirling around in sheer excitement.

Was it because she seemed to bring back the distant days of lost youth?

Lost, because his world wasn't quite what it used to be, and he couldn't always summon up his happy memories.

But, sometimes, if he relaxed hard enough, he could relive those faraway years before the Great War to liven up those days when he felt despondent about life.

He looked back, now, over his long life, in the same way that he gazed down the valley to the distant ruins of Old Tokyo, with a bittersweet longing for a time he could never retrace, closed his eyes for a moment, and conjured up those very happy days in the countryside.

The freedom to enjoy himself, chasing and working, showing off in front of his lovers, the complicated simplicity of country life, with its rich, earth exploits, and always in the background, the man working hard.

***

Masahiro, too, had worked hard for most of his life, not just in the country, but in a munitions factory on the edge of Tokyo. At first, he'd felt strange, lost in the city, but soon he'd found a friendly niche at the factory, as many country folk had been drafted in to work the factories.

He had been proud to be part of the huge war-effort, and working to save mankind was a necessity more than a noble effort.

In a sudden swell of nostalgia, Masahiro wondered about his old friends, Tenzo and Yako, and … now, whatever happened to poor Sadako? He missed the cheerful companionship, and he hoped they were all resting peacefully like himself.

Now he was alone. Masahiro wasn't lonely, not in the true sense of the word, just content to now be able to savour the peace and quiet. Work had certainly been arduous, but he was glad he'd done his duty.

Proudly, he lifted his head again and looked at the sun's comforting warmth. Now, with the slower pace of existence, there was so much time to watch the grass grow, free of the constant stress and strife.

Although Masahiro's soul was a little more battered and weary, it would still carry him along, and he lived like a real survivor if a little melancholy at times. That sharp, napping sorrow had troubled him, when the memories swirled around, reminding him of how long he'd been around and what he had seen.

The breeze quickened, and the warm scent of meadows filled his nostrils… It was strange how smells still felt far more evocative of life than sights and sounds. He'd never taken much notice of what people said, as they reminded him that he wasn't working the fields no more.

In the noon quietness, he missed the factory banter, the jokes played even in the direst times. Masahiro paused. Yes, he was reminiscing. Very reminiscent.

He thought back to the evening strolls he spent with Shizuka. She shared all her dreams with Masahiro, and although he didn't share her innocent optimism, he comforted her with old stories from the country. So young and brave, she made his sentimental old heart yearn to recapture days long gone.

Then he shook himself out of his reverie. "Why, you silly, romantic old fool!"

Machines had put a halt to romantic liaisons. It is estimated that 1.3 million people in the Tokyo conflict had died instantly. Immediately followed by entire districts being taken by Humanoid troops. And not just in ground wars, the skies above the Japanese front were another battlefield, with A.I drones taking control within hours. Casualty rates on the Japanese Front alone had been unimaginable.

Masahiro's factory had been decimated within the first hour of the conflict. The battle for supremacy had been quick and efficient. Humanity had lost… almost immediately. Only a futile resistance force lingered.

This new world was to become a mechanised domain, where drones and humanoids searched through the rubble of the old cities. Seeking destruction and easily finding it.

His days of taking walks with Shizuka were long behind him. Masahiro had been deceased now for sixteen years, and his life was now spent lingering on the hills near Old Tokyo and passing time in the sunshine.

The Fat Goblin

"That goblin is getting fat," Mrs Brun from the village said. "You should stop feeding it between meals."

"Actually I don't," Tracy protested, looking down at Andre - the young goblin - who was waddling himself around her legs and grinning so hard she could feel his cheekiness emanating.

She had to admit it was looking a little porky these days.

"He gets just what you told me to give it, and no more," Tracy told her.

Tracy reached down and patted the rough, matted-haired head of the goblin as it rubbed up against her touch.

"Well, you'll have to be careful. I do hate to see goblins getting fat."

Mrs Brun was the local Goblin Rescue Co-ordinator, and her nearby farm had become a sanctuary for needy creatures who were awaiting re-homing.

Half the families in our village had a goblin, many of whom had, at one time, been cared for at the sanctuary. Andre himself had been there until six months ago and Mrs Brun still liked to keep an eye on her fostered creatures.

"I'll try and cut down his portion sizes," Tracy said.

Tracy picked Andre up and gave him a big hearty hug, before putting him back down and watching him run off to play somewhere in the house.

He did feel heavier than he used to, it was true. If he had been a dog, Tracy would have been concerned, but he wasn't. He was a growing goblin.

"Maybe it's because he's not getting enough walks? Tracy mused.

"Possibly. But I think it's simply getting too much to eat."

Mrs Brun nodded to her and went on her way, leaving Tracy to take the village magazine she had brought, and my cheeky accessory, back into the house.

So Tracy put Andre on a diet. She measured his meals - three small bowls of stew a day - and she brought a washing-line toy that an online pet-store recommended.

Tracy played with him every evening when he came in, getting him to jump and pounce and leap about after the balls that Tracy threw about her lounge.

At the end of the month, Tracy weighed him. Andre had gained a few ounces.

"Fuck sake," Tracy muttered, already hearing the condescending words from Mrs Brun.

"It must be muscle," Mr MacCallen from the village suggested. "Don't they say muscle weighs more than fat?"

"You're still feeding him too much," Mrs Brun insisted. "And remember: there are to be no snacks between meals."

Tracy cut his food down again and cut out snacks herself, so that she wouldn't be tempted to "just let him have a nibble" of the cookies or scones or a few granola bars.

***

At the end of the month, Andre hadn't lost a single pound, but Tracy's clothes seemed to fit a little easier, so she weighed herself and found that she had lost nearly half a stone.

"Well, Andre, your diet seems to be working wonders on me," She told him, measuring out his supper and putting it down on his small table. "I think I'll carry on with it. And while I'm at it, we'll change from dairy milk to Almond milk."

"Goblins shouldn't be drinking milk at all," Mrs Brun remarked when she popped around for a coffee and her eagle eye noted the glass of milk I had given Andre. "Milk isn't good for Goblins. Gives them terrible heart-burn."

She went over, took away the glass, and poured the milk down the sink.

"Goblins just need water, they don't need anything else."

Tracy caught the spiteful glance that Andre was giving Mrs Brun, and she tried to stifle a giggle.

Mrs Brun glance went towards the bottle of pineapple rum on Tracy's worktop and she knew what Mrs Brun was thinking: the poor lonely woman whose husband is away at war, drinking indoors all alone…

"Andre hasn't been drinking the rum," Tracy assured Mrs Brun and they both laughed together.

Mrs Brun was a nosy woman by nature, but Tracy knew that the woman meant well, and the local creatures of the wild did very well by her actions.

The village always gossiped about Mrs Brun and her nosy ways, but she was a feature in the community and was really very sweet and kind underneath the abruptness - and the determination that every creature should have opportunities of love and comfort.

When she had gone, Tracy looked at the bottle

of rum. Maybe she had been drinking too much recently, Tracy checked the calendar.

When her husband came home in three months time, she wanted to be looking at her best, and fitting into the sexy dresses she had brought in the New Year sales.

The rum wouldn't help her to lose the weight, Tracy knew, and really it was only there on the side because her friend had brought it around the other day.

Neither of them were big drinkers, but Tracy hadn't wanted to seem ungrateful by not accepting it.

"Right, then, Andre, that's the booze in the cupboard and it can stay there until special occasions."

Actually, Tracy was talking to herself: Andre was, as usual, scurrying off out someplace.

She'd no idea what goblins do with themselves all day, but her furry companion quite often went out in the early morning and didn't return home until the evening.

Tracy was a little relieved at Andre's absence today, because Mrs Brun no doubt would have had another moan about his weight.

Andre didn't arrive home for supper. Tracy waited and waited, but only next door's tabby cat showed up in her back garden.

When Andre didn't turn up by dusk Tracy was starting to get worried. Was he making mischief someplace? Had he found another goblin to muck about with? Had he gotten himself injured somewhere?

Tracy would have to go searching around the village in the morning.

It was a long, long night. Tracy kept stirring every time a noise rattled near the house, thinking it was Andre returning home.

**

Tracy felt anxious and weary the next morning when Andre had not put in his appearance. She had woken feeling exhausted, fat and depressed. There was no lingering doubt that Andre had probably gotten himself lost someplace, and Tracy felt gutted at this prospect. She made some breakfast for him and left it on the table, then went off to work at the local care home, but she came home at lunchtime just to check.

No Andre.

"He'll turn up," friends said. "When he gets bored. They always do."

After work, Tracy checked her house again and then rang around the veterinarians and animal charities to ask if they had had any injured goblins brought it.

Fortunately, they hadn't. But, although that gave Tracy a moment of relief, she then decided to take a look around the village and see if she could find him.

Tracy looked around the playgrounds, the graveyards, the local woods and called and called. She thought the locals probably assumed she was mad.

No Andre.

She went back home and slumped in a chair. She was aware of a quickened heartbeat and a weary feeling, as if someone had given her a good shaking. This always happened in stressful situations. Her vision started to blur. She could feel her emotions jumbling and her mind trying to hold off a panic attack: Jesus, don't say she was going to be sick. She could do without cleaning up vomit all evening. Taking herself to bed, her thoughts always lingered on poor Andre.

Was he lost? Had he been injured? Had someone snatched him and was now selling him off someplace? Was he dead?

Her fragile young goblin.

She turned uneasily through the night, trying to get comfortable. Her pillow felt hot, the bedclothes felt heavy.

She finally cried herself to sleep and then kept waking up imagining that she could hear him returning home. Another restless night ensued.

He hadn't turned up at home in the morning. Tracy started making up posters and flyers with a photo of Andre and his description, and she started putting them up on the village notice boards.

Then, outside the local post office, Tracy met a retired lady who read Tracy's flyer and nodded.

"That very distinctive mole on his chin? That's my brother's goblin, that is. You can't have lost him."

Tracy was lost for words, and just stared at him for a moment.

"No, I got him the Goblin Rescue a few months back," Tracy said.

The old lady nodded.

"Simon lost him when he got taken into hospital. He just started turning up again one day like a nuisance. It must have been eight months later.

"Right glad, my brother was, to have him back, but every night he disappeared off making mischief and only came back the next day for meals."

"Oh, for fucks sake," Tracy blurted out,

thinking about regular Andre was his outdoor disappearances, setting off after breakfast each morning.

"My brother got moved into a care home," the old lady went on. "He went in a few nights ago, so I took the goblin over to the county zoo, so that they could re-home him some place."

"Fuck sake," Tracy repeated. And she told the lady her story.

They sat down on a bench and ended up laughing about the whole ordeal, but Tracy was already tapping away on her phone.

She went online and searched for addresses and phone numbers, and made a call the county zoo.

The guy there was charming and suggested that Tracy make her way over so that could identify the crafty goblin.

Tracy's new friend, Mrs Gallach, went with Tracy "just to help out and to keep Tracy company".

***

Andre was looking very guilty, walking about his pen at the county zoo.

He recognised Tracy at once and went waddling over to receive a head rub.

"Hello, Andre," Tracy said.

Tracy longed to open the cage and hug Andre, taking him out to take home.

But she had to prove who he was before the zoo guy would let Tracy do that.

"Hello, trouble," Mrs Gallach said.

Andre just gave her a sheepish look. He was well aware of the trouble he had caused.

"How much trouble am I in?" he seemed to be

saying.

"He's micro chipped," Tracy recalled. "Mrs Brun from the Rescue centre did that for me when I got him."

Mr MacGiobain of the County Zoo checked with a scanner he found.

"Yep, this goblin is definitely yours," he said, looking at Tracy's passport details and matching it to the details on the microchip.

"You little shit, Mr goblin Andre!"

"That accounts for his weight gain," Tracy mentioned, thinking of all the meals he had been cramming in between the two households.

"Mr brother will be glad to hear this news."

Mrs Gallach gave Andre a friendly rub.

"My brother adores this fella and he was very upset when he realised he would have to accept him gone this time."

Mr MacGiobain was unlocking the cage and he attaching a collar for Tracy.

"He might wander again," he warned Tracy.

"You would be best to put a collar on him with a name tag, just in case he gets lost again. Folks will then see where he belongs -"

"And maybe he won't get more meals than he should!" Tracy added, to which they all laughed at. All accept Andre, who looked very sheepish.

Tracy leaned down and kissed Andre on his forehead.

Vancouver Voodoo

Immaculate in her new navy blue suit and posh shoes, Ali couldn't resist popping into the neighbourhood coffee shop where she'd worked since finishing college. She waited in line, then beamed a smile at the familiar barista.

Megan, an old friend, raised her eyebrows.

"Wow, Ali. You look great. They've got to hire you looking like that."

Pre-job interview nerves jittered in Ali's stomach.

"I just hope I'm doing the right thing."

Her friend made Ali her usual soya latte and scoffed. "You'll be fine. You need a bit of excitement and adventure, and it's such a famous store that you'll bound to have lots of interesting things going on. Though we'll miss you here. We had some laughs."

Her friends had thought she was joking when she'd told them she intended to work at the Voodoo store.

"It's kind of a shame that I left," Ali said with honesty. But she needed a career change, and a store manager job at the Botanica was a big step up.

"I might not even get it," she warned.

"Oh, go on. They'll love you!" Megan hugged her. "You'll be fine. And don't let the ghosts rattle you!"

Ali chuckled as she walked along the sidewalk on West Fourth Street. The old Voodoo store was steeped in local history, and was supposed to be haunted. Well, she wasn't the kind of woman to be worried by daft local folklores and ghosts.

She didn't have to walk far. The Voodoo Store

was in the same neighbourhood as the coffee shop, in the part of Vancouver called Kitsilano. An old hippy neighbourhood from the 60s, Kitsilano still has plenty of cool hangouts, but more and more its apartments and houses are now occupied by young urban professionals and families.

So, there she was, full of anticipation. She felt in a very 'upbeat' mood, partly because she had hopes that this job would be 'the' job, partly because it was a blissfully warm day. Spring in Vancouver had always been her favourite time of year.

Thirty-five minutes later, and sipping the last dregs of coffee, she walked through a tatty car lot that had a couple of rusty sedans.

It was an impressive store set back against the car-park, the outer walls smothered by colourful graffiti and old wooden advertising boards imported up from Louisiana.

On a dank day in Vancouver, with rain and fog, there could be an eerie feel to it. Especially with rumours of ghosts still lingering around in local gossip.

She shook herself. No such things as ghosts. It was the stuff of nonsense.

Checking the email she'd received asking her to come for an interview, she reminded herself that she was here to meet Mr Moreau.

Ali took a deep breath, brushed herself down, and walked nervously into the store.

The counter area was glass panelled, bordered with dark oak frames, shadowy after the bright sunlight outside. Three grandfather clocks stood against one wall, the small of the three in the middle. Framed paintings of exquisite portraits hung on the walls. She had never seen a place like it before, except in old movies. She was instantly charmed. The store must have been more than a hundred years old.

The other walls were all shelved and had small wooden cupboards. It looked like a store you'd see on a set from an old western film. There seemed no bell to ring for attention, so eventually Ali called out, rather sheepishly.

"Hello! Anybody about!"

"Hello to you, my dear."

Ali spun around, startled to find an old gentleman standing right behind her.

"Oh, hi."

The old gentleman smiled. He looked to be about seventy five with black afro locks and dark crystal eyes that held a mischievous twinkle. He was black as cocoa, flat-nosed and solid built.

"Sorry, miss. I didn't mean to startle you." He had a heavy accent, part Cajun and part African. He was as mysterious as he was dark.

"I'm Kasper Moreau. You must be Ali Jenson."

Ali held out her hand, warming to the old gentleman immediately.

"Yeah, I'm Ali. I'm here for the job interview." She saw he was dressed in old tatty clothes that looked dated and period-dress. "I love your outfit, it looks perfect for the shop."

The old man smiled. "It's what the customers expect. It creates an ambience. Now, tell me a little about yourself." He clasped his hands behind his back and smiled at her.

Ali had been expecting a formal interview, but this was just a friendly chit-chat. No different from chatting with her customers at the coffee-shop.

Finally, he clapped his hands together. "You sound like you might be perfect for the job.

When will you be available to start?"

She was taken aback in astonishment.

"You're offering me the job? Just like that?"

The old man laughed. "I'm assuming you still want the position?"

Ali flustered.

"Oh, yes. Very much so."

"Perfect. Renee will deal with all the details; salary, holidays, that kind of stuff," he added. "Now, would you like a little tour?"

Ali nodded, keen to see the rest of the shop.

"The Moreau family are very proud of our ancestral store," he said, strolling towards the back of the shop.

Ali hurried after him.

"Are all the paintings of your family?" She could see the likeness in many of the portraits, although none had such character as Mr Kasper Moreau.

"Yes, they are of our family. Some from Louisiana, some from Africa. We go back some centuries now."

"Fascinating. What a heritage," Ali stated.

"It would be good for you to meet some of the staff," Kasper Moreau said. "The back rooms are just along here."

Ali laughed. "You make it sound so mysterious."

His smile juddered slightly.

"Well, we are an odd bunch here."

***

Ali loved the old fashioned back rooms. Mr Moreau led her through down numerous corridors, past glass display cases filled with antique silver cups and ornate wooden boxes. Battered chairs and scuffed stools filled the corners. It was like walking into a history book. No sign of the twenty-first century in sight. The walls had been lined with dark wooden panels. She tapped on one with a knuckle as she passed. It was strong and thick.

There were two middle-aged women working away with jars of herbs. They too were dressed in costumes and dated clothing.

They both had warming smiles, and Ali guessed they were Mr Moreau's family members. All added to the grandeur of the place.

She smiled.

"Hi, I'm Ali Jenson, and it seems like I'm going to be the new store manager."

Both women nodded and smiled.

"That's wonderful," said the youngest of the two women. "I'm Yolanda, and this is Beatrice."

Mr Moreau touched her arm.

"I must go and deal with other matters. Can I leave you in Yolanda's capable hands?"

"Yes, that's fine" Ali replied.

Her hand was grasped by the youngest of the two ladies and she was pulled towards the cellar rooms.

"Want to see the curios?"

"I don't want to be a nuisance…"

"Nonsense… come on."

The staircase to the downstairs rooms was dark and her feet echoed on the bare wooden floorboards. She felt slightly spooked down the amongst the rooms, and she felt nervous. She noticed a strange sensation at the top of her back in between her shoulder blades. It wasn't an itch, but rather a tingling sensation. She had to fight the urge to look behind her, but in the end she turned. Of course, there was nobody in sight but Ali felt it momentarily quite unnerving. She didn't know if she was becoming somewhat neurotic or supersensitive to *something*, and certainly felt a relief when she saw the stairs.

"So they offered you the job, eh?" Beatrice's Benin accent was heavy.

Ali had not noticed the older lady had followed them and she glanced back over her shoulder.

"I certainly hope so. Mr Moreau said I was good for the role."

"You must be very brave."

Ali cast her a puzzled expression.

"Why would I be brave?"

"Because of the spirits that dwell here."

"Shut up, Bea!" Yolanda quipped.

"It's alright. Go on, please," Ali pressed, curious.

"The last manager left because he said the ghosts unsettled him too much. Don't be surprised if you're writing out another C.V by next week."

"Stop it, right now!" Yolanda snapped. "Don't go scaring her."

Ali smirked.

"I'm sure I'll do okay. I don't easily anyhow," she joked.

Yolanda tugged at Ali's hand.

"We have lots of regular customers. Folks coming in to buy good-luck spells, or protection mantras. People like to come here because of the honest feel, and because of the tales of ghosts."

"Ah, yes. I bet that kind of thing brings in the crowd," Ali reasoned. "So, either of you two seen any spirits."

Yolanda and Beatrice both exchanged a look.

"Oh yes," they answered in unison.

"Weren't you scared?"

Yolanda just shrugged her shoulders.

"It's kind of weird, sure. It's the old spirits from the Congo heartlands that make me nervous. "

"But they haven't scared you enough to make you leave" Ali stated.

Yolanda scoffed a little.

"This is our store. Anyhow, I like the tension it brings sometimes. You don't get that at JC Penny or Java Coffee."

Ali wandered along in the shadows of the woman, realising that her assumptions about the women were right. These women were probably priestesses, or at least Beatrice probably was. And they obviously shared Mr Moreau for the theatrics.

Beatrice gave Yolanda a wink.

"We should be getting on."

Ali nodded and stopped walking.

"You'll be okay to just look about on your own, okay?"

"Oh. Yeah, sure."

They were off, one following the other down the short corridor. Their feet echoed on the wooden floor long after they were out of sight.

Ali chuckled to herself. She couldn't wait to join the staff.

***

Ali eventually made her way through the rooms down in the basement and back up the stairs to the main store front. A middle-aged man was writing up tickets beside the till.

Putting him somewhere in his forties, he had a peculiarly inexpressive face that hinted at a guy who kept his emotions on a tight rein. Lean, charismatic with pale eyes, the man looked preoccupied.

He flinched at the sound of hearing Ali approach and turned to face her. His dark features made her smile - she saw the resemblance to Kasper Moreau immediately. Maybe a son, grandson.

"Oh, hello. Can I help you?"

"Oh, hi. I'm Ali Jenson. The new store manager."

His eyebrows arched.

"Oh, really. Whilst I admire your confidence, should I not have interviewed you first?"

"Your father interviewed me… and offered me the job. Well, I assumed he was your father." Rosie flustered on not really knowing what was occurring. "I seem a little confused."

"My father?"

"Kasper Moreau, an elderly man, with the raggedy hair and wide smile. He was wearing his elaborate outfit."

The man's face went from quizzical to deathly pale.

"You spoke to Kasper Moreau?"

"Yes, and he introduced me to Yolanda and Beatrice."

The man looked blank.

"They look like priestesses," she said, half-jokingly. She wondered why the man looked so puzzled and perturbed.

He rubbed his chin, then slumped into a wooden chair by the counter.

"Those blasted people. They always want to visit and interfere with the store's business."

Ali had no idea what he was talking about, but was starting to doubt the idea of working at the store.

"Is everything all right?"

He heaved a sigh, then got out of the chair and started to open the drawer under the till. Pulling out a large log book, he dropped it on the counter and started flicking through the pages. He waved Ali over to him.

"Miss Jenson, come take a look at these paintings. Tell me if you recognise anyone?"

Ali took a brief look at the first few pictures. It took only a few moments before she saw a portrait of Kasper Moreau. He was stood in front of an outlandish plantation house that looked like it was in a New Orleans setting. Although his statue wasn't as grand as in real life, there was no mistaking him.

"That's the gentleman that I just had the interview with. Is he your father? Grandfather?"

The guy chuckled.

"Actually, Kasper is my great-grandfather. Born 1725. Died 1782."

Ali felt the hairs on the back of her neck tremble. The man pointed to the wooden chair. "Sit if you have to."

"So… the man was a s-spirit?"

He nodded.

"But he introduced me to Yolanda and Beatrice." Her mind churned with daft notions. "Were they…?" She didn't hide her bewilderment or unease.

He nodded again.

"Still want the job? It's quite an adventure."

Ali was trying to make sense of all the connotations. It seemed absurd. Yet, she had experienced it all. She didn't really believe in all the Voodoo mumbo-jumbo, yet…

Although the experience had been startling, it

had not been scary or frightening. The characters seemed harmless enough, though a little dark.

She suddenly felt reassured in herself, and that she might be able to manage the new situation that had presented itself.

She took a deep breath.

"Yes, I think I still would like to work here."

He smiled. He had a lovely manner. Truth be told, he was quite handsome in a way and Ali was slightly smitten by him.

But also, Ali needed the job. Having handed in her notice at the coffee shop, she was in need of employment.

After a long-term relationship had ended, Ami had felt cut adrift. For a while she had been in limbo, allowing life to dwindle along without any direction. She had quickly come to realise that what she needed was a complete change.

The advertisement for the job at the Botanica had been just the push she'd required.

"I'm pleased the others haven't scared you off. If you wouldn't mind waiting here, I'll go find some paperwork."

While he was gone Ali wandered around the main shop room, glancing at the old shelves that held the jars of herbs and dried flowers. It all piqued her interest. Her gaze fell on the small portrait that hung behind the till. She saw the resemblance to the man she had just been speaking to. He looked even more grandiose in the painting. She read the name plaque beneath the portrait.

Marshall Moreau...

The hairs on the back of her neck stood up. She took a step back, unable to free her gaze from the painting. She felt spooked and mesmerised at the same time.

Marshall Moreau. Born 1750. Died 1815

With a shudder of disbelief, she felt the chills going up her spine. Her mind just began racing.

Ali made a dash for the front door, knocking herself against some display units. A young man was just coming in the front door, and Ali almost stumbled straight into him.

The good-looking guy held open the door, but as Ali passed by she paused. She saw the Moreau resemblance immediately. He looked a distinguished gentleman, quite tall, with piercing eyes.

"Are you Ali Jenson? Come for the manager's job? I'm sorry I'm running late."

She raced out onto the sidewalk, not wanting to look back. The cold, electrifying sweat of panic and fear prickled on her shoulders.

Sometimes you can have too much adventure!

The Phantom Robot

On a late March evening, Chris Owen was out walking his terrier, Frank. Chris' trailer was not far from the old military base and he loved to walk along the edges of the dilapidated runways. One could see plenty of wildlife and, besides, it was a perfect place to walk Frank. He could be safely let off the leash for a bit and he just adored running into the undergrowth for a scamp. Chris shivered and pulled his jacket tighter around him.

The cloud cover was pulled down like a window blind in front of the distant Welsh mountains. The old airbase was still dark, overcast, spitting snow, with sharp winds snapping across the moss-covered runways.

Chris often took the path that went by the old military laboratories, now just ruins. He seldom saw anyone else apart from the other occasional dog walker, like himself, or perhaps a horse rider but there were not many of those around these parts of Welsh hills.

This suited Chris. He was a solitary man by nature, especially since his wife, Mary, had died seven years back. Mary and he hadn't had any children, so when Chris was made redundant from the Royal Air Force as a biomechanic he had moved from the military-lodgings to the trailer, where Chris still now lived. It wasn't perfect, but it suited Chris well enough. He was a man of few needs. After Mary's death he had found himself heavily melancholic, so he had brought Frank, then a bundle of ragged fur and energetic mischief. Frank kept him busy. It was the terrier that had warded off the depression of grief that lingered. No matter what, Frank could always bring a certain clarity to Chris' world.

Frank was now a full-grown, rather chunky terrier. He had been barking at the trailer door for a good few minutes, which, of course, meant that it was time for a walk. Frank was a clever dog, and Chris believed that he knew every word that Chris said to him. So Chris would often hold lengthy conversations with Frank, about whatever he was feeling glum about. They made good companions.

So off they went on that dank spring evening. Chris unleashed a rather over-excited Frank as they got a little way along the perimeter of the old airbase. A gentle drizzle had started to descend from the hillsides around the base. A few crows took flight from the rough grass as Frank came snuffling along, trying to find a rabbit to chase for a few minutes. A blackbird sang farther along the path, a magpie called out in annoyance, before taking to the wing. Chris smiled as he listened to the birds. It made a stark contrast to when the airbase was operational, and the noise was of robotic testing and government assignments. He also noted that small shrubs and trees were sprouting where once buildings had stood. Nature had begun to reclaim.

The airbase now bore little resemblance to his memories. The entire base was filled with boarded up buildings and cracked runways and lopsided roads. There was never a soul to be seen. There were mounds of junk by the sides of the old hangers.

He couldn't understand how things had got in such a state. Years ago this had been the post to get, working for the military and having free-reign on bio-mechanics and an endless budget. Lots of people and top secret projects. And there had been an American Cyborg department hadn't there? And a mini-village? Now the place was a wasteland.

He was so upset that he walked past the three main hangars and continued to the far end of the runways. He passed a collapsed control tower and some gutted brick buildings with weeds growing over them. He passed an abandoned six-wheeled truck and a line of rusty and discarded buggies. Everything appeared bent with exhaustion and endowed with a certain dishevelled sadness.

He was already headed back when he heard an odd noise, one that seemed out of place.

He stopped in the middle of the path. No one else in their right mind would be out walking in this weather, he thought, it's far too miserable. So why then did he have a feeling of anxiety in his mind?

The mist had combined with the drizzle. He realised that visibility was down to a few hundred yards. Instinctively, Chris called Frank to heel, although there was no reason for concern. Not much harm could come to him on the disused base, and he was a little scrapper anyhow. Frank reluctantly sought out his master, looking askance at his master, as he was usually allowed to run on ahead regardless. Chris pulled up his collar against the foul weather. The mist and drizzle were slowly soaking through to his first layer of clothing.

"Shall we have bean burgers for supper, Frank?" he asked. He did not know quite why, but he wanted to hear the sound of his voice, even if it seemed daft. There was something oddly sinister about the mist. It was nothing specific, just a feeling he had. A shudder rippled across the back of his neck. He looked down at his dog. It was reassuring to feel his warmth and aliveness. "You love those burgers from the butcher's, don't you, fella?" His voice sounded somehow nervous, muffled in the misty rain.

As they neared the path that turned off towards the ruins of the old hangars, Chris thought that he heard what sounded like scraping footsteps coming from behind the crumbling walls. He stopped to listen. Frank stayed to heel beside him, tail wagging as per normal, waiting to scamper after some poor unsuspecting birds or critter. Scrape. Scrape. Scrape. Slow, but sure footsteps. He could see nothing through the damp vapour but the sound was too obscure to be that of a person.

For fuck sake, thought Chris, it's probably local kids larking around with the scraps or rubbish left behind from the Air Force. He knew that there was probably some dangerous materials lingering around. Government bodies never cleared up after themselves properly. It was too dangerous for children to be larking about. His annoyance rose. How daft can kids be! He had never met anyone on the base before but it definitely sounded like nothing made by birds or critters. He expected to see any moment, a local lad dragging a length of metal or roof rafter, not realising how dangerous it could be. He felt slightly more comfortable with these thoughts than the creepy ones that had earlier made his neck hairs shudder.

It was then that Chris realised that Frank was nowhere to be seen. Anxiety swept through him again. He must have scampered off, startled by the foreign noises. Chris called Frank's name again and again. He realised that there was no way the dog could see; the mist turning thick and dank. He would have to rely on Frank hearing his voice. Chris was now glad that he had trained Frank well, and that Frank was an obedient, responsive terrier. He was anxious to get him on the lead before he barks and scares the children.

He felt a wave of sick anxiety. His mind struggled to reconcile the primitive reflex of running for dear life with his more rational tendencies. It was then that he turned and saw a rust-covered robot, coming towards him. The robot slowed. Now it seemed to be looking at him, studying him. His mind whirled in a strange, panicked dance of logic and emotion. He felt the flutters of fear. The airbase was deserted. He thought, That robot is coming for *me*.

Chris froze. He opened his mouth but did not scream. The world around him went thick with the sound of his own blood pounding in his throat, in his temples. Chris had never felt so vulnerable. A shiver took hold of him and he willed himself to calm down.

The robot was obviously struggling to function properly, and Chris wondered whether it was a left-over from the military days. He was cautious.

"Frank, come!" he shouted. "Nothing to worry about, old fella." His voice trailed away as he looked closer at the robot. There was something peculiar about it. It had a strange look to it. The *X-Files* came to mind.

He turned again to call Frank. He knew that it could not be far. Frank hardly ever left his side for long. He turned again, expecting the robot to be closer by now. But to his disbelief, the robot was nowhere in sight!

He stood in a paralyzed state, scared beyond all

reason. Fully awake, fully conscious. There was no fuzziness in my thinking, no debate about whether or not he was dreaming. He was not dreaming. He tried to move but to no avail. He couldn't turn. He could barely breathe. There was a pressure on his chest - an all-encompassing, revolting pressure - that would eventually spread over his whole body. He was terrified and confused.

His heart started to race. He broke out into a cold sweat. How could this be? He was a rational man; he searched for some kind of rational explanation. There was none. The robot had simply disappeared! It was then that fear dawned on him. His pace quickened. He began to run homeward, frantically calling for his dog as he went. For fuck sake! Frank, come on! He almost felt annoyed at his dog. What on earth was going on? The thick mist was relentless, veiling everything in his path.

Chris bolted through the dank Welsh air. The pounding of his sneakered feet against the rough ground was the only sound in the quiet of the misty mountains. He nervously scanned the airfield, looking everywhere but at the steps in front of him; it's proof of luck that he didn't fall and break his neck.

By paths and tracks, along a strip of tarmac bisecting the vacant lots, through a drainage culvert dank and dirty, and then to the section of spare runway, he made his way to the trailer at a brisk pace.

It was the utter silence that unnerved him most. With no birds, no wind in the distant trees, and his own breath muffling his footsteps, all he could hear was the panicked thumps of his heartbeat. Easy to believe how something like a phantom could haunt the airfield without detection. He felt like a robot himself, slipping between the margins of the world, unnoticed and solitary.

He found Frank, at last, huddled and cowering behind the wheels the trailer. Frank was overwhelmed to see him, jumping up, trying to clamber around his feet. Chris quickly put him on his lead and he virtually dragged him into the trailer. Chris felt in a state of shock. At length, he started to recover his breath and nerves. He felt exhausted and very alert, as if having recovered from a fever, as if in a daydream. He spluttered, floundering behind the trailer door.

Chris managed to catch a couple of deep breaths before collapsing. He didn't know how long he had been lying there before he heard movement in the far end of the trailer, and could only look up numbly as Frank appeared.

He cradled Frank in his arms. "We had a scare, eh?" he said. "Listen, we're just gonna sit here for a while."

Unwilling to risk an encounter with the phantom, he began to wonder how long Frank and him would have to huddle in the trailer. He'd never be able to take a walk here again. He would either have to hide out for the rest of his life or find a new place to live.

For days afterwards Frank would not go for walk and certainly not at the far edges of the airbase. Chris, too, found it hard to regain his nerve to walk that way. There would always remain a feeling of dread that went with what he had witnessed on the old disused airbase, in Wales.

The Komi Cannibal

The sound of a clapped-out old van slowing on the track made Elena glance out of her kitchen window.

The bonnet of a white van appeared at the end of her long driveway, then pulled away again as soon as the driver saw that the little refrigerated-cart by the roadside was empty.

Elena sighed. She'd never seen the driver because her rusty ATV blocked her view of the cart, but she recognised the van as one of her regulars. A regular that would feel let down again.

"Are you still there?" a voice said in her ear.

"Oh, sorry, Iskra."

Elena turned her attention back to the phone. "I haven't put any fresh cuts out again, and just saw someone pull up looking for some."

"You not done much killing?" her friend asked.

"No, not really. I know I should… with winter approaching and all." Elena sighed. "It must be the full moon cycle or something. I can't seem to summon any enthusiasm."

"Do you want to come visit for a few days?" Iskra asked. "Kristina's home from the city at the moment, but I can still find room."

"No, you're busy enough at the moment, without having an extra houseguest. If I can get through last winter without Pavel, I can get through an autumn."

"I still can't believe that prick tried to stitch you up," Iskra said.

Before Elena could answer, she heard Iskra's doorbell in the background.

"I'm sorry, Elena, that will be -"

"No problem. You go. I'll call you later."

They said their hasty goodbyes and Elena turned back to the kitchen window, with its views of the autumnal trees and stark farmland. Birds were flocking across it, exploring for bugs and worms where fields had been recently cultivated.

Wariness was her default setting these days.

The rule book of her life was down the shitter.

She stood for a long time, lost in her own thoughts after the white van had long disappeared from sight.

It had been the strong spirit of hers which had first attracted Pavel to her; a strong wildness which had captivated him. Yet the things which had first drawn him to her had become the wrecking attributes in the end.

She couldn't help feeling just the slightest bit of envy for her old childhood friend's busy life in the town. Living in the flatlands of Northern Russia was had enough, but alone can be real tough, and not just physically. Live could be bleak in the Komi Republic.

***

The next morning, as the roosters woke the countryside with their alarming cock-a-doodle-dos, Elena pulled on her quilted jacket, stuck her feet into some old military boots and went out into the back yard.

Growing up in the countryside, she'd always been an early riser and knew the morning chill might help shift some of her weariness.

Selling meat from a cart add significant income to the farm, but melancholy and seasonal blues had made it easy to neglect the task for the past week.

The money her customers dropped into the honesty box was keeping the place afloat, and Elena knew that she'd soon have to go out and hunt for some prey. She looked over at the slaughterhouse that had not seen use for a month or so. She couldn't survive on eggs and chickens, after all.

"Come on, Bunin," she called to her boxer as she took in the empty shelves from the cart.

In the distance, she heard the rasping of a chainsaw where her lover Astrid was taking down a few old larch trees at the far edge of the farmstead.

The sun was climbing slowly, throwing weak, grey light across the fields. The ground smelled fresh and the air clean. The landscape around her farm made her feel small and inconsequential to be surrounded by so much countryside, the massive unending sky reaching away to a distant horizon.

Elena knew that Astrid would have been up before dawn. She was a true countryperson - like herself in many ways.

There was still some lingering of overnight rain in the cloudy sky.

"Winter building," her pa used to say.

It had already been a dank enough summer for Elena's liking. She felt like she had been living under grey clouds for months.

At least it was dry for the moment, she consoled herself.

Before she left the house, Elena had penned a note that she pinned up on the cart: *Apologies. Sorry, no meat lately. Will rectify soon. Please bear with me. Thanks.*

She briefly wondered whether the note was a bit much. Would anyone actually care that much if she had meat to sell or not?

Her little farmstead was on a quiet track with virtually no passing traffic, and she knew from experience that people often drove a considerable distance out of their way to buy her produce.

She knew the annoyance herself. There was a stand outside the priest's house in the town where she regularly picked up jars of fresh honey, as well as a wheelbarrow full of seasonal herbs.

It was always somewhat disappointing to drive out for some honey and find she'd left it too late in the week and the stand was sold out.

Elena didn't like the thought of her regulars making a special journey to her farm and going home empty-handed. Regulars of hers were hard to come by. Her unique meats were not the sort for everyone.

She'd noticed the white van make two fruitless trips in the past couple of days and felt the need to leave the note as an explanation.

It was funny, she reflected as she headed back up the track with Bunin darting around her. When she was growing up, she had led a very solitary life, but now she seemed fraught with regret by letting others down. Maybe she was getting soft in her age?

Elena had never met the people she bought honey and herbs from, and didn't really know the people who bought her meats, but she felt a connection to them, even though the only connection was anonymous money deposits in a jar on her cart.

Mahmut swayed when struck with the taser, then steadied himself against the side of the van.

He had been fixed on the bleak road stretching out in front of him, and was humiliated by the absurd fact that a man in his forties was having to hitch-hike. And this wearisome nudging had been irking him when the woman in the van had pulled in just a few feet ahead of where he had been standing.

"Pleased to meet you," he beamed, busily buckling himself in as if they were about to embark on a fun adventure to the countryside. He had a faint Turkish accent, altered by his years in Russia.

He regarded the middle-aged woman before him, taking in her shapely body, the slim legs. Improper thoughts swept over Mahmut.

She was smiling broadly, and it was this delightful smile that distracted his mind from the fact that she was bringing up a taser from beside her seat. It took a moment for his thoughts to register.

His eyes stared blankly, his mouth open in surprise but no words coming out. Mahmut barely had time to register anything that was going on. He stared intently into the woman's eyes and saw evil, and curiosity, and the desire for pain.

And anger? Yes, perhaps just a little.

Immediately, he had started to panic.

He had tried to struggle, but he felt his limbs flop about with numbness. He grew weaker by the second, and his fight-instinct began to fail him, the shock stealing him away, little by little, relentlessly thieving all his pride and strength.

One moment there had been space and tranquillity between them, the next there was none, but he had been caught off-guard. He himself was muttering words but he was weak and disoriented and just head himself repeating the same words over and over. He still did not really understand what was going on.

Surprise showed for a brief instant in his face, then true shock took hold.

He lifted a hand to strike her, his thoughts tangled in fury and frustration. She caught his wrist and held it, twisting until he uttered a cry.

He sat there mumbling incoherently as she reached for him again.

"No, wait -"

Desperately he reached out for the door handle, once, twice, making several agonizing attempts to grab the door. But each time he thought it was within his grasp, he missed it and he knew he was slipping into a void of nothingness. Fuck, he thought vaguely, I'm fucked.

A second severe shock made him gag and lose consciousness.

His slumped body had been shoved back into a sitting position.

The shock-induced sleep wore off into nothingness, and the guy began the agonizing struggle back to consciousness. A dim and hazy light greeted his slowly opening eyes. He hung dead-still for several moments, forcing his mind to regain control of his thoughts. It was unreal, a nightmare, he tried to hell himself upon awakening. It had to be some kind of horrifying nightmare. He fought the sudden urge of terror in himself. Terrified beyond all reason, he began screaming - screaming insanely. His heart strained in his chest and he struggled desperately. It was useless - his ankles chained tightly to the roofing rafters.

His stomach twisted. It was the truth of a fear that lurked in the back of his mind. He twisted to try and work loose, but the chains kept him swinging locked in place.

He was trapped, screaming and howling, beating at his binds. His whole being was frantic. It burned his muscles. He felt his mind tumbling, spiralling through space, bustled by shame and sorrow and a sense of regret that would never end.

After an hour or so, he heard footsteps in the barn. A door opens, and the woman appears. She had been elsewhere when he woke, and now she was here. She ran her hands across his nakedness and face. She stood beside him and flicked his limp cock, seemingly just to add humiliation to the horror.

No shadow of expression touched the woman's face, not even a flicker of intent.

He drew back involuntarily, waving his feet and kicking his legs to keep his pride.

It was a nightmare, he thought as he tried to wriggle himself away from the horror.

His panic was steadily winding up into a feeling of outright fear bordering on hysteria.

He caught a glimpse of the knife in her hand. Within a second, the panic radiated through his mind and body, where it started to squeeze his heart.

The woman terrified him. It wasn't just the knife in her hand, although that was bad enough. The woman conveyed a sense of implacable evil, a desire to inflict pain that was beyond reason.

"Calm yourself," she had said. "You'll spoil the

meat."

He stared wildly about him, an act of blind terror. "You have no reason to kill me!"

It was this panic that meant he didn't feel the slow cut made across his throat. It was the warm floods of blood over his face, into his mouth that told him the horrifying truth. His breaths were bubbling and choking. His mind reeled in the knowledge of what had just occurred. His breathing became shallow and rapid.

After a time, she left, and he never saw her return.

His breaths got shorter and shorter. He was fully aware that he was losing too much blood. His chest heaved in and out. Blood bubbled out of his mouth and his body went into a seizure like convulsion. As if in slow motion, he could feel himself; seeping away like an untied sailboat on a choppy lake. He tried to move but was limp.

***

The following week, with a chilly dusk already falling on the stark fields, Elena walked down to the meat cart to collect her takings that her customers had left.

The walk had eased her head, and the time spent outdoors had brought her a little peace.

After a depressing day rounding up invoices and receipts for the taxman, she was glad to get some fresh country air into her system. People didn't realise the amount of paperwork involved in running a farm.

The strain had seemed less when Pavel had shared it, and she wondered briefly if getting rid of him so quickly had been a wise move.

Astrid was a good companion, but she had her own life to lead and would be leaving come winter time to go seek out adventures in Turkey.

When Astrid left for the winter and Elena was alone for the stark months, the farmstead felt empty and melancholic.

At the cart, she stopped, bewildered. Propped in the lid of the fridge was a postcard with bright sunflowers on it.

She took it out and looked over at it. On the back, she read: *Sorry to hear you're struggling. Hope things improve. (Meat always delicious) Eduard.*

Elena smirked in surprise, and even took a bewildered look around as if the scriber was going to be standing nearby. She didn't know anyone called Eduard.

Realising that he was probably one of her anonymous customers, she headed back up the track home with a befuddled grin.

So someone was bothered whether she provided meat or not! For the first time in ages, she felt a light buzz of purpose.

***

Vanya was a 32-year old mechanic and single father of two sons who had hired a babysitter on a Friday night and had enjoyed a rare evening out with a group of friends.

He had been cycling home along the main country road when he had passed the woman by an old blue postal van. At first, he had not given her a second thought, but as he rode by he saw that she had the bonnet open and appeared to be struggling with the engine.

Under regular circumstances, Vanya would have cycled on. He was not prone to helping others. It was not in his nature. Quite the opposite, most of the time.

But it was late. It was a lonely road. The woman was alone. When he had looked over she looked frightened, as well she might. It was a desolate stretch of road, used mainly by the rural folk making their way to and from town. On a night like this, with clouds looming and a brisk breeze teasing at possible rain.

He opted to help her, and he did not yet know if he was stopping for reasons of goodwill or drunkenness.

He turned around and peddled up to her.

"You look like you're having some trouble," he had said.

Because of the darkness, he hadn't been able to instantly see what the problem was, but he was sure he'd source it in good time.

The woman looked relieved that he had stopped. She came forward, the nervousness of approaching a stranger apparent on her face. He had hung back, waiting until he was motioned to look at the van's engine.

He perched on his bike and had an initial peek. All seemed in place. But while he peered at the engine, he did not notice the cattle taser in the woman's hand. He didn't even notice it when she stuck it beside his neck.

The strength went out of Vanya's legs almost instantly, and he clattered with his bike to the floor, the woman standing over him now as spasms sprang from his body, with a pain that had flared throughout his system slowly reducing to a dull, awful glow.

Vanya slumped rooted to the spot. Shock froze

him and he knew, somewhere on the surface of his mind, that he was in terrible trouble.

He struggled against the rising panic that his dizziness was turning something more serious. He fought for control. His face was white and his mouth opening and shutting like a goldfish. Fragments of memory from the last few minutes hit him in bursts, making him flinch and fumble.

Vanya tried to get up, failed as pins and needles crippled his arms and legs, and settled for trying to crawl away. His chest heaved as his lungs fought to extract what little oxygen they could find; his head throbbed like a balloon being squeezed. This was madness. He was going to die, He had to get away.

It was the second jolt that put him unconscious.

When he woke, he instantly wished he were unconscious again.

His mind tried to make sense of the surroundings and his position, and it took a few minutes to realise he was inside an industrial barn. It took the same amount of time to also realise he was hanging upside down by his ankles, chains running up to the ceiling holding him inches from the floor.

His thrashing about was frantic.

His legs and back ached, his head hurt like hell, and now, the anxiety done for a moment, in the sparse barn, the horror rushed back into his mind.

He bobbed his head about trying to see what was happening, and then out of the corner of his eye, he saw his assailant approach.

She was slim, her hair light brown and shining, thickly draped over her shoulders. Against her pale, almost porcelain, skin, her hair flowed like hillsides over untilled fields. Her black, sparkling eyes gazed at him unrelentingly.

He should never have stopped for her - not even a woman alone - what he suddenly realised.

He should have left well enough alone.

If he hadn't been so drunk and, yes, even a little pervy, he might have woken in the comfort of his bed - safe and sound.

He saw the butchers knife. His body tensed. Horror pinballed in his mind. Jack-knifing his body, he fought for breath, and with his final efforts, his reserves of strength diminished until he was close to complete exhaustion.

Everything went suddenly quiet.

Suddenly he knew how it would all play out.

Vanya opened his mouth to speak, but her blade entered him so swiftly that all that emerged from his throat was a painful gurgle.

Her expression was a mixture of calm, secure superiority, and something else that he couldn't fathom. Evil, was the closest description his fearful mind could grasp at.

She almost smiled as she sliced him for the last time, while he was alive anyhow.

***

The next week, still feeling the tingle of the hunt, Elena gathered her packets of fresh meat cuts and headed down the track.

Stuck down with tape on the cart was another postcard with her name on it.

The postcard fluttered in the breeze as she turned it over.

Dear Elena. I noticed the meat selling has begun again. Hope this means everything is going better. If you need anything, call me. Eduard.

He had scribbled his number in the bottom right corner. It was a town number.

Elena raised her eyebrows. Did strangers still offer help to each other? Even if it were the countryside where such habits came naturally. She wondered if he was from the authorities. Were they onto her?

Reading the postcard again, she was surprised how much the offer warmed her, especially when she'd been feeling so low.

She liked the way he'd respected her space and left the card in the meat cart, rather than coming up to the house and pushing it through her letter-box. It felt considered and respectful - the way country folk normally conducted themselves.

As she carried the card up the track, she wondered who the mysterious Eduard was.

***

That evening, as she prepared some vegetable broth, with the radio turned down and almost redundant in the corner, Elena gazed at the two postcards she had propped up on the windowsill. She thought of the phone number penned in the corner of the latest one. She hated to admit that it had piqued her interest.

There was no way she was going to call him of course. In a way, she found the offer a bit suspect. It wasn't as of she was an elderly lady in need of caring.

The more the cards drew her attention, though, the more she felt the need to acknowledge the stranger's kindness.

As soon as she'd finished cooking, she took a bowl of soup and went into the lounge. She rummaged in her desk drawer for some scraps of card. Did anyone swap notes any more?

Dear Eduard, she began. *Thank you for your kindly words.*

No, that was far too soft! She crumpled up the note and tossed it into the fireplace. She found another piece of card and started again.

Dear Eduard, Please do not concern yourself. I am able to manage. Thanks.

Elena stared at her words and sighed. Could she sound any cold-hearted? She didn't want to sound a bitch.

She felt like she'd been a recluse for too long. She had a need to be a little open, even if it were to a stranger.

Thank you for your note. I was feeling a little down at one point, but your notes have cheered me up. Thanks. Elena.

She wondered whether that was going too far in the opposite direction, but it sounded sincere. She was still slightly uneasy though. He was a stranger who bought meat, not a distant relative or old school friend. She folded the piece of card, popped it in an envelope and sealed the flap before she had second-thoughts about the whole venture.

The next morning, she propped up the note at the back of the cart with *To Eduard* written on the front. She didn't think anyone else would take it.

From the way her customers left their money in the jar, she reckoned they were an honest bunch. Or perhaps they were wary of her?

That evening, Elena took Bunin for their usual walk along the local paths and along the farm tracks.

Autumn had passed, and although she knew it

was too early to pass judgment on winter, it was one of those chilled dark days with a pewter sky when she could almost feel the approach of snow.

Would this winter be better than last, she wondered. Elena was numb to it all.

The months before Pavel had been despatched hadn't been easy. Looking back, she realised she could have handled things differently. Ignoring the cracks before they grew too big to fix had been a major flaw on her part.

She always thought their problems would be solvable. It was annoying to believe she had to take him to the slaughter house.

Pausing under the line of stark elm trees at the top of a ridgeline, she looked down at the farm, laid out like a child's play set, with its patchwork of fields and farm buildings.

Slap in the middle, her little white house looked tiny. For a family, it was a confined space. For one, it looked lonely and empty.

A movement in the distance caught her eye. The shape of a dirty white van slowing between the hedgerows piqued her interest. She wondered if it was the mysterious Eduard.

She'd check the cart before she went back to the house and see if his card was still there.

The van stopped long enough for someone to pick up some meat, but the raggedy hedges blocked a decent view of who it was.

As the tatty van cruised away, Elena wondered what the future was going to hold.

* * *

A few days later, Elena took Bunin down the

track to the cart to pick up any money that may have been left.

Propped up at the back was a colourful envelope with *Dear Elena* on the front in Eduard's handwriting.

A smile spread across her face as she took out a card with big red roses on the front.

It was so long since she had felt fluttering of romance, and it felt odd that she was even thinking of romantic connotations.

Surprised, she glanced up and down the lane to see if anyhow was there, watching her in readiness to tease or laugh, but the country lane was deserted. She nevertheless stepped a little sheepishly into the privacy of her track before opening the card to read.

Dear Elena. I hope all is well. I wondered if you would like to take a break from the farm and join me for a coffee in town. Give me a call if you'd like. Eduard.

***

"Oh, a secret admirer. What fun, eh?"

Iskra teased when Elena spoke to her on the phone that evening. "Lucky you, my fella never bothers with cards, even on my birthday!"

Elena, as often she was, seemed impervious to the sarcasm.

"What makes him think I'm available?" Elena asked. "How would he even know what I look like?"

"Who knows? Maybe he's seen you around the farm when he picked up the meat," Iskra guessed. "Maybe someone mentioned you in town. You know what it's like in the countryside."

"You don't think he's a weirdo, do you?"

"Oh, let's hope so. Liven things up a bit," Iskra joked.

Elena sniggered. "I don't know anything about him," Elena told her.

"Well, you won't know unless you give him a call."

"I'm beginning to wish I'd never replied to his first note."

"For fuck sake, listen to you!" Iskra laughed. "It's just a coffee invite. What have got to lose?"

"Maybe."

After she finished the call, Elena gazed at the cards, and the roses one in particular.

Of course, she couldn't tell Iskra about all the problems and risks that would come of having a man about the place. How would she tether the darkness that swelled within her? Could she replace murder with romance? Was the evil part of her DNA, or just a horrid habit that could be kicked?

Once again, though, she felt the yearning for love and admiration surfacing. She ached at the idea of leaving the invitation unanswered.

Taking a deep breath, she found her pile of scrap card and began to write a note.

Dear Eduard. Thanks for the invite, but I don't even know you. Makes me nervous.

Did that sound too harsh, she wondered. Too honest, she questioned.

To lighten the note, she added a small smiley face in the corner.

***

Two days later, there was another envelope in the cart. A letter this time.

Elena's pulse quickened as she opened it. She took out a photograph and straightened her back, impressed.

Eduard was a slender, muscled man in his mid-forties, with light-brown hair cropped close to his skull and a lean, square face all jaw and cheekbones under a Viking-style beard. He looked, how Iskra would describe as, a man's-man. Stoic and sturdy.

"Well, he doesn't look like an inbred," Elena commented to Bunin.

She took a deep breath to steady her mind. It was all she could do not to start grinning. She hated to feel anxiety. But the moorings of her life seemed to be coming loose, and the unease throbbed in her chest like a physical ache.

Unfolding the letter, she sat down and started reading.

Dear Elena. I know that it's kind of quirky these days to be sending notes to strangers, but I saw you outside the honey stall in the town and asked about you to the woman who runs it. Hope that doesn't make me sound a stalker!

If you'd a coffee, or a drink of something else, in the town, then please feel free to call. If not, I won't be offended (too much!) GSOH. Yours in hoping. Eduard.

***

"Should I chance it?" she asked Iskra when she rang the following morning. "I'm still not sure."

Elena had not been on a date for decades and she was nervous about the idea. What if he didn't turn up? What if the whole thing was a total flop and she just ended up feeling depressed and more annoyed than ever?

"It's ok, Elena," her friend replied. "Just go for a coffee at least. I think it's time you spent more time away from the farm and started enjoying yourself again."

"Suppose he turns up and doesn't like the look of me?" Elena laughed nervously.

"Of course he'll fancy you!" Iskra said. "He's already seen you in town anyhow, and that's why he's asked after you. I'd feel flattered."

Elena was worried she was letting her heart take over from her head and was in danger of allowing possible love to run amok.

She was too old to be swept off her feet, too anchored in her darkness. Wasn't she?

Why did it suddenly feel that some sunshine had spilled into the grey coldness of her life and was warming her soul?

One step at a time, she thought. She was embarking on a journey she had never expected.

Elena wasn't sure. The idea of suppressing her darkness seemed too much an ordeal, maybe an impossible one. She'd already dragged one partner over to the slaughter house, and didn't think she could face it again. With strangers, it was different. When she had invested her heart into a relationship, it was difficult to bring it to a violent end.

She gave herself a few days to get her courage up and think about it properly.

***

Waves of anxiety and excitement flooded her. Elena felt confused. Part of her felt like a teenager to whom someone had sent a valentine's card.

Another part of her was riddled with caution and uncertainty: she had lived a life of darkness and anger that she wasn't sure how she would adjust to trying to form a new relationship.

The rest of her simply liked the idea of having company and sex through the dark autumn days and cold winter months. Eduard had brought much to think about into her life.

The next few nights she could hardly sleep, but by the third day, she'd made her decision.

She took a deep breath and wrote the last note she'd leave Eduard in the meat cart.

Dear Eduard. If you're willing to give me a chance, then the least I can do is meet you in person. Perhaps we'll have an exciting time. Elena.

The Abisko Adventure

From where Lucas lay, the sun shone across the hills above him and made slow shadows on his bare arms and legs. He watched the patterns drifting, changing as a westerly breeze blew the clouds across the Swedish countryside.

He could hear his mother talking from inside their cottage, and away in the distance the hum of a boat chugging across the Tornetrask Lake. He felt peaceful lying here almost asleep in the June sun. He felt the aches and apprehension seep from his body, and the pains in his limbs seemed to ease a little.

What a view he had! Above and beyond him, rolls of barren hills and arctic tundra from around the lakeside. Small birds and lemmings chirped and there was a constant scurrying and shuffles of tiny creatures. During the morning, the mists that had ensnared the countryside began to clear, and by lunchtime, the sun was shining brightly again. He listened to the dreamy sound of birdsong drifting on the air. It was as if it was trying to cheer him up with its hope of better times to come, he thought, managing a smile.

In front of him, the hills rose up, fields that had a scattering of goats and reindeer making their silly, fussy noises that always made him chuckle.

Sometimes they would come to the wire fence by the cottage and stare at him lying on his chair in the back garden.

He wanted to cry out, "If I wasn't a cripple I would be off into the mountains exploring!"

But, of course, he could not cry out, and he thought that if goats could think, they would wonder at the eight year old boy sitting in the sun all day.

His mother came out of the cottage with his sister, Elsa, carrying a drink for him.

"Hello, Lucas. I expect you're ready for a drink. I'll pull you a little into the shade."

She held the cup while he sipped away at the straw, then sat beside him chatting. She smiled at him and sat on the grass picking at the wildflowers.

His mother told him of the donkeys she and Elsa had seen that morning - one donkey so blond and groomed and beautiful she must have been going to a show, and an old donkey so ragged that Elsa wanted to buy him and bring him home to groom.

-

Lucas sat and looked at his mother's face as he listened to her soothing, cheerful voice. He loved her dearly, loved her for knowing this place was just what he needed in the tiring weeks of rehabilitation ahead, loved her for knowing instinctively that they had to talk about nature.

He could recall the bus accident, only the moments before, knowing with a sickening fear that the driver could not control the bus on the icy road. That was all. He could remember the bus leaving the road and down into the deep ditch, where children lost lives, or where he had crawled by his fingers from the tangled wreck.

Lucas had woken to a pain he could even fathom, in a room so sparse and white he thought it something out of a sci-fi movie. He had been lucky, he was told - a passing motorist and saved nine children, Lucas included, whereas eight had perished at the scene.

But the weirdest, and most frustrating, thing of all was discovering that although he could understand what was said to him, his own speech seemed unable to come.

At first, only his mother had realised he could understand perfectly all that was being said to him. Doctors had done scans and confirmed brain activity.

She fought to have him home in Abisko with family, and, with the help of a nearby nurse, organised his rehabilitation day after day. Mother tended to him carefully, ensuring his basic needs were met as the weeks passed and the days slowly grew warmer and brighter.

Lucas knew he would not normally have been so lucky were it not for the constant nagging and strength of his mother, and she had brought him here to this remote landscape to work out and heal.

"My dear Lucas," she would whisper. "It's only an illness from which you can get better. Body and mind will heal with time."

He had smiled inside, the frustration easing to an almost acceptable level. Even at eight, he understood the power of love and nature.

After a while, Lucas's father returned from working at the harbour, and joined them all in the back garden. As they talked gently together, Lucas fell into a comfortable doze under the warmth of the gentle arctic sunshine.

-

When he stirred from his sleep, it was to the chilly diffused light of late afternoon, and the land was still and silent. He had been pulled away from the shade so the later sun could keep him warm. He moved his body in a test of his abilities, stretching his legs with the casts on them, trying once more to move his toes. He was almost sure feeling was coming back, that it did not pain him quite so much as it had yesterday.

His right arm, the one that had remained unscathed, fell over the arm of the chair and came into contact with fur.

Surprised, because he knew they had no pets at the cottage, he turned his head and looked down by the side of his chair.

He must be still dreaming, he told himself, for enjoying the sunshine beside him was a small goblin. He laughed, closed his eyes, and opened them again.

The goblin was still there, grinning at him, panting beside him like a ragged dog, regarding him with beady brown eyes.

Lucas could not believe it! He moved his hand to touch the matted fur, and the goblin stayed exactly where it was, letting itself be stroked.

Amazement flared in Lucas - he found he was trying to sit up and turn to the house to call for his mother.

Sweat broke out on his forehead with the strain, but no energy came. The goblin, catching the frustration, got up, shook itself and patted itself down, then at a movement from inside the cottage, turned and scuffed away to the gap in the stone wall and began to move away towards the hills.

Lucas watched until it was out of sight. Was it the same goblin that the village elders joked about in tales? Why had the goblin dared to come into the village and right up to him?

-

When his father came out to check on him he moved his right hand and nodded his head at them.

"What is it, son? What is it you're trying to tell me." His father leant closer, and Lucas gestured with his hand towards the hills, but there were only goats and birds - the small goblin had long gone.

Scowls of annoyance and frustration flushed across Lucas' face. He thud his hand into the ground with anger, then felt guilty at his display and waved his in an apology.

His father smiled and scoffed at the emotions being shared.

Over the weeks a closeness had developed between father and son. Bonded now by his trauma, they were airing their feelings openly rather than bottling them inside each other.

His father placed his hand on his son's shoulder. "Good, Lucas. It's good that you're trying to tell us something. Never stop trying. One day, we'll chat and never stop. Believe me."

But at that moment, in the heat of frustration, Lucas did not hold his father's beliefs, and he felt himself crying.

***

Now, each afternoon Lucas waited for the goblin, and every afternoon it came. Hobbling over from the wall, the goblin was short, a little ugly humanoid that stood just over two foot tall, with a scrawny body, oversized head, big ears, beady yellow eyes and lots of matted brown - unwashed - hair. Though startled at first, Lucas noted the friendly smile and cautious approach. It was obvious that the goblin was more afraid of Lucas than the other way round. Lucas watched it coming closer and closer.

Then it would meander around the stone walls, only to reappear by the gap in their wall and move cautiously through the lengthening shadows to his chair. It would sit watching him.

Lucas longed to show it off, but it never came when anyone else was in the garden. Lucas stayed awake for it and tried to form words in his head for it. The excitement of the goblin coming to him never lessened.

Sometimes Lucas would doze with his hand on its fur, and it seemed to doze, too, hidden from the cottage by the hospital chair. Lucas would try to sort the words in his head, and the words began to form like a refrain - "Goblin, Goblin, Goblin."

One afternoon, his sister approached from the lakeside, saw them together and rushed into the cottage calling, "Mother, Mother! Quick, there's an odd animal near Lucas!"

His parents came racing out, but the goblin had gone, quick as a shadow. He caught a glance of his mother's face. She looked weary and tired.

Lucas was annoyed - now they would watch him and the goblin would not come. He glared his anger at his sister.

His mother looked thoughtful.

"Don't be annoyed at Elsa, dear," she said. "A village dog, was it?"

"No," Elsa said. "It wasn't a dog. It was mangy looking."

"A goat?"

"It was brown and muddy-looking. I didn't see it properly, but it was odd."

His parents exchanged looks and sent Elsa inside for some drinks.

"A little artistic licence, I think. Maybe she's been reading too many of those fairytale paperbacks," his father said. "She's turned into one of those Bizarro types."

The word was jangling again and again in Lucas' mind. It was going to burst in his mind like a bubblegum balloon.

"Goblin! Goblin!"

It came in such an explosive sound that all of them were taken aback in shock.

"Lucas! Lucas! What did you say? Come on, son. Say it again," his father encouraged.

"Goblin." His voice was shaky and croaky, as if coming from someone else. "Goblin. Goblin."

For a moment they both stood and looked on, surprise then incredible joy on their faces. His mother burst into tears, and both his parents were hugging him, and laughing and crying together.

His mother cradled his hand in hers. "You're doing it. Oh, Lucas."

"Like a goblin, was it, Lucas? So Elsa may have been right," his father joked.

"Goblin," Lucas said again, suddenly feeling weary.

Still smiling, his father picked him up. "Goblins don't come this far west, old son, they live in the forests of Finland mainly. Come on. Time you were in resting. You look very tired."

The words were not a jigsaw in his mind anymore. Lucas didn't understand why but they were beginning to form correctly.

When resting on his bed he prayed that the goblin wouldn't desert him, that it would come back to visit. He had come to enjoy its visits.

-

The following day, Lucas was struggling with words again, and he was still very tired. After his morning exercises, he slept most of lunchtime on a rug on the grass so that he could move his limbs more freely. The summer sun was gloriously warm in a part-clouded sky and unknown, unseen wildlife chattered and scuttled in the rocks and long grasses.

The goblin came later that afternoon, quietly, as dusk made an approach, and it sat beside him on the rub breathless a little.

Lucas noticed his matted fur and dirty skin for the first time really and knew that the goblin was living in a poor state.

This evening it was restless, and padded about near him looking for a sunny spot. Eventually, it collapsed beside him seeming weary.

Tentatively, Lucas reached out and patted it, and he felt it begin to relax.

Goblin, he thought. My goblin.

His mind kept racing to the odd event, searching for something significant, for explanations, possible reasons for what had happened over the past few days.

Lucas looked out over the lake. A late breeze wrinkled the water.

Then Lucas dozed again.

He woke to lots of hushed voices, and felt the goblin rushing away from beside him. Looking up, he saw his family at the back door of the cottage.

They were beaming smiles.

"I'm sure it was goblin! What else could it have been?" his mother said. "Didn't you see his pointy ears and big eyes?"

"I thought goblins were wild. Why's it creeping into our backyard?"

"It is odd."

"It's very odd."

They walked over to where Lucas was sitting.

"It is a goblin," he said in a muffled voice. "My goblin."

"Oh, Lucas!" They laughed. "Just listen to you. It's so good hearing you speak."

As they reached him, someone called from over the end wall and looked into their garden. She was an old lady wearing tatty gowns and big military boots.

"It's only Maya, from the next town," she called. "Sorry to intrude, but I'm looking for Aslaug. It appears to be lost."

The family looked at each other in a mix of bemusement and confusion.

Lucas though realised in a flash.

"Your goblin?" he said in a croaky but steady voice.

The old woman smiled at Lucas and it felt that somehow they had an instant connection.

"Yes. I run a sanctuary up at the far end of the lake. I thought Aslaug may have ventured down these parts."

"A few times," his father said.

"I guess it's found a companion here, as it?"

"So it was a goblin?" his mother said.

"I didn't know you could tame the wild creatures," his father added.

"Goblins are my life," the old lady explained. "Benn running the sanctuary for six years now. Collecting the waifs and strays. I've cared for them until they are ready to return to the wild.

"The trouble is, some get used to being in these parts. Don't want to go back being wild in the forests."

She waved her stick in the direction of Finland - east.

"Seems Aslaug likes it in these parts of the lake," she added.

"It certainly likes it here," his mother said softly.

—

    If the old lady heard the comment she didn't acknowledge it, merely turned her attention back to Lucas.

    "You'll have to come visit us when you get back to your feet, won't you?"

    He stared at her. "Yes… but… does that mean it won't visit here again… to me?"

    He felt crestfallen and trembled with his words.

    The old woman held his gaze. "No, young man, maybe it's time you visited Aslaug. Seems only fair, no?"

    He smiled thinly, and Lucas nodded. He figured what the woman was doing. Bringing him encouragement.

    He gritted his teeth and moved his feet across the rug. It hurt… hurt a lot, but suddenly he was sure he might be able to manage it.

    He didn't see the beaming smiles his parents exchanged with the old woman, before she moved slowly away back out of the garden and into the hills to find her goblin.

PING

It was alone. It was low on energy. It was
unwanted. It was a fascinating little robot with a
friendly face and a shiny white exterior. The blue
trim around the edges of its panels matched its
eyes with distinction. Made of titanium and
plastic, it had a robust body that had ensured its
longevity.

It looked across the empty lots and disused
building site, the piles of dumped local
household items and under a sky marked with
looming clouds. All this was new and terrifying
territory.

It felt that everything was wrong in some
indefinable way - that it had found its way into a
world that was unfamiliar, malevolent.

The two teenagers had taken it out on their
bicycles two days before. Excitement mastered
it, for this was a regular activity that its owners
often did, and, for a fortnight, it had been
forgotten.

In happier times they always took it out for
adventures to different locations around Tokyo
and on vacations, and they all returned home low
on power and covered in dirt and dust. Then it
would sit on charge in the back room and listen
to the city reverberating around it.

Once they had been eager voices and they had
played with it gently. Then they grew bored and
were weary and less interested. It, too, was left to
languish in the back room for weeks on end.

Designed as a ground-breaking humanoid robot
to be used as a teaching aid for use in robotics,
systems and control, and social sciences, it soon

fell out of favour to more powerful A.I machines.

The word 'Boring' was mentioned more and more often and seemed to make the teenagers even more frustrated and uninterested.

It tried to keep itself functioning and amusing, always to perform if requested, but sometimes the teenagers gave her bizarre tasks that seemed almost doomed for failure even before started.

It was neglected, but it was never told why.

***

That morning they had not driven to the downtown sights. Instead, they drove to a small district out by the harbour, and placed it beside a large pile of disused wooden pallets.

It was used to that, though. They would leave it someplace and go off to play exploring or seek adventure in the old factories or warehouses, and then they would come and find it again, and it would sit with them while they ate or chatted.

But that did not happen this time - something was different. Lorries and workers hurried past it and it was afraid.

It crouched down against the cold sidewalk, and then looked up in disbelief as the boys drove away, leaving it behind.

It called out their names, reminding them that they had forgotten it. Its forlorn bleeps followed them as they accelerated away, and finally, confusingly, the blur in the distance was gone and the street was empty.

Nobody came for it…

It rested for an hour, trying to conserve energy, desperate, and when it felt comfortable, walked along the windy harbour-side, trying desperately to find the only humans it had known in its short existence. It didn't understand why they had gone - or that they were never coming back.

It looked down the empty harbour-side road hoping desperately that someone would come along and help it.

-

It was the young men on motorbikes who saw it first. They had spent the last hour racing up and down the empty old quay, and their blood was up.

When the leading biker saw the startled robot, he gave an excited whoop, revved his engine and came screaming to a skid towards it. Without pausing to think, the other biker did the same.

Cautious and scared, the robot raced into an old warehouse, away from the street, and into the darkness of disused machinery and skips. Here it was able to dart and dodge, but the relentless bikers had followed on foot, and soon there cane searching calls and hollas, loud voices and the hurried scuffs of footsteps.

Worried calculations whirling in its mainframe; strained working from its limbs; fear dominating every thought.

Dusk was sighing into darkness of night. The sky was dusted with stars. The footsteps and voices no longer pursued it, but it carried on moving anyway - too cautious to stop and rest.

There was a wind in its face, a spiteful, biting wind, whistling through the empty warehouses and neighbouring factories. It was not used to being outside in the darkness and to the night-time ways. All about the space, carpets of weeds and bushes. There was something sad and forlorn about the whole of it.

It had been loyal at home, but this lonely unease

of the unknown was new to it.

Its existence till now had been calm, regulated by routine and in a comforting environment that it had been programmed to understand. The only enemies it had known were those times where new people and places had been introduced, but now its world had been turned upside down.

There were concerns behind every corner, in every shadow, down every dark street or in a desolate building. It knew the city was no paradise; it had shabby streets and faded glory. It treated the dank streets with hostility and suspicion.

It was nervous and uncertain in the harbour district. It was used to the bustle of downtown and lots of people. It loved the smell of vehicles and the sounds of shops, cafes, and the machinery that came with the urban environments. Existence had been fun, once, it recalled.

Here the ground smelled salty and musty and the sidewalks were dusty and wet and scattered with litter and dirt. The wind swirled and roared, and unseen shadows flickered down the empty streets.

Still it wiggled and waddled along, its listening tuned for danger, its eyes seeking out possible concerns; scared alone and low on power. So far, so worrying. A moment of good fortune was all it needed.

***

When it reached the edge of the Narashino district, it stopped. It could go back into the harbour district or take the path that led along to the houses.

It did not know of humans were to be trusted ever again. Humans had abandoned it. There had been noisy humans behind it, intent on some game that it did not understand.

Tree branches rustled in the wind and a drizzle began to drift in a steady, miserable onset. Its mind was made up.

Where there were houses, there might be shelter It trotted warily down towards Narashino. The street twisted down the side of the harbour, and lingered beside a stream. Here the trees grew close to the water, and the banks were sodden with overspill. Cruel brambles caught at it, tearing at its legs. In the background, it could hear the murmuring of people and the barking of dogs.

The ghost of a moon soared up the sky, silvering the woods, and still it strolled on. Away from the harbour, away from the terrifying chase and away from the place where the people it loved and trusted had left it to its fate.

Pausing for energy, it took time to recalibrate that took power from less-important tasks and back into its energy pack.

It felt as though it had been walking for hours, days. A battery life of time. And even as it totted along, dodging the uneven sidewalks and pot-holes, it knew the walking would end soon.

But for now it walked, so great was the will to seek help and sanctuary.

Its body needed cleaning and oiling and its programming struggled for stability, but it knew there would be none.

There was a bite in the night air, and, harsh on the cool breeze, it caught the sharp tang of a wood fire, as it cautiously skirted the Narashino

District.

It was nearing the edge of the garden of the first house, an outlying deckhouse, stood alone, smoke pluming from the chimney. It looked around for a moment.

Everything seemed daunting somehow. Though it wondered if it was giddy due to its depleted energy levels. Everything seemed too much - the desolation, the betrayal, the confusion. The things of the world in all forms loomed into its circuits, making it weak and barely functioning.

Was there safety there? Or was there more to fear?

A van swished past, sparkling in the street lamps, and it turned into a narrow alley, instinctively seeking quieter streets - wary of people.

The street seemed endless.

A scrawny fox hissed and spat and ran. It trotted on, slower now, the energy levels dropping down by the critical twenty percent level.

The ghost moon brightened and shone on the streets, shining on a gateway in a high brick wall - on a gate that stood ajar.

It slipped through into a small, well-tended courtyard.

The curtained light of a window cast faint shadows across the yard, and a door stood open as an old man went out to lock his bicycle.

There was no time to react. It was close to complete power-loss; sanctuary was imperative.

The old man did not see the robot as the machine slunk behind him and into the bright hallway. But when the man came back indoors and caught sight of the intruder, he gave a startled gasp.

The man seemed uneasy, not quite sure of what he was supposed to do.

The robot flinched and the man bent down to it stiffly, his voice comforting.

"It's okay, fellow. I won't harm you," he said and held out his hand for the robot to reach out and touch.

Sensing no danger, the exhausted robot followed the old man into the gently-lit room with curtains drawn and a wood burner crackling cheerily in the corner.

The old man picked up his book and watched the flames flicker.

Only slightly reassured, the robot crept to him, and sat down by the man's feet.

It could tell that the old man was both proud and awkward - traits that the robot identified as positives.

"You seem depleted, fellow," the old man told it. "We'll get you fixed up in no time." He reached over to his side table and opened his laptop. Finding a USB cable, he plugged one end of an extension lead into the laptop, and the other into the robot. For a moment, the robot just sat still, and then slowly felt the swell of electricity charging up its systems.

"I lost my dog last month," the old man told it. "Thirteen years I had that Boxer, and I miss his company so much."

The old man would never admit that he was lonely, since he had long ago decided that 'lonely' was a negative word. But he used the word 'solitary' to describe his state, thing being in his view a positive word, since it is possible to choose 'solitariness', whilst 'loneliness' was more an infliction. Surrounded by the teeming city, he felt himself to be apart and different. He had begun to feel constricted by the swelling city, and hemmed in by the urban populous.

The old man felt that as a single old gentleman he was restricted and that his days and his retirement were becoming repetitive.

The voice was soft and compassionate. The robot bleeped as its energy level rose to twenty-five percent.

"He went suddenly, did my dog," he continued. I found him asleep out in the garden."

His eyes misted over and he swallowed, then, with a stoic shake of his head, he sighed. A pained look crossed his face.

The old man shrugged, forlorn, and spoke in a halting voice, explaining how he had expected to live alone till his end-days.

He was a slight man, with a soft, grandfatherly face and close-cropped hair that had a few streaks of grey in it. The robot registered with a pang of knowledge that the old man's dark, piercing eyes had dimmed, becoming milky and glazed, as if adjusting themselves already to a world beyond life.

They looked at each other and lapsed into silence.

Gentle hands touched the robot. "By the looks of you, maybe I should give you a wipe and clean." His face brightened as a thought struck him. "Maybe we can become friends…"

***

Nobody came to claim it.

As the years went by, the old man often sat in the local park, the robot, whom he named Ping, stretched out beside him.

His daughters were told of the night that the little stray wandered to its sanctuary, and gained a home. They laughed gently at their father's belief that this was meant to happen.

Ping often sat out under the trees and stared out over the park. Far away and long ago it had another life, but that was forgotten now.

Adjusting itself to a new life had been a delicate, fragile process, but its processing was no longer panicked. Its existence was suffused with the ease of security, of feeling wanted and useful. The hope of happiness replaced the feeling of loss.

The sight of them both trundling along the sidewalks always amused and entertained.

Soon, the neighbourhood looked for them on their daily excursions; the old man walking proudly, the little robot with the red plastic panels and white trims wandering at his heels - never once wanting to stray from his side.

Pat's Pet Shop

Pat's Pet Shop read the sign above the door as eight-year-old Adam O'Neill pushed the door open and wandered inside.

There was nobody in the store, just Mrs Leary, a large rosy-faced woman with bushy hair and glasses. She looked up from her paperwork and smiled in Adam's general direction. "Morning, dear," she muttered. Adam nodded a shy greeting and started to look about the store, holding the envelope that held the pocket-money his granny had given him for his birthday. Adam was very excited because his mum had agreed to him buying a pet. He was planning to get tortoise… or at least that was what he had thought.

Young Adam was mesmerised by the numerous animals that were in the shop. He had walked by this store many a time when out in with his mum shopping in Dingle, and they wandered by Pat's Pet Shop by the harbour when they watched the Atlantic waves coming in to crash against the wild west coast of Ireland. Though passing by so many times, he had never imagined all these animals inside the shop. There were wall-to-wall cages containing cute and cuddly creatures; rabbits, gerbils, guinea pigs, ferrets and amazing fluffy kittens. On the counter sat a large fish tank with impressive gold-fish. But there was very little sign of any tortoises, in fact, he couldn't see *any* tortoises.

Mrs Leary sighed loudly, obviously distracted by Adam's wanderings, and put aside her paperwork. She walked out from behind the counter. A startled Siamese cat jumped out of the way and scampered out back.

"You looking for anything in particular?" she asked the small, timid boy.

" I was looking for a tortoise really?" Adam asked in a meek mutter.

Mrs Leary winced as she already knew the sad reply she would give. She nervously rubbed her forehead. "Ah, sorry my love. I've not got a tortoise I'm afraid."

The young boy looked crestfallen. He had built up his hopes too much. Anything else seemed second best.

"We've many interesting animals outside though," Mrs Leary nodded towards a door at the back of the shop. "Out back."

Adam started to wander towards the door, already feeling disappointed and miserable.

His mum had given him strict instructions to buy a tortoise and nothing else, but once outside, stood in the courtyard out back and surrounded by so many amazing and wonderful animals, Adam found himself thinking what it might be like to own a snake, or a big spider, or a grand parrot or in fact all three.

Since his dad had left them, life with just his mum and him had been rather a struggle. His mum had cried a lot. Alone in his bedroom, he had cried a little too. He never had many friends and sometimes he wondered whether he ever would. The local doctor had told his mum that he had Asperger's, and although Adam knew he was slightly different from the other kids, he never knew what being autistic really meant. He'd always been known as a bit of odd-boy, which is the kind of reputation that can follow a boy around. It wasn't as if he was especially weird or anything. He just had the sort of mind that liked to drift away and, once it got drifting, always seemed to lead him into daydreaming.

Nobody really gave Adam a second look, except of course, the local bully, twelve-year-old Paul Connolly, who teased him mercilessly. Adam imagined what life would be like if he owned a tarantula. Would he be able to train it to scuttle after Paul? Would having a parrot get him some best friends?

"You like the big spiders do you?" asked Mrs Leary. She looked enormous as she stood beside the shy boy. Adam looked up and nodded nervously. Mrs Leary gave a small chortle and smiled. "They are interesting. But they also very expensive I'm afraid. I'm not sure if you have enough pocket money," Mrs Leary told him, pointing to a worn price label fluttering in the breeze.

Adam sighed and felt a sinking feeling in his stomach. If the animals in Pat's Pet Shop were breathtaking, which they were, then their price labels were too. He thought of the money in his pocket. He knew he'd never have enough to buy anything too exotic. It appeared all poor Adam could afford was a bedraggled gerbil or a weary rabbit. He sighed and made his way out of the courtyard.

Mrs Leary smiled to herself and called after Adam. She then looked sheepishly about, and whispered to him. "Of course, if you're looking for something really unusual…"

Adam turned to see Mrs Leary beckoning him towards some wooden cages in the far corner of the courtyard. She stood there and pointed toward a small gage in which there sat, right at the back, a small, nervous, furry creature.

"What is it?" whispered Adam, peering into the cage.

"That, my young fellow," said Mrs Leary proudly "is a baby goblin."

Adam scoffed at the idea. He knew goblins were only the stuff of tales and children's stories, and he was well aware that they had a reputation for causing mayhem and mischief. However, the more he looked at the timid creature, with its pointy ears and googly eyes, and its bundles of brown fur; he supposed it did look like a goblin, a tiny one of course. It certainly didn't look like it would be troublesome.

Mrs Leary tapped the mesh front and the creature looked up at them and looked at Adam straight in the eye.

"It needs lots of love and affection," said Mrs Leary, "But you look like a kind lad."

"I am," Adam said, blushing. Usually kind meant soft or wimpy but Mrs Leary used the word as if to be kind was something worthy and special.

"How much is it?" asked Adam, rustling in his pocket for his money, and fearing the worst.

"I'll take whatever you can afford," said Mrs Leary, "I'll just have to write you down some proper instructions and then you can take him away."

Adam was flabbergasted, he had had his very own goblin! He said thank you, paid Mrs Leary, and grasped the little cage tightly under his arm and stuffed the care notes into his back pocket. Then, just as he was leaving, a thought flashed into his mind.

"Does it have a name?" he called back to Mrs Leary, expecting to be given a weird or wonderful name.

"I called it Graham," said Mrs Leary, casually flicking through some of her paperwork on the counter.

–

Adam walked back home through Dingle town and up to the hill where he lived with his mum. Thankfully she was still at work, so he rushed straight upstairs and tucked the cage under his bed.

"Never mind," said Adam's mum when she came home from work, "perhaps they'll have a tortoise next week." Adam nodded, trying his hardest not to grin or let out his secret.

Graham had to live under Adam's bed with his old socks and forgotten books and tatty teddy-bears, but it didn't mind. His new owner was very kind, fed him twice a day, and in the afternoons took him out to play in the back garden. Adam would often sit with Graham and talk about his day at school.

School had been fairly uneventful that week. He had only fallen over in the corridors three times, his form teacher had forgotten his name twice, and he had only been bullied once for his tuck-shop money so things seemed to have been better this week. It was Friday afternoon and Adam was just leaving school when he noticed a new poster pinned to the board by the main entrance.

'PUPILS AND THEIR PETS COMPETITION' Adam read. The poster announced a show-and-tell contest that was to happen in school the following week and that there would be a prize for the best talk.

Adam would have normally shied away from such a public competition. His babbling and embarrassment would have only brought laughter and teasing from the other children, but he suddenly found himself writing his name down on the sheet and where it said 'Pet' he wrote in capital letters GRAHAM.

-

The following week soon arrived and Adam watched nervously as the other children filed into the school assembly hall. He sat and watched the parade of different pets being shuffled about. He was very nervous as he waited to be called, but the moment he stood up in front of the school with Graham sitting quietly on a leash, Adam forgot all his nervousness. Everyone listened, captivated, as he talked about Goblins in general and then introduced Graham, who entertained them by doing handstands and roly-poly's that Adam had been teaching him at home. It was over all too soon and the whole school, including the teachers, were all clapping and beaming smiles. Adam had never known such warm and friendly attention. Even his classmates, some of whom probably didn't remember his name, were smiling.

He sat back down and watched the others. There was Amy with her sheepdog, Paul with his white ferret, the Rowan sisters and their odd-looking rabbit that was huge and took up nearly the whole table, and a whole host of other animals that looked pretty ordinary and timid. All the animals looked nice, but none looked as impressive as Adam's goblin. Finally, the head teacher announced that Adam was the overall winner and congratulated him on an entertaining talk. First prize was a gift voucher, it was the first time he had ever won anything at school.

Of course, Adam's mum was over-the-moon to find out that Adam had won a competition at school, but rather disappointed that he had not told her about his odd pet. Because there was only the two of them, his mum had always insisted they not keep secrets between themselves. She wanted a home built on honesty and love, but she understood that Adam didn't mean any nastiness or dishonesty by it. He was just a shy child that found it hard to be open sometimes.

"Yes, it is a cute creature, Adam," she said, "But it is not a tortoise." At first, she had suggested that Adam take it back to the pet shop but when Adam explained how much happier he was recently, his mum agreed that it would not be nice to return it and that perhaps Graham could live with them. So the little goblin was allowed to stay, provided Adam looked after it properly and didn't let it affect his school work. So Adam kept his promises. He did his homework on time, helped his mum with chores, and still managed to play with Graham in the back garden. Since the competition at school he was beginning to get by in classes, he'd made a couple of friends, the teachers no longer referred to him as 'that boy', and even Paul Connolly had stopped bullying him for his tuck-shop money.

At the weekend Adam and his mum took the bus into Tralee. They travelled up the N86 through the lush green countryside of Co. Kerry. Feeling slightly skittish to be leaving Dingle for a while, they sat on the top-deck so they could see over the country hedgerows. Undulating rocky hills and fields fell away to reveal the sweep of the coastline beyond. Even from inside the bus they could smell the gorgeous spell of wind and sea and hillside sweetness.

They took their time wandering around the town of Tralee, walking down the long streets of bright coloured little shops and houses. They huddled on a bench to share a bag of chips, and enjoyed the morning sunshine. His mum slips her arm through his. Adam leans in against her, and all is well. They went into a book shop to spend the gift voucher Adam had won at school. Naturally, Adam was looking for books of goblins, but could only find books on myths and fables. Then he spotted a book with a picture of Graham on the front - well a creature very much like him. Adam opened the cover and found the odd creature was, in fact, a dog - a cross-breed called a Goberian: a mix of Siberian Husky and Golden Retriever. He'd had a dog all along, okay, maybe a weird and small looking one, but a dog anyhow. Well, fancy that! He wondered whether Mrs Lear had known all along that her unusual pet was nothing more than a dog. The Adam of last month would have been upset and probably would have cried, but not this Adam. Goblin or not, Graham had brought him comfort and friendship and he was the best pet a young boy could ever have.

A Robot Called Ramone

"Please, Mother, please say we can keep it."
Three faces grinned hopefully at their weary
mother. But this morning, faced with the little
machine that was bleeping away in Yoshi's, her
eldest son, arms, Mother was feeling far from
amused or forgiving.

Zhao Xun pegged the last of the washing on the
line and picked up the empty wicker basket.
Turning a stern eye on all the wishful faces, she
said, "I've already told you, boys. We are not
having a robot, and you best take that machine
back to the old man."

Zhao felt most annoyed with the neighbour
down the road who was trying to pass off his
unwanted robot on to her mischievous sons. The
boys looked dejected as she began to walk back
into the house, but Yoshi was not to be out off so
easily.

Followed closely by his younger brothers, he
hurried on behind his mother.

"Mr Kun said if he can't find a home for
Ramone soon, he'll have to scrap it."

Ignoring the bleeps and eager whistles from the
robot, she turned to Yoshi.

"You can't appeal to my better nature, Yoshi
Xun. It won't work on me. I'm quite sure Mr
Kun will find someone to take it," she said, with
an air of stoic conviction, and she went on inside
quickly before they saw her sullen frown.

When Zhao came back out again with a broom
to sweep the yard, the boys were still grouped
around the robot, making a great fuss of it and
promises they could not possibly keep.

Ramone was happily spinning and wiggling

about with all the attention.

"Come along now, boys," she said impatiently, "do as I asked."

Yoshi turned pleading eyes to his mother. "Why can't we keep it, mother?"

"Because I have enough work keeping house with you three boys, that's why."

"We'll look after it, won't we?" And two eager voices hastily agreed with him. Chow, the baby of the family at five, grinned and said stoically, "I promise too."

Zhao sighed, put the broom to one side and placed her hands on her hips. She looked at each one of her three sons shook her head in exasperation.

"For how long - maybe the weekend at the most? Then who'll be left to ensure it's not left outside in the rain, and to put him on charge every night? Me. No! And that's the end of the matter."

***

The boys went into a huddle at the far end of the garden. When their mother had finished sweeping out the back porch, Raymond, Zhao's middle son, tried his luck. Yoshi, the eldest at almost eleven years was, by mutual consent, the spokesman for his brothers, but nine-year-old Raymond was the one with the charm.

He now turned its full power on his mother. "We promise, mother, to take full responsibility for Ramone. We have all sworn to take turns at looking after it, taking it to get systems restoration, even if there is thundering and lightning…" And everyone knew how scared

Raymond was of thundering and lightning. "…
And put him on charge every day. We promise."

Chow wasn't going to be left out. Once again,
he beamed a huge grin. "Me, too."

Zhao clapped her hands over her eyes, then
slowly dropped her arms to her sides. She looked
down at the three hopeful faces - four if she
included Ramone - and shook her head.

She loved them all but she was determined to
stand her ground.

"Listen to me, all of you. We are not going to
take in a robot, now or anytime, so stop wasting
your time. And don't start moaning, Chow -
sulking won't do any good. Take that robot back
- immediately!"

Knowing they wouldn't sway their mother's
thinking, the boys gloomily trailed across the
yard with Ramone trotting beside them quite
unawares.

"You're not to take Chow with you this time,"
Zhao called out, "and remember to close the gate
behind you."

That evening when she told her own mother all
about Ramone and her firm stance to the boys'
pleas for a robot, she quite expected her to say,
"Absolutely right. Absolutely right."

But instead, to her amazement, she heard her
mother say, "I don't see why the children
shouldn't have a robot if they want one. It's good
for children to have a companion. It'll teach
them to be responsible and understanding. We
had a pet when I was a child."

"That was different," Zhao snapped. "You were
only a child. Grandmother didn't have three boys
to look after."

She wished immediately she hadn't said that
because she knew that her brother had been lost

in childbirth. Her mother had often told Zhao
how lonely it had been growing up as an only
child. Well, she thought dryly, none of her boys
could make that complaint. Zhao apologised to
her mother for her flippant remark.

The following day was Saturday and Zhao was
woken by her mother standing beside her bed
with a cup of tea in her hand.

"Mmm, I love the weekends," she said sleepily
and took the tea from her mother.

"Well, the sun is shining bright today," her
mother added, "The boys are up early this
morning, except for Chow - he's still dozing in
bed."

"That's unusual for them," Zhao said pensively,
but she forgot about it once she was up and
preparing breakfast for the family.

Grandmother went out to the early market for a
couple of hours, promising to take the boys out
when she got back.

"Have a chat while I'm out with the boys - I
mean, have a chat with the boys while I'm out -"
She giggled at her fumble and Chow, who had
gotten up for his breakfast, laughed with delight.

***

After her mother had gone out, Zhao soon
discovered why her sons had been so keen to get
up early that morning. She walked through the
door in time to see Yoshi and Raymond opening
a back window to trail a USB cable outside.

"What are you two doing with that?" she asked
suspiciously.

Two guilty faces looked back at her and she
knew instantly.

"You didn't take it back, did you?"

They shook their heads and Chow got down from the table, breakfast scattered down his front, and crept in between his brothers. "Ramone needs charging up," he said.

Ramone was in the back shed at the end of the yard. Yoshi had just come in from cleaning it and had only just opened the back window.

He coloured when he saw his mother and only had to see her expression to know what was going to happen.

"Immediately after breakfast, Yoshi," was all Zhao had to say and he knew what she meant.

The boy turned on his heel and walked back out into the yard. His brothers, without a backward glance at their mother, followed him.

Zhao's legs wobbled like jelly as she climbed the stairs to make beds. Was she being too hard on them?

From her bedroom window, she could see the boys having their last play with Ramone before Yoshi and Raymond took it away.

***

She finished the beds and had another look out of the window. It took a moment to scan the garden and realise that Chow wasn't playing in the yard, as he had been earlier. Her flesh went clammy. The back gate was swinging on its hinges.

Zhao ran down into the yard and met Yoshi and Raymond coming back without the robot.

Yoshi was scuffling his feet listlessly as he walked beside his brother. Raymond was humming away to himself to keep his mood from breaking.

Zhao heard Raymond mutter, "I bet Mr Kun will be surprised when he comes back and finds Ramone back in his yard."

Zhao's heart twisted at the sight of her sons' dejected faces but right now she was more concerned for the youngest brother. She was experiencing a parent's worse nightmare: losing a child. "Have you seen Chow?" she gasped. "Someone left the back gate open and he's gone."

Yoshi turned to Raymond and said, "You go with mother to the playground in case he's on the swings."

Grandmother was home by the time they all met up again and there was still no sign of Chow. "Maybe we should call the police," she suggested and Zhao nodded numbly.

The boys huddled together on the sofa, white-faced and worried. Chow had wandered off before but he had never gone off for this long.

Their grandmother was just about to go down the police station when Raymond cried out, "Here he comes - and look who's with him!"

They all crowded in the doorway and, with sighs of relief, Yoshi rushed out into the back yard with Raymond hard on his heels.

"Well, I never…" Zhao muttered in disbelief.

Walking slowly up the back path came Chow, holding the hand of an elderly gentleman. "It's Mr Kun, mother," cried Raymond, "and Ramone."

***

Mr Kun leaned heavily on the stick he held in

his hand and Ramone trotted beside him. They stopped in front of Zhao, and Mr Kun freed his hand from Chow's clasp and held it out to Zhao.

"Your son brought me here, Mrs Xun." He spoke with difficulty and had to cough before he could continue.

"Chow, he said his name was. I remember he came with his brothers." He nodded his head in the directions of her other sons.

"I've returned with young Chow here because I want to thank you for your kindness in looking after Ramone for me and I'm sorry for the trouble he might have caused.

"I found him in my front yard when I returned from the doctor's. Chow arrived just after I did.

"Please accept my apologies for the inconvenience that Ramone may have caused you."

He patted the robot's head and went on, "It needs the company of youngsters, like your boys here." He smiled at her sons all clustered around Ramone.

"It's… it hasn't been too much trouble," Zhao lied. She looked at Mr Kun and saw that he was sincerely troubled by Ramone and it's future.

"I'm struggling to look after it, too be honest. Your boys tell me though, that you're not keen on the idea?"

Zhao felt herself blush. Truer words had never been said, but she felt bad at her impulsive reaction to the idea.

"Well…," Zhao mumbled, "I was thinking about maybe reconsidering."

Yoshi picked up on the positive vibes and nudged Raymond.

"If you would give the idea another thought, I'd be very relieved," Mr Kun muttered. "I'm going into a retirement home next week and I was getting worried."

"What if we give it a trial period?" Zhao suggested.

"Thank you all."

He turned to go and Zhao found her voice and pleaded with him to come inside and have a rest while she made them all some tea.

Mr Kun shook his head and thanked her. "I must get back. I have a lot to do."

The boys saw him to the street and promised to come and visit him at the retirement home. Then, with Ramone stood beside them, beeping softly, they watched him go until he was out of sight.

They came back to find their mother busying herself in the kitchen filling a teapot with boiling water. Her cheeks were flushed and she hastily wiped her eyes with the back of her hand.

"Mother…?"

She nodded. "Yes, Yoshi - but remember what you all promised…"

The promise was renewed with lots of shouts and jumping about by the boys as they all rushed about the robot, who had sensed the excitement and was bobbing about on the spot.

Grandmother crept into the kitchen and put her hand on Zhao's shoulder. "I suppose this means we'll have a big electricity bill?" she teased with a smile. "With all that charging every night."

Zhao's answering laugh was a little weary but as she laid her head against her mother's shoulder she knew she had made the right decision.

The Robot Tattoo

Simon waited till she had finished her second glass of wine before breaking the news to his wife. As he had expected, she went bloody mental.

"For fuck sake, Simon… you went on a three-day conference to Japan, and you came home with a bloody tattoo!" She almost spat out the last two words.

Her face went as dark as the claret she was drinking. Despite buying her the duty-free at the airport, the news that timid-shy guy Simon had broken character and got a two-inch-high robot tattoo on his left shoulder had not been eased by the gifts.

He tried his best to make it a tale of amusement and mid-life stupidity.

She didn't seem like she found it funny at all.

"Why the fuck did you get a robot?" she scoffed, rounding on him to sit glaring and bemused. "It's just odd." Her neck was already experiencing a furious rash.

"What is? The robot, or getting the tattoo?" Simon joked.

His wife raised an eyebrow. "Now's not the time to suddenly take up stand-up comedy as well. Just… just why?"

Simon shrugged. He didn't know, really. He was in the Yokohama area of Japan, and had read in the hotel brochure about the famous tattooist, Nakahara3rd. With the engineering conference finishing early on the last day, he fancied using the free time to go against his, normally shy, nature and to go get a tattoo. It was a daft notion he had harboured for years, and it seemed the perfect time.

But perfect timing wasn't always his best attribute, as he was currently finding out. He knew his wife wouldn't like it, and he knew the problems it would cause, but once in the tattoo studio, he didn't really care what his wife would think. In fact, he was getting sick and tired of how his wife dictated his life.

"You never stopped to think it was a stupid idea?"

"Apparently not."

"For fuck sake, don't let the kids see it."

"You think they'll hate it?"

"No, just the opposite," she said. "That's what I'm worried about."

She took a second look at it. A small red, boxed-body, robot. What the fuck, she muttered.

-

The mood calmed by the second bottle of wine, and Simon popped a pizza in the oven and kept his fingers crossed. Her words 'It's just not you' resonated in his mind. He grinned, silently enjoying the chaos he had caused. He was a forty-five-year old man who had a wife that nagged him like he was one of the kids. Her constant bitching had made it simple to jump at the chance of going to Japan. It was a blessed relief to escape for a few days.

He was silent for a few seconds. Despite the resentment he held for his wife, he did love her. It was this love that brought the regrets for his recent trip. His drinking, his tattoo, the drinking and excursion to the mystic shop. His Japanese friend had taken him stumbling, laughing hysterically into the dim, dark shop with the cute witches.

With the gallons of alcohol swishing around in

his system, he couldn't deal with two things at once. Daft decisions took precedence over future complications.

The tattooist had listened to Simon's woes and, as he shaded in the red colours of his tattoo, had mentioned the mystic shop to his friend. Revenge and anarchy had been joked about amidst the reckless drinking. Money and morals had been very loose that day. Everything about the place had made him uneasy, but the heady mix of drink and bravado had helped quash his apprehension.

It was while he was away that he realised he had developed a sudden, deep-seated dislike for his wife, and he didn't really know why. A strange malevolent impulse began to reveal twisted emotions, and, indeed, he was slightly fascinated by it.

The smell of burning pizza woke him with a jolt, like being shaken from a vivid nightmare.

Stranger and stranger: He let out a long sigh of weariness, with a thin rattled tinge that seemed to express a sense of feeling harassed.

He was somewhat relieved and satisfied to be back home with his family, living his quiet and timid life. Hopefully, a good night's sleep would do them the world of good.

-

With the mood heavy with guilt, he kissed his wife and snuggled beside her in their bed. He felt her warmth and wished his trip had just been a dream. Tomorrow, he thought, he'd book a family holiday to the seaside and try to erase the legacy of the disastrous trip.

He needed space and time to evaluate what he wanted in life, and to figure out how he was going to get there. He loved his kids, but not his wife. What a situation he found himself in.

–

Simon's wife woke to the incessant beeps of her husband's alarm, stretched across his sweaty body and silenced it. 'Fucker's stone deaf this morning,' she thought, giving him a shove. She considered elbowing him. Getting no response, she reached up and peeled back the duvet.

Sleeping through his alarm was unusual for him. Tiredness slowed her reaction time.

The sight that met her eyes was so shocking that it was seconds before her screams began. Simon lay on his back, his eyes wide open, his mouth in a frozen cry, his lifeless body like a horrifying statue. A ripple passed across her face as realisation began to sink in.

She began to tremble uncontrollably and fight the anxiety in her chest muscles as she struggled to grasp the panic-stricken emotions. The adrenaline of shock overcame her tiredness; she suddenly started to think practically and how she was going to deal with the problem.

Kneeling beside him, and fighting back nausea, she looked around the bedroom trying to understand the sudden horror she had found herself in. Fumbling about for her phone on the bedside table, she tried to figure out what she was going to say to the emergency response operator. There seemed no obvious explanation. Except for the terror that was etched across his face, there were no signs of injury or malice.

She shuffled back from her lifeless husband, stood by the bed and fought against her shaking and notion to start panicking uncontrollably.

But when she saw the robot tattoo wink at her, the bedroom filled with her screams.

The Professor and the Robot

Sunday morning dawned even more slowly and drab than the previous day had gone. The very concept of 'dawn' was a joke. The darkness seemed to be holding on, holding back the feeble sun, until well into the official daytime hours.

The old military airbase just outside Macau had been deserted for eight years, and the lingering mist made the place seem like a set from a spooky movie. It felt exposed and melancholic, on that dreary morning. The old runways were monochrome and deserted, save the weeds and shrubs that were pushing their ways through the cracks in the tarmac. The morning cold pressed itself in.

The young lad squatted on his haunches like a small frog in front of the open warehouse. "Muck about with that robot and I'll thrash you!" Mr Cheung's weary face was contorted with suspicion as he materialised from the shadows at the back of the warehouse.

The young lad leapt up and took a few steps backwards. "Sorry. I wasn't doing nothing, honest I wasn't. Just being nosey, that's all."

Mr Cheung walked over and stood in front of the old metal table that was scattered alongside wheeled-tool boxes. He patted the half-built humanoid robot and the robot stared back, unblinking, head slightly shifting side to side.

Satisfied that no harm was going to come from the young lad, he turned on the lad again.

"You shouldn't be here," he said. "I won't have you larking about here." His mouth twisted up with impatience.

"I was only looking," the boy said sullenly.

"What are you doing here anyway?" He pointed to the scattered bits of robotics on the table. "And why's he's got no legs?"

Mr Cheung's left eyebrow lifted slightly. "I'm building a vacuum cleaner," he said sarcastically.

"Out of a druid?"

"Why not?" Exasperation rose to the surface.

The lad scowled. "Shut up - you're having me on."

"Maybe?" the old man said. "Well, lad. I'll tell you what I'm not teasing you on that. I don't want you here. There are lots of dangers around here."

The young lad wondered how the man had ended up living like an outcast in the middle of a disused airbase. He looked over at him and caught his gaze and smiled.

"What do you do all day?" The young lad asked.

"This and that," Mr Cheung replied, shrugging. "Fix stuff. Keep out of the way of anyone that comes this way?"

Almost instinctively, the young lad looked about. "You see a lot of people?"

"Enough to get by," he said, huffing at the questions.

Mr Cheung thought. In the past, the question about his day would have been easy to answer, but now? His days now had an empty, melancholy quality to them, despite the fact that he had tried to maintain his military routine to help him adjust. He woke at dawn as he had when working, made tea and toast, and pottered-about till dusk forced him to retire back to his lodgings. What he did in between, he wasn't quite sure as of yet.

The recollections made him bristle. "Just scoot,

and I don't want to see you about here anymore," he muttered.

The lad wiped his brow and made a face. "It's not your warehouse," he said. "Are you actually supposed to be here?"

Mr Cheung surveyed him for a moment, then, reaching out for an old sponge, he threw it towards the lad.

The lad took off and didn't stop running until he was away from the old airfield and back on the country lane that led to his town.

A few days later, Mr Cheung came out from a second hanger and into the clearing with a box of robotic panels.

Seeing the lad once more by the warehouse entrance, he stopped short. "What you doing here? I thought I asked you to stay away from here."

The lad ignored the question. "What you doing with this druid?"

"That's no druid."

"What is it then?"

Mr Cheung walked over and stood beside the lad and looked at the mechanics spread out on the table. "It's a robot."

"Brilliant!" the lad said. "It looks like something out of a sci-fi film."

Mr Cheung plonked his box on the end of the table and started to unpack a couple of titanium feet. The lad looked on with interest.

"Do you think it'll ever walk?"

"I hope so. That's the idea."

"You're crazy. It'll never work." It was said thoughtlessly - a knee-jerk and absolutely honest response from a child whose attention was gnawing itself with looking about and being inquisitive.

"How long will it take to fix it?"

"You ask too many questions, young man. And come away from the table. I don't want you knocking anything off the table."

The young lad stepped back to a respectful distance. "What's it made of?" the lad persisted.

"Plastic, mainly. But titanium and metals," Mr Cheung said.

"Fantastic!" the lad said. "Where do you find all the bits?"

"I just find them."

"Yes, but from where?"

"I just find them here on the airbase, all right?"

The lad was silent for a moment, then he gazed up at Mr Cheung with big dark eyes, his messy hair flopping over his forehead.

"Where'd you get the robot?"

"Over in the main hangar." Mr Cheung nodded his head. "At the far end of the base."

"What do you call it?"

"I don't call it anything. It's a machine. You only give names to things that are living, you know, pets and people."

The lad considered the logic of the man's reasoning for a bit. "What's your name then?" he said at last.

"You're very nosey, aren't you?"

"I just wanted to know what to call you."

"You've not to worry about calling me anything."

"You've got a name in the town," the boy persisted.

Between the frown and frustration, there was a small twitch of his mouth that might have been a smirk. "What do they call me?"

"They call you 'the mad-professor'."

"The mad-professor, eh? And what else do they

say about me?"

The lad hesitated. "They say you're miserable and dangerous."

" Dangerous?"

"They say that anyone who has gone through what you've been through must make you dangerous."

"Do you think I'm dangerous?"

The lad shrugged. "I don't know," he muttered.

The old man leaned forward, hands on knees, looking down at the boy. Mr Cheung's first reaction was strong annoyance, before he caught himself up.

"Well, now listen here," he said quietly. "I am a bit miserable, that's true enough. I'm not really dangerous, but you should know that and not come back here again."

"Your mother wouldn't like it if she knew you were hanging about the old airbase."

"Ain't got a mother."

"No Mother?" Mr Cheung straightened up, taken aback with the lad's revelation.

"Not for a few years. I live with my grandmother."

"All right, then. Your grandmother wouldn't like it then, would she?"

"She wouldn't mind, not if she knew I was visiting you." He hesitated. "We could be friends."

Mr Cheung scowled. "I'm not your friend. I hardly know you. Haven't you got friends your own age."

"Not many twelve-year-olds about this town."

Mr Cheung stared at the boy in exasperation then turned abruptly and started walking off to the neighbouring hanger.

The lad scuffed his feet in the dirt. "Hey,

professor," he shouted after the departing figure. "Can I help you with stuff?"

Mr Cheung spun round angrily. "No you can't," he huffed. "It's private. Now get yourself off this airfield and stay off."

He turned away once more, calling over his shoulder. "And don't let me catch you visiting again."

-

The morning breeze whistled through the valley, amid the lonely shacks, old hangers and crumbling buildings. It was an eerie landscape. A desolate, secluded place.

In a neighbouring hanger, Mr Cheung was building a new workshop. It was a large construction, with several disused rooms having been knocked through to make fewer, but larger, rooms. The remainder consisted of a locked observation room.

The materials he had obtained from the numerous ramshackle hangers and warehouses that had once been the hub of the airbase.

Mr Cheung whistled tunelessly as he collected all the wooden struts for the new internal walling.

The young boy arrived and hovered about nervously by the hanger doors until eventually his curiosity overcame his anxiety and he called out, "What you doing, professor?"

Mr Cheung sighed and muttered a few quiet cuss words. He straightened up and took a deep breath. "I thought I told you never to come here again."

As if not hearing, the lad pointed to the construction work. "So what's all that about?"

"Never you mind."

The lad looked sullen. "I only want to know what you're building."

"Yes, well," said Mr Cheung, never one to apologise if he could avoid it.

"I was only trying to be friendly."

"You're too nosey by half," Mr Cheung observed.

"What is wrong with you?"

"What?" Mr Cheung enquired, not know where this chat was going.

"I don't think I've seen you smile."

Mr Cheung rolled his eyes and look dismayed.

"Well, it's none of your business. Stop getting involved. Go back to town."

The lad shrugged his shoulders and made a face to suggest he hadn't taken on board what Mr Cheung had just said.

"You don't care about other people," the lad added. "You don't seem to care about yourself." The lad took a moment to look about at the rubble and rubbish.

Mr Cheung looked at him and saw the boyish charm had mixed with a devil-may-care grin.

The lad added, "I'm worried about you."

Mr Cheung felt slightly foolish and pathetic, seemingly having to answer to a child. But social situations unnerved him, and always had. The prospect of having a heart-to-heart conversation with the young lad was too odd for comfort.

"I'm worried about when this conversation is going to end," huffed Mr Cheung.

The lad looked downbeat. "Don't you have anything to be happy about?"

"My wife died. My colleagues are dead, and I live in a disued air-traffic control building."

"We all struggle Professor. And I can still

smile."

Mr Cheung didn't know whether to laugh or get even more annoyed. He could not help but like the lad's audacity. "Yeah, well, maybe I don't have a lot to smile about right now. I've little to care about."

"Then why are you fixing up the robot?"

Mr Cheung sighed. "Because it's all I can do." He kept his temper in check, his face stony and impenetrable. He could feel the youngster studying him while he tried to look away in the slim hope that the lad would lose interest and leave him be.

They both stood about in silence for a few agonising seconds.

"Anyhow, shouldn't you be at school?" Mr Cheung said, trying to break the melancholy. He brushed dirt and dust off his trousers and watched it float off away in the breeze.

"I hate school," the lad said.

Mr Cheung raised an eyebrow. "Don't want to go? What will your grandmother say when she finds out?"

"She won't. She's too busy running the guesthouse. I don't like school."

He pointed at the laboratory inside the hanger. "What's that for?"

"It's a laboratory."

"What's it for?"

Mr Cheung huffed in disgust. "You don't have any common sense, do you? If you went to science class at school a few times, they'd teach you things about laboratories. It's for the robot."

"For him to live in?"

"Don't you ever stop asking questions?" Mr Cheung wiped his forehead in exasperation. "If I tell you, will you go away and not come back?"

The lad nodded, and Mr Cheung pointed to the lab.

"The robot is almost fixed. But to test it, you have to have a secure space that is immaculately clean and safe. You don't want dirt or dust to affect the testing."

"When the testing is over with, the lab can be an area for the robot to charge and rest," he said firmly, unscrewing the top off his flask of tea. He poured a cup. "You can't fix up a robot and then have it just sitting about in the dirt or outdoors. It needs a clean area to remain when not in use." He took a sip from his tea, "and that is all I've got to say about it."

The lad was not so easily put off. "Did you fix its feet yet?"

"How old are you?"

"Eleven. Nearly twelve"

"You're very annoying... even for an eleven-year-old. Hasn't anyone ever told you about your chattering?"

The lad grinned. "Grandmother has. She always says I talk too much."

Mr Cheung turned away to smirk. "I know how she feels," he muttered under his breath.

"Do you think you'll properly fix it?" the lad asked.

"Me and science together."

The lad nodded with a smile. "That's pretty cool!" the lad said admiringly.

Mr Cheung dropped his screwdriver. The lad darted forward, scrabbled about on the floor and handed it back to him, but made no effort to leave.

Mr Cheung sighed heavily and handed him the screwdriver. "Here," he said, defeated. "Pass it to me while I put up the door."

He caught a reflection of himself in the glass of the door - a pale withered face, warped by rough living and shadowed by the poor light in the hanger. The reflection staring back at him seemed strange, at odds with his past stoic statue of the military days, and Mr Cheung realised with a sullen feeling how he must look to the young lad. He tried to mask his emotion by fixing his thoughts on the work at hand.

By late afternoon, the main structure of the internal laboratory was complete. The walls, door and ceiling boards were all fixed in place. While Mr Cheung did the heavy stuff, or the fixings that involved dangerous tools, the lad swept up, carried out trash, then helped move some supplies.

They worked together for a few hours, Mr Cheung doing the construction, the young boy fetching tools and attachments needed. He tried to catch Mr Cheung's eye from time to time, almost unconsciously. The realisation that there was a connection between them was bubbling somewhere inside him, warm and auspicious.

The rhythm of the work settled his thoughts; they began to soften and dissipate. He was no longer where he was; time went by differently: old love, the bustle of the old days and the warm summer evenings. His mind had the brief respite from melancholy.

When finished, they stood together and admired it. "Is it ready for the robot?"

"Few more days yet. I need to lay the flooring first, then put in a filter system," Mr Cheung said firmly, and he started to collect up his tools and put them back in his mobile toolboxes. "Here," he said suddenly, "you said your grandmother doesn't know you're not at school."

The lad nodded.

"You've got to promise me something before you ever come back," Mr Cheung said. "And properly promise this time. You've got to tell your grandmother where you going - understand?"

"Why?"

He rubbed the back of his neck. "Because," Mr Cheung said wearily, "I'm a stranger and it's not safe for children to be visiting strangers. Your grandmother might not like it."

"Yeah... but you're not really a stranger now though, are you," stated the lad, staring up at Mr Cheung.

Disconcerted, he rubbed his forehead and rolled his eyes. "I'm not your friend though, am I," he muttered and wheeled his toolboxes up against the hanger wall.

"Besides, I'm the mad-professor. Dangerous, also." A slight smirk appeared.

The lad just laughed. "Yeah, but you're not though."

"Your grandmother might think so."

"No, I'm sure she won't."

"Tell her, okay," Mr Cheung persisted, "Or no coming here."

The lad sighed. "All right then."

"Promise?"

The lad sighed again reluctantly. "Okay. I promise."

"Mind you do."

Mr Cheung nodded curtly outside, tucked his tea flask under his arm and disappeared in the direction of the dilapidated air-control tower.

-

Mr Cheung waited all the following day for the boy, but he didn't turn up. At the end of the afternoon, he studied the robot and then decided to leave it where it was until the following morning, when he transferred it carefully into the laboratory.

For the next few days, Mr Cheung watched and waited for the quick, cautious movements through the edge of the airbase that would herald the lad's arrival, and found to his surprise that he felt a keen sense of disappointment when he didn't come.

So, he thought, he's told his grandmother and she's told him to stay away. He feels a heavy sinking in his stomach. He has realised that he has been too long in silence, too long in solitude, too long in the past. He tried to settle his thoughts, then gave it up and fell asleep out in the sunshine. He didn't wake until most of the day had passed.

Stirring from his nap, he felt the sting of loneliness hitting him as he realised that maybe the young lad wouldn't be coming back. It was too much. Frantic to exorcise the melancholy, he pushed a nearby tool trolley as hard as he could, welcoming the burst of noise that broke the reverie.

Early in the morning of the third day, however, the young lad arrived on the airbase, his face grinning with anticipation.

"My grandmother wants to meet you," he announced breathlessly.

"Whose idea was that?"

"Grandmother says. She wants you to come back to the guesthouse this afternoon when I get home from school and have some tea with us."

"And suppose I don't want to?"

The young lad looked surprised, as though such a thought had never crossed his mind.

"I figured you might like to spend some time away from here. Say you'll come."

Mr Cheung turned his back and stared into the laboratory. Not long now, he thought, and the robot will be fixed - then he'd be bored again.

"You'll visit, won't you?" The lad stood beside him, looking up at him.

Mr Cheung huffed and wandered away a little. "All right, all right," he muttered. "I'll come. But only for a short time. I don't do socialising.

***

Down a long, narrow lane where undergrowth threatened to over-run the road, and farmland had been gouged out from the wooded hillside, Mr Cheung found the guesthouse where the lad lived with his grandmother.

The woman was a timid lady, wearing a bulky dark-blue dress. She was a plump, pale woman and clearly not very interested in putting on a beautiful impression, although she was pretty under the unkempt hair and dated-clothes.

She's about my age, Mr Cheung thought, surprised. He'd expected a grandmother to be much older.

Mr Cheung was grateful that the tea was a no-nonsense affair, just steaming green-tea in delicate cups and some homemade cookies.

"The lad enjoys them," she said simply.

He nodded. "They are very good."

"My grandson tells me you live alone on the airbase?"

"Yes, just me and the ghosts."

The lady smiled at his remark. "You must get lonely."

Mr Cheung shook his head and took another sip of tea. He had learned it was best not to dwell on the melancholy of his life, so he feigned a smile as best he could.

The lady took the hint, and tried to lighten the mood. "Look at me, asking personal questions. I'll be turning as bad as the young lad."

He, in turn, didn't know what to say, so he smiled, noticing her kind, caring face and warm smile with just a hint of weariness behind her eyes.

Mr Cheung drank his tea and looked around the kitchen in the guesthouse. A door hanging loose and a cupboard door swung open, the latches broken. The room was stuffy and cold, and the floorboard creaked under his foot, so noticeable that he felt guilty with every creak so kept his feet perfectly still as to not embarrass the grandmother.

"I don't have time to fix everything," she said defensively. "There's never enough time to do it."

She nodded in the direction of her grandson. "He helps out when he can." She smiled at the lad and he grinned back.

"After school, mind," Mr Cheung warned.

"School's finished - it's the holidays."

Mr Cheung's beard twitched and he bid his goodbyes and goes back out into the country lane, back towards the airbase.

-

The young lad came each day, sometimes twice, and man and robot grew used to his presence. Soon he was allowed inside the laboratory to help put the finishing touches, admiring the robot and how it was coming together.

When it started to stand on its new feet, the lad beamed wide smiles with delight and even Mr Cheung would allow himself to feel a little glow of satisfaction.

The fixed robot stood still for a moment, head to one side, listening, then suddenly it took a step, then followed it up by another. Mr Cheung and the lad watched on with glee. There was a brightness about himself that Mr Cheung hadn't felt in a long while.

"It won't be long now."

"What won't?"

"Till the robot will be finished, and we can put it to use."

"When? This week?"

"Maybe," the man said. "Depends on the tests I'll do in the next few days."

"Will you sell it?"

And Mr Cheung grumbled at the lad for his ignorance and the boy said anxiously that Mr Cheung shouldn't let it go until he was there, too.

The old man paused, taking in what the lad had said to him, and couldn't help but smile. He wasn't sure what, but the request had found itself to his heart. Mr Cheung thought it was because he recognised something in the younger man - pride, a flourish of determination - that reminded Mr Cheung of his own personality.

Mr Cheung grumbled again, but he didn't say no to the request...

***

The robot sat on the edge of the low table as Mr Cheung and the lad unplugged it from the electrics.

Carefully he pulled out the USB charge cable and took a breath. Quietly the lad ran his hand across its back, until Mr Cheung began to type instructions from his laptop.

It slowly stood up and took a first step. It then looked around the hanger, and began to walk slowly out towards the entrance. It stood in the doorway and looked about, trying to gauge the surroundings.

The young lad's eyes widened with wonder as they both watched the robot assessing the situation it found itself in.

For breathless minutes, the watchers gazed onwards, until at last, with a stoic stance, the robot slowly walked outside and began to step into the weather.

Mr Cheung maintained a quiet demeanour and was rewarded with genuine joy. "You're amazing," said the lad admiringly.

"I'm very nervous inside," Mr Cheung admitted.

There was a strange comfort in speaking those actual words, and he realised it was the first time he had been so honest and open with the lad. He felt suddenly lighter, exposed.

The lad looked on for a long time after the robot had walked away. Then he rubbed fiercely at his eyes with the back of his hands and a small, sullen sigh escaped from his mouth.

Mr Cheung put a hand on his young shoulders and squeezed gently. "Reckon we'll and make some tea now," he said.

"We never gave it a name. We must have known it long enough to give it a name."

Mr Cheung considered. "Okay then - how about Jonnie."

"Jonnie," the lad repeated thoughtfully. "Why

not. Sounds okay."

Mr Cheung stooped to pick up some old cables. "Here," he said, "Catch hold of these. We'll find a drawer for them."

The lad did so, and together they started to tidy up the tools and workshop.

Mr Cheung had noticed that a sadness seemed to descend on the lad, and he took a heavy breath as if to ward it off, and Mr Cheung suddenly understood the fragility in the youngster.

"I suppose you don't need me to come and help anymore," the lad said in a small voice. "Not now you've fixed up Jonnie."

"I've been thinking," Mr Cheung said. "Maybe your grandmother would like me to do some odd jobs round the guesthouse for her. I wouldn't want paying - I'd do them as a friend."

The lad looked puzzled. "Whose friend?"

"Yours, of course."

"I reckon she'll like that." The young lad looked relieved.

Mr Cheung strode out of the hanger and paused. The young lad followed along side, now and then skipping the extra step to keep up.

Shyly Mr Cheung glanced sideways as they stood together.

"You see that old hanger over there," he said, pointing towards the neighbouring dilapidated building.

The young lad glanced around him - dusk was already settling in around the handful of old buildings scattered around the airfield. He nodded.

"It's filled with old bits and bobs," Mr Cheung added. "You fancy helping me have a clear out? Maybe we could even find some robotic stuff and build Jonnie a partner."

The young lad watched Jonnie slowly walking around the disused airbase, trying to calculate it's surroundings. He then looked up at Mr Cheung. For the briefest instant their odd friendship and the twists in fate had joined them together in achievement.

And somewhere in amongst Mr Cheung's beard there was a slight quiver.

The young lad grinned. The old mad-professor might have even had a smile...

The Cornish Cottage

The old flint cottage stood in a fold in the hills at a point where two lanes met. Meadows and pasture stretched as far as the eye could see, edged with straggling hedges of blackthorn and hazel.

The cottage, long, low and rambling, its ancient walls bleached by time and weather, and chimney pluming smoke, was surrounded by small yards with ramshackle outbuildings and patches of nettles and weeds.

"We dare you," Tom and James said. "Knock on the door and say you're lost."

Martyn looked at his older brothers and tugged nervously at the brim of his old white baseball cap. A little gnawing churn rumbled in his stomach.

With giddy legs, he skipped across the front yard, stood by the old wooden door, cast a nervous glance back to his brothers, and knocked. Both his brothers stifled their laughter.

The door creaked open and from where they hid, Tom saw his little brother go inside.

"We never saw anyone inside," James told his parents as they stood outside the cottage a few hours later. Tom was red-faced with worry and guilt.

"This place has been abandoned for years," the local policeman said. "See?"

The officer pushed open the rickety door by giving it a hefty shove with his shoulder. Dust and cobwebs flitted everywhere and made everyone cough.

"I'm sorry, officer," their dad said. "My boys

are just playing at idiots. I'm sure Martyn is hiding out someplace."

Nobody noticed the drag marks by the old dusty fireplace.

The Rusty Robot

The Burke's lived on a pleasant farmstead in a quiet corner of Minnesota; overlooking hectares of cornfields, of course, but now all was shrouded in a haze of late afternoon summer sunshine.

Jarvis paused for a moment before he pulled open the rusty barn door. It seemed wrong to be doing this on his father's birthday. But when his father had brought up the subject over lunch Jarvis hadn't been able to resist having a peek to see how the robot had fared after so many years being stored in the dusty old farm building.

Salvo the robot had been newly built and gleaming navy blue the first time Jarvis had seen it. His father had been so proud as he'd showed it off to his family. Even though that was nearly 45 years ago, Jarvis remembered his father's comment.

"One day, Jarvis, this robot could be yours. I hope you'll come to look after it someday."

A smile touched Jarvis' lips now as he remembered the summers of his youth.

For years the robot had been a great source of income to the family. He and his father had toured the heart of America with their seven-foot high humanoid robot, competing in amateur Robot-Boxing tournaments. Back in the day, Salvo had made the family some serious money as they competed against others from all around the country. The underground robot-boxing scene had flourished at one time, before the fad had died out to the fringes of county fairs and local conventions.

Those memories brought a sigh from his mouth

as he looked at the rusty hulk of the robot. Especially as that long-promised day had never really ever arrived. He coughed back the sadness welling inside him.

"Bit of a poor state, isn't it?" His mother had come out from the house to join Jarvis, peering over his shoulder into the dingy old barn. Broken farming equipment, rolls of fencing-wire and some old fridges and cabinets filled the shadows.

"It's a bit sad." To see the robot in its dishevelled condition was depressing. It was a stark reminder of a childhood long gone.

"You're not actually thinking of taking it, are you?"

Jarvis paused. He knew his ideas were borne from sentiments of old. "You don't really want it languishing out here, surely."

His ma cast her eyes skywards. "Look at the state of it. And what will Tami think when you cart it home?"

Jarvis scoffed a little. He could picture her frown and glare of annoyance. He knew he would have to sugar-coat the revelation somehow. She harboured no sentimental notions. There would only be one way of finding out.

"I'm sure if I put it in the garage, out of the way, she won't mind really."

"I could just call Uncle Stevie's Scrapyard," his mother suggested. "Get them to come and collect the bloody thing."

Jarvis gave a heavy sigh and shook his head.

"I wouldn't want to upset the old man."

"He is a daft old fool," she noted. "He spent years talking about restoring the hunk of scrap, but I guess that time has flown by quicker than we all realised. But certainly, I think out-of-sight out-of-mind might stop him dwelling on the past."

"Seriously? This is your inheritance?" Tami joked as Jarvis pulled back the tarp on the back of his truck.

Jarvis cringed. He had pictured this moment and almost chuckled. Two people couldn't be more different. He, so staunch in the old country ways, so reserved, being chastised by Tami, the model of the wary 'Dakota' woman, flamboyant and outspoken, blatantly sarcastic.

"Yeah, yeah. Very funny," Jarvis said. "I'll just shove it in the corner of the garage," he tried to assure her.

Tami sighed. "Great," she muttered sarcastically.

"You sure you don't mind?"

After a brief laugh, she paused and then shook her head.

"I know how much that chunk of metal means to you. The history an' all."

"Where's Dane?" he enquired.

Their teenage son would surely be interested in the old robot. Dane was around the same age that Jarvis had been when his father had brought the old fighting Robot home for the first time.

Not that he'd shown much interested when Jarvis had shared some old photos from back in the day - his concentration had remained firmly on the game console he had been playing on.

Tami scoffed.

"Good luck with that," she chuckled. "If it's not plugged into a T.V or monitor, he ain't gonna be interested very much."

Jarvis sighed and his shoulders sagged. The relationship with his son had always been a tight bond growing up, but now he was a teenager and forging his own personality, the dynamic had fractured slightly.

"He needs to get away from that damn computer."

She could feel her husband's eyes on her, waiting for a response. After a moment, she sighed and gave in to him. "I agree," Tami said. "But good luck trying to persuade him of that."

***

Once Tami had returned into the house. Jarvis began unloading the truck. Just handling the old rusty parts reminded him of old happy childhood summers spent with his day. Feeling a twinge of sentimentality, he remembered the months spent travelling through South Dakota, Nebraska, Kansas, and even down as far as Oklahoma. Their robot, Salvo, had sparred with many opponents, but had also featured in many a side-show of one kind or another. They had never made millions or travelled the world, but they had found the love between father and son that many never experience.

A trickle of sadness ran down his spine. He felt pangs of nostalgia as his recollections jolted his mind back to the care-free days being on the road as a kid. Impromptu trips to neighbouring States proved to be wonderful experiences through some breathtaking American countryside.

A silly sentiment washed over him. He daydreamed about taking his family across country, and visiting local fairs and fates to show off a revamped animatronic robot. Looking down at the pieces of rusty metal in his hands, he broke his nostalgic reverie. Little chance of repeating history - this poor old robot would never be pristine again.

"Pa?"

"Out here, son!"

Dane appeared out on the front porch. He looked at his old man carrying junk into their garage.

"Ma said you were needing a hand," he said, not seeming all that interested.

He stepped off the porch and joined his pa by the trunk.

"What the hell is all this stuff?" He picked up a buckled metallic limb.

"Grandad's robot."

"Really?" He laughed. "He had a frigging robot?"

Jarvis scoffed. "Yeah, I know." He smiled at his son's bemusement. "This was the robot he had when I was a youngster. It's ours now, I guess."

"This is the one you showed me pictures of?"

Jarvis smiled.

"Yeah. Grandad had it stuffed in the back of his barn for some time, but now he's thinking of moving, he won't have anywhere to put it."

Dane picked up a dusty limb and gave it a quick inspection.

"Looks like it's seen better days."

"You're right."

Dane was quiet for a moment as he took in the awful run-down state of the robot.

"What are we going to do with it?" he asked at last.

"What do you mean?" Jarvis didn't understand, though he was pleased to see his son taking an interest.

"It's a shame to leave it like this."

Jarvis brushed scatterings of dust and perched on the end of his truck bed.

"I agree. But I don't know what we can do it. Grandad was always going to rebuild it, but it was in a much worse state than he thought."

"I dunno, Pa. People renovate stuff all the time. Folks are rebuilding cars and bikes all the time."

Jarvis considered.

"It could take some time. And it won't be cheap."

"I suppose." Dane slumped against the truck, the excitement seeping from his eyes.

Jarvis immediately realised his mistake. Dane hadn't shown much interest in anything for some time. This might well be the diversion that would lure his son away from his gaming.

And if they managed to do a good job, maybe their relationship would improve.

Surely it was worth a go? Who knew whether anything would come of it.

"Why don't we see if we can rebuild the robot together?"

"Seriously, Pa? We could work on it?"

Dane was grinning now, and Jarvis couldn't help but feel a slight warmth inside.

"Yes, seriously." Jarvis was thoughtful for a moment as something occurred to him. "Just don't mention it to grandad just yet. I don't want him getting excited over something that might not work out."

"Won't he see it when he comes to visit?"

Jarvis shook his head.

"He never looks in our garage."

After all, Jarvis figured, he'd barely shown any interested in the robot when it was in his barn.

Dane nodded and grinned wickedly at him.

"I get what you're saying. It'll be a surprise for him later."

Jarvis hoped it might be.

It took five months of toil but, with the help of the town mechanic, online manuals, Jarvis and Dane eventually managed to get the robot started.

"Looks good," Dane said when they brought the robot out into the afternoon sunshine.

Jarvis smiled. He was starting to feel a scattering of success. There was still a little way to go, but progress had certainly been made. It seemed as a proper restoration might actually be possible.

"Now we need to do something about the paintwork. There is still a bit of rust to clean off. Maybe some new feet might not go amiss."

"I've been looking on the internet," Dane said. "There is a second-hand dealer in Florida that has plenty of robot parts. We could see if he has any feet for our robot."

He smiled, and Jarvis felt they were connecting again. Somehow his days spent lounging in his bedroom and playing first-player shoot'em ups had been put to one side amicably.

The enthusiasm in Dane had not waned at all over the past few months. He no longer seemed the weary teenager he had once been. These days his time spent on the internet wasn't for gaming and social media.

As the worked together, Dane began to talk to Jarvis about local events, thoughts about their farm, planning trips to neighbouring states. It seemed all the teenager had needed was some quality family time - and they both had found a zest for life.

Most importantly, they had been there for each other, sharing the successes and their failures freely.

In the beginning, Jarvis had been sceptical. But Dane had been so engaged in the rebuild that Jarvis was put at ease straight away. Jarvis had begun to detect a certain confidence and maturity that belied his son's age.

They eventually managed to restore the robot to its former glory. A programmer from Minneapolis was brought in for a few days to reprogram the old circuits. When the robot was pristine and gleaming in a new coat of paint, Dane invited some of his mates from town to have a look at it.

"We rebuilt it from scratch, me and my Pa!"

***

"Where's Dane?" Tami enquired the following weekend. "It's time for us to get ready."

"The kid's probably in the garage with the robot!" Jarvis scoffed. "I'll go see where he is."

His hunch was right. He found his son polishing the front plates of the robot.

"My mates were asking what we are going to do with Salvo," Dane stated. "Are you thinking of selling it?"

Jarvis sighed and wiped his brow. In truth, he hadn't given it much thought.

"No idea. What do you think we should do?"

Dane paused for a moment. "I reckon we

should hold on to it. Maybe we could display it at local fairs?"

"Maybe we could take it on show to the State fair?"

Dane's expression was disbelief.

"You mean we could tour with the robot?"

Jarvis smiled.

"Sure. Why not? With all the work we've put into it, I reckon we should have some fun with it. Of course, we'll have to convince your ma."

Dane laughed.

"Sounds great!"

Tami popped her head around the garage door.

"We'll need to think about leaving in a moment. Dane, you need to go and get changed. Grandad's probably already got the bbq going by now."

It was another Sunday lunch at the family farm, and still, Jarvis had to tell his pa about the robot. They'd managed to keep it a secret this long, but today was the day to reveal all...

It was with a grin that Jarvis opened the back of the horsebox he had borrowed for the day. "What on earth...?" his ma started, then she saw Jarvis open the back and smiled. "Sweet lawdy. I can't believe it!"

Jarvis gave a sly wink at Dane.

He glanced at his pa, wondering what kind of reaction he would get. Then he saw the older man's grin. A lump rose in his throat. Jarvis was put at ease straight away.

His pa held his hand to his forehead in amazement.

"I kept dreaming about restoring the old robot, but I could never find the enthusiasm. And then time just kinda slipped by. I can't believe you've actually done it."

Jarvis' ma put a comforting hand on her husband's shoulder.

"It looks amazing. Doesn't it?" Her heart had lurched as she gave her son the sweetest smile.

"It was Dane really," Jarvis admitted, patting his son on his back. "He did the most work… tracking down parts and doing the grunt work."

Dane gave a little shrug, then got his camera out.

"We should get a family photo with Salvo." He started to usher grandad into position.

"What do you think we should do with it now, grandad?"

Jarvis' father gave an awkward shrug.

"I don't know. I'm so taken aback by it all." He heard his voice crackle with emotion.

Dane glanced at his pa and Jarvis, touched by the warmth, nodded.

"We were thinking about going to the Iowa State fair later this summer. We were wondering whether you'd like to come with us?"

Grandad laughed, then paused when the realisation sank it. "Really?"

Jarvis nodded. "Sure. Why not? Relive some of those old summers we used to have."

"Well, I could hardly say no to that! Sounds fun."

Tami grinned. She could see the joy in all the generations.

"It's just like old times," Jarvis' ma said, almost to herself. Then she turned to Tami. "They used to go to just about every show and fair at a moment's notice."

Tami smiled at Jarvis.

"I've got the feeling we may have resurrected a family tradition."

Jarvis gave a light chuckle... and didn't deny it. He gave a quick look to Dane.

"Let's do it," Dane said.

"Are you sure you'd want to?"

"Yes," he said. "I'm totally up for it."

Robot 451

I could not control my frustrations and annoyance when my parents sent the robot back. Both Ma and Pa tried desperately to explain their reasons for shipping it back to the manufacturers.

At first, it was about the baby's safety. Then it was about costs and upkeep. Finally, they told me that I was lucky for having not spent too much time with it because it may have harmed me.

When I complained that I was now going to be bored without my robotic playmate, they tried to soothe my anguish by suggesting they might buy me a pet instead. Maybe a dog... maybe something exotic like a creepy-crawly or bird of some kind.

Scoffing at the idea, I began to kick up a fuss by insisting that they try and get another robot... or better still, work at getting the old one back. I kinda had a soft spot for ol' 451.

Apparently, that suggestion was simply out of the question. The tales they told me about the robot made me question their sanity. They started by telling me about the neighbour's dead dog, then went on to tell about me about the bleach tablets left in the baby's crib, how the gas stove was left on in the kitchen, how Mrs Levy from no.26 had found her two cats dead in her backyard pool, and finally, how robot 451 had discarded a broken glass tumbler by their bedside while they slept.

I stood very still and watched a storm front of conflicting emotions play across their faces as they recounted their horrific tales.

They stated that I would just have to occupy my

time with hobbies or homework. Maybe find a new friend in the neighbourhood or stay behind after school and join a sports team. They suggested enrolling me in the local Scouts, or even joining a Warhammer club at the comic store in town. I'd be brought a new bike so I could cycle to these places.

Suffice to say, their ideas and guilt-driven bribes didn't wash with me though.

However hard I pleaded though, my wishes to get the robot back fell on deaf ears. They were seemingly steadfast in their resolve. At present, there would be no returning of robot 451.

You cannot fathom how much I hate it. It means I have to pretend to be good until I can find other ways of concealing who I am... and what I do.